Pride and Pemberley

A Novel Inspired by Jane Austen

Dee Garretson

Dee Garretson

This book is dedicated to Jane Austen, for all the enjoyment I've received over the years from reading her works, and for all I have learned about writing from her, though there is much work for me to do.

Contents

Chapter 1

Countdown to the Raine Randolph/Stefan Andris

Wedding

30 days

To Do List:

Finish fixing damaged plaster in the dining room

Choose paint color for it - either *Fredericka's Blush* pink or *Lyme Sea* blue-gray

Negotiate with the mice to vacate their hideout behind the wall

"IT'S DECIDED," I said. "We'll use the *Fredericka's Blush* for the dining room paint." I looked down at Betsey from my perch on the ladder and she meowed at my decision. I took that as a sign of approval. I needed approval, even if only from a fluffball.

The paint color was such a deep rose, I felt a bit sorry for the poor Fredericka who had given her name to it. Since I blushed too much at the worst times, I had great sympathy for the other blushers in the world.

Betsey meowed again and I realized it was her "I've brought you a gift" meow.

"What now?" The move to Pemberley from North Carolina had been hard on the cat, and she spent the eight months since we'd arrived stealing items from my little sister Kiki and bringing them to me, as if trying to bribe me to take her home.

This time she had a pair of black thong underwear between her front paws. Not mine. I didn't own any, but Kiki did. "Oh, Betsey baby, not again."

I'd hoped Betsey would take up mouse hunting instead of cat burglary since so many of the little creatures had moved into Pemberley when it was shut up. From the skittering sounds I could hear behind the wall, the entire dining room mouse clan seemed to be holding a country dance party, but Betsey was totally uninterested. She rolled over on her back and tossed the underwear between her front paws as if subduing her captive, because thongs held so much more danger than mice.

More skittering. "Libby Darcy, you know there are actually very few mice here," I said out loud to convince myself as I felt a shudder ripple through me. "And they are just small creatures who want to live in peace with us." This was Kiki's mantra, which she repeated every time I asked her if she was hearing the mice too. "Deep breaths. It is silly to be bothered by mice."

Except it wasn't. If we were going to make Pemberley work as a wedding venue and a bed and breakfast, we couldn't have mice. Not even one. They needed to move their fuzzy little butts and beady little eyes and tiny scrabbling feet outside to commune with nature, not traipse about in the wreck of the house we were scrambling to renovate. I was not going to creep back to the U.S. with another lack of accomplishment to add to my life-long list of failures because of a gang of rodents. I was going to find something to be proud about.

I almost launched into a pep talk and then realized I'd been spending too much time talking to myself. It was one thing to talk to a cat, but a totally different thing to carry on constant solo conversations, even if they were my version of stress reduction. Instead, I went back to finishing the plaster repair. Somebody had to do it and I came cheap.

A breeze wafted in, bringing with it the scent of the only Blanc Double de Coubert rose that still remained along the outside wall of the dining room. The poor thing was so old only a few scrawny branches survived, but the flowers did have an incredible scent.

My grandmother had loved that variety of rose dearly. I remembered her telling me one time, *Rose breeders keep trying to make roses have bigger blooms or have more of them or bloom for a longer period of time, but then they find they've bred the fragrance right out of them. Without the scent, are they really even a rose?* I had tried to think that through but she didn't wait for an answer. *An old-fashioned rose like this teaches you to live in the moment. When it blooms, you delight in it, even knowing it's not going to last long. "Gather ye rosebuds while ye may." The poets had it right. Remember that, Libby.*

Most of it had made no sense to me as a child, though I'd grown to understand it even if I didn't practice it. I was terrible at living in the moment, and it had only gotten worse since I'd come to Pemberley. I had too many lists filling my head of things that had to be done. "So I should try to enjoy this plastering, right, Betsey?" She had tossed the underwear aside and sprawled in a patch of sun, totally exhausted by the battle of the thong. At least for the moment, Betsey was living in her own moment and not yearning to be back in the States.

I murmured the instructions from the plastering video one more time to myself. *Smooth the final plaster coat on thinly and gently like you are applying a calming mask to a lover's face.* Right. I probably shouldn't have chosen that particular video to learn about plaster repair because my attempts were not going smoothly at all. I was rushing, so thinly and gently weren't happening.

A motion outside the window caught my eye, a car speeding up the long drive. We weren't expecting anyone. I had a brief moment of panic that it was William, even though I had told him over and over I didn't want to see him and we were done. But since he never listened, every phone call or text message gave me a tinge of worry. I could imagine him flying over to England to come see me in person, thinking I'd weaken in his presence.

As the car stopped, Mr. Mackenzie, the old gardener, came into view pushing a wheelbarrow with a small tree in it, moving so slowly I was sure the tree would outgrow the wheelbarrow before it got to its destination. I wasn't sure moving trees around was the most efficient use of Mr. Mackenzie's time, given the grounds were more like a wild Alice in Wonderland fever dream than a proper English garden. We were lucky our first scheduled bride claimed she liked the wildness, but I didn't think many wedding couples would want the abandoned vibe.

I stopped thinking about the gardener when I took a good look at the car. It was gorgeous. I usually don't care a whit about cars except that they run, but this one was dark green and gleaming and even in my ignorance I could identify it as a vintage Jaguar. It couldn't be William. He'd never rent a vintage car.

The man who emerged from the car was definitely not William. Far too tall with a lanky easygoing way of moving William had never displayed. Unfortunately for William, he always moved too slowly, with his hands clasped together as if he were leading a funeral procession. This man wore a suit that fit him so well it brought back too many memories of the sleek polished lawyers I'd come across in my brief time interning at Lloyd and Lawrence, and in dealing with my stepmother's attorney and the attorneys who hovered around William and his father and their mega church. When the man reached in and pulled out a briefcase, I wanted to go hide in the attic with the upstairs mice clan. I'd gotten to the point where I actually preferred mice over lawyers. It also annoyed me that the visitor looked like he belonged to the house, far more than me. If someone saw the two of us together, they'd think he was the owner and I was the scullery maid.

The man surprised me with his next move. Instead of walking toward the house, he went over to the gardener and clapped him on the shoulder. The two launched into a discussion as Mr. Mackenzie pointed at the tree, before pointing to a hole I hadn't noticed he'd dug near the drive. At least that meant the gardener had a plan for the tree, instead of just wheeling it about to show it the scenery.

The visitor's next move surprised me even more when he set down his briefcase, took off his jacket and handed it to Mr. Mackenzie, then took over the handles of the wheelbarrow and pushed it over to the hole. He lifted the tree out and placed it in the hole, then brushed his hands and took his jacket back from the gardener. They chatted some more, as the man waved his arms around like he was talking about the property. The man clapped Mr. Mackenzie on the shoulder again and then retrieved his briefcase, before moving toward the house.

I shifted away, nearly falling off the ladder, though I knew the visitor probably didn't see me watching him. As he walked toward the front portico, the resident black swan I had inherited with the property came into view, ready for its usual attack on any invaders. The swan was named Palmer, though after the creature had charged me the first time, I contemplated changing his name to Darth. Palmer spent most of his time in a small ornamental pool on the right side of the drive, even though he had a perfectly good pond he could use far away from the entrance. I think the creature preferred the pool so he could keep a sharp lookout for anyone trying to come close to the house, having given himself the job of guard swan.

I watched as Palmer gave a loud squawk, spread his wings and charged the visitor. I'd run the first time the swan charged me, but the visitor stood his ground and actually smiled at the demon creature, reaching into his pocket and pulling out something that might have been a cracker or a cookie. He tossed it at the bird, who caught it in its beak and then waddled off like it hadn't ever considered pecking the man to death. Who was this brave soul?

A screeching noise nearly made me fall off the ladder yet again, the kind of screeching only Kiki could make. A word in the shrieking sounded like "Ghosts! Ghosts!" My sister came dashing through the door, not paying attention to the drop cloth on the floor. She slid as soon as she put her foot on it, waving her arms and continuing to screech as she came crashing into the ladder and me. As the ladder tipped, Kiki caught hold of it but I dropped the plaster hawk tool. It fell into the bucket of plaster, making wet plaster splash up. Betsey yowled when some bits hit her. She leapt straight up like she was on a spring and then dashed out of the room, leaving the underwear behind.

I got off the ladder. The way the day was going, it seemed a prudent move.

Kiki stopped screeching. "There was a ghost! A real ghost!"

"Excuse me." A man's voice came from the doorway, the visitor.

He had put his jacket back on and was looking like a lawyer again. "I hope you don't mind me walking in. The door was not closed all the way and I heard screaming. Is everything all right?"

"Ghost sighting," Kiki gasped out as she motioned out toward the hall. "Old woman in a giant nightgown and a night cap wandering around the hall. She was calling out for someone or something. I really wanted to see a ghost but now that I have...well, it was weird. I couldn't breathe for a minute and then she was gone, just like that." Kiki gave what I thought was an overly dramatic shudder. She was good at drama.

The man stared at Kiki like she was speaking in tongues. That happened often because she spoke fast and tended to natter on and on.

Kiki looked back at him and I could see the exact second she became aware that we had a very good-looking person standing in our house. She flipped back her ponytail, gave him a dazzling smile and turned on the flirt fountain. "But I'm not really scared of ghosts. It just surprised me. I'm Katherine Smith." She held out her hand. "Kiki to my friends." Her voice held all the sweetness of a peach pie. She had learned to flirt from our other sister Lyra and often went a little overboard with it. I wanted to point out the man was too old for her, at least my age if not older, but I held my tongue. There would be time for that later if she expressed a real interest in him, which I doubted.

A bemused expression appeared on the man's face. Kiki had that effect on people. She had the same warmth as her father, my stepfather, though his had diminished over the years as our mother had worn him down with her complaints.

The man took Kiki's hand, becoming a little less lawyerly. "How do you do. I'm looking for Libby Darcy."

"That's me," I said.

He turned back to look at me. I hoped I didn't have plaster spattered on my face.

"You're Miss Darcy?" From the disbelief in his voice, I must have really resembled that scullery maid.

"She is." Kiki replied before I could respond.

Who was he expecting? "I really am."

"I'm Davin de Bourgh." He moved closer and held out his hand to me, speaking as if the name should mean something to me. It didn't. When he spoke again his voice was distinctly frosty. "I tried to call, but the number I have doesn't seem to be working."

He sounded irritated that he couldn't get in touch with me. I didn't feel like explaining we hadn't reconnected the land line because of the cost or that I'd changed my cell phone number to avoid calls from certain people I'd left behind in the U.S.

"Davin de Bourgh," he repeated. "I'm the landscape architect. The one your grandmother wanted to help you fix up the place."

"Oh, right." At the time we learned the details of that part of the will, my mother had been in a huff about it. *Why did your grandmother feel the need to set aside thousands of pounds for flowers? She should have left it up to you how you spend the money. And why this company? Who are they? I smell a rat. Undue influence, probably.*

At that point, my very expensive attorney had been fending off my stepmother's attempts to challenge the will, and I hadn't wanted him to take on yet another costly battle.

"We're so occupied with fixing up the inside, I haven't had a chance to think about the outside," I said.

"Yes, I understand. I thought I'd stop by so we could discuss a timeline for the repairs. I'm sure you've noticed you've got some real drainage issues outside, especially by the northwest corner of the building. I did a complete survey of the grounds before you arrived." He held up his briefcase. "I have a report in here we could go over, but the drainage problem is pressing. I'm afraid if we don't deal with that soon, it will undermine the foundation on that section of the house."

Deal with that soon. I could feel a bubble of laughter building up, not a ha ha kind of laughter but one of despair. Every single person who'd been through the house with knowledge of some aspect of building repair had used some version of that phrase. Everything needed to be dealt with soon, immediately, urgently, etc., or the whole house would fall down.

"My immediate problem is the conservatory," I said. "It's a mess and it's leaking and we need to hold a wedding there."

He raised an eyebrow. "You're getting married?" There was so much disbelief in his voice, I could feel the heat in my cheeks rising and knew they were flushing. He sounded as if he had never heard anything so unbelievable.

"No, I'm renting the place out for weddings, and we've already got one scheduled. Soon. That's why I need the conservatory fixed up."

"Oh, I see. Unfortunately, conservatory repair isn't really part of what my firm does," he said. "It's very specialized work."

"It's got plants in it," I said. "You deal with plants, right?" I knew I was sounding like an obnoxious American but I couldn't help it. I was still smarting over his reaction to me.

He ignored my obnoxiousness. "I could recommend a few people if the structure needs repairs."

I didn't want that. The estate had already set aside money for him and his business and it couldn't be used to pay other firms to do the work.

The smell of something burning made my nose twitch. "Kiki?" I turned to her but she was already dashing out the door.

"My pickle scones!" she cried.

I sniffed the air. Over-roasted pickles would explain the strange tint to the burnt odor. I hoped Kiki got to them before they caught on fire. She was a remarkably creative cook but still trying to learn how to work the massive range that ruled the kitchen.

"Did she just say pickle scones?" Davin asked.

"Yes, she's working on a new recipe, a savory scone with pickles and cheddar cheese. They're quite good, actually." It was silly to get defensive about Kiki's recipes but I always did. I felt like I was allowed to criticize some of her attempts, but I didn't like it when anyone else hinted that she might be making something too weird. Kiki needed at least one advocate. She'd been punched down too many times already.

"Hmmm...Interesting," he said. He paused and then added, "You don't remember me, do you?"

Chapter 2

Countdown to Raine Randolph/Stefan Andris

Wedding

30 days

To Do List:

Finish fixing damaged plaster in dining room

~~Choose paint color = either *Fredericka's Blush* pink or *Lyme Sea* blue-gray~~

Negotiate with the mice to vacate their hideout behind the wall.

Fix the front door lock so door will stay shut and random handsome strangers can't walk in and find me a mess

Tell Kiki to keep her underwear locked up

REMEMBER HIM? I was sure I'd never seen him before. I'm met any number of British people when I'd done a study-abroad year at the

London School of Economics, but his face didn't seem familiar, and I surely would have remembered. It had only been ten years ago. No one from then could have changed so much I wouldn't recognize them.

"No...I'm sorry, I don't."

"When we were children," he said. "The whole group of us who used to play on the grounds here."

I remembered the children of course. They had been one of the reasons I'd loved coming to visit. My grandmother encouraged them to run all over the place, saying she liked the sound of children's voices. We'd set up elaborate imaginary games and made hideouts in the woods and dug for treasure, though we'd never found any, much to my disappointment.

"Right, the village kids." I'd been close friends with Samuel, Mr. Mackenzie's grandson who had lived with him. Samuel shared my interest in birds and in drawing and I'd had a bit of a child crush on him. But this man wasn't Samuel. Samuel married a woman from Australia and was living there with her running her family's vegetable farm. I studied the person in front of me. "You're...you're not Robin, are you?"

I couldn't believe I hadn't seen it before. The rest of his face had finally grown to match his nose and his ears. Back then, they'd all been far too big, though they had matched his large feet. And there was no more cowlick in his hair, or he'd at least tamed it. I remembered he'd been willing to go along with most of the games I thought up that involved imaginary worlds or time travel, but he'd also been bossy, acting as if it was his right to be the leader of the group, no matter what we were playing.

He nodded. "Yes, that was me."

"But...but you said your name was Davin."

He finally smiled. "Robin wasn't my real name. You didn't know that? Robin was my nickname because of that silly game we played."

The game. "Robin Hood and his merry men. Of course." Robin, Davin, carried around a bow and a quiver of arrows all the time, and some days he brought a burlap sack with him, a sack full of items we'd place around the yard and then pretend to sneak around and steal to give to "the poor." Some of the items were so fancy, I'd worried he'd get in trouble bringing them from his house, but he always waved off my worries. I'd been Maid Marian, or at least my version of her, someone who also had a magic wand and extra powers. "I didn't realize your name wasn't really Robin." I felt my face flushing again. How stupid of me not to have known that.

Even if I hadn't recognized him, why hadn't he recognized me? I hadn't changed that much, though back then I had been undersized for my age because of some medical problems which hadn't yet been diagnosed. I suppose it was because I wasn't one of those people with features that others remembered. No beautiful eyes (just your basic blue gray), no amazing hair (your basic curlyish brown), no pronounced cheekbones (average), no memorable features at all, though my skin wasn't bad since my anemia was under control. He really should have known who I was.

"So that's how my grandmother knew you," I said. Kiki and I had wondered why she had specified a particular landscape architecture firm in the will. My grandmother must have been thrilled a village child grew up to run his own company. "I remember now. You helped Mr. Mackenzie in the garden sometimes." That explained why Davin had been so friendly with the gardener when he'd arrived.

"Yes, he taught me so much," Davin said. "I'm indebted to him. And to your grandmother. She was very good to me." His expression changed. "I hope you know how much she loved the place."

"Of course I know that. I'm sorry I didn't recognize you." I started to motion to his face and then I caught myself, but not before he realized what I was doing.

"Yes, the ears and the nose," he said. "They are what people remember. I'm glad they aren't my most noticeable feature now." The frosty look came back. "I didn't think I'd ever see you again," he said. "I was surprised when I got the news you were coming back."

I thought I knew why he'd said that. The last day I'd visited as a child, the day my father had come to collect me turned into a huge fight between my grandmother and my father. She'd wanted him to move his new young second wife and himself back to England to help her with the estate and he'd refused because his wife was determined to become a successful New York actor. There had been so much shouting and then my father had cried and it had been terrible. I hated seeing my father so upset, because he was the only buffer I had for my mother, and I knew he had a bad heart and wasn't supposed to get agitated.

I'd gone out to the boys and said I'd hated the place and I never wanted to come back. I'd cried too, though I'd made a point of never crying in front of them before that. I was furious at myself for doing so. I hadn't been back to Pemberley since then, until I'd learned my grandmother had left it to me in her will.

Davin cleared his throat and I realized I hadn't responded to him. Was that really why he was being so cold to me? Because of something I'd said when I was ten? If so, that was extremely annoying.

I shrugged. "Things change."

He looked at his wristwatch, which had the same vintage appearance as the car. "I can see you are busy," he said. "Shall I leave my survey report with you and then we can set up a time to meet?"

"You can leave it but I'm not sure when I'll get to it. We really are slammed." I almost launched into an explanation of the deadline I was facing, but then decided it wasn't really any of his business.

My phone rang and I had to fumble around to find it. It was my friend Emmaline, the wedding planner. "Sorry, I have to take this. Can you wait just a moment?" I didn't wait for his reply before I hit the accept button.

"Libby! Good news and bad news! What do you want first?" she asked.

"Can I call you back?" The words 'bad news' made it sound like a conversation I didn't want to have in front of anyone else.

"Yes, if you do it fast. I've got a meeting in ten."

I became aware that Davin had taken a sheath of papers out of his briefcase. "Okay, I'll call you right back."

"I'll just leave these with you then," Davin said, looking around for a place to put them. It was then he noticed the underwear on the floor, which I had forgotten about. He gave a little start but didn't say anything.

"It's the cat," I said, feeling my face get extremely hot, sure my cheeks were the same color as Fredericka's Blush paint. "I mean, not the cat's underwear, of course. That would be silly. The cat is upset about being here and she brings me things. Those aren't mine." Why was I telling him that? "Sorry, I was trying to get the plaster done before it hardened and I didn't pick them up...I...I..." I reached out for the papers. "I'll just take those."

He handed them over. "I'll wait to hear from you then," he said.

"Yes," I put the papers down on the floor and I picked up the plaster tool. "I should get back to this before the plaster hardens. I'll call you."

"Goodbye, then," he said. As he left the room, he turned back and said, "Your grandmother really did love this place. It does need the right sort to keep it from falling down."

Right sort? What did that mean? Was he implying I wasn't right? There was no reason for him to think that. I was here, and I was working on the place.

Before I could come up with a response, he was gone. "It's not going to fall down! Just you wait and see!" I said to the empty air.

The phone rang again. Emmaline again. "It's me," she said. "I'm about to go to my meeting but we really need to talk."

"Tell me the good news first." I needed a bit of good.

"The bride has increased the guest list. We'll have twenty more so that's more money!"

That was more than good news, it was excellent news. With twenty extra guests, I'd be able to pay off a few more of the renovation bills that had come due. I worried we were already charging too much per guest but Emmaline had convinced me it was the right price. She'd said, *You don't want to seem cheap. Raine and Stefan have oodles of money and they are willing to spend it.* I'd have to tell Kiki right away. More guests meant more food for her to prepare.

"Yes we can handle that. It is good news. What's the bad news?"

There was a pause. "Now don't freak out. Promise?" She didn't wait for me to reply. "The wedding has to be moved up, just one week though. Raine needs to be on set for her new movie a week before she was originally scheduled."

It took me a moment before it sunk in. "No! We'll never be ready in time. It was always going to be a crunch for the 28th. Moving it up just

gives us three weeks. No way! The place is nowhere close to being ready."
I could feel my jaw clenching up, something it had been doing so much
lately, a headache was always ready to spring on me.

"You promised not to freak out," Emmaline said. I was going to tell
her I hadn't been given time to promise but she kept talking. "Nobody
will be looking too closely at every little bit of molding and flooring.
You're obsessive so you notice, but other people don't."

"I think they'll notice if bits of plaster fall from the ceiling and
plink into their glasses of champagne." Visions of plaster bits falling like
raindrops filled my head.

"Just don't let people in those rooms. I'll get you some velvet ropes
like they use in museums to block off rooms you don't want people to
see. The guests won't think that is the least bit strange. Anyway, we have
no choice. Hold on." Her voice grew muffled. "I'll be right there." Then
louder again. "I'm not going to let you back out for both our sakes. You
need this and it would be the death of my wedding planner business if
you cancel. I'll come down and help do whatever you want. Put me in
painter's overalls and give me a brush."

"Oh, I can just see that." Emmaline wore only the latest fashions,
always with high heels, and she never had a touch of makeup out of place.

"When is your friend from the church arriving? Eleanor, right?"
she asked. "And when will your other sister get there? I'm sorry I can't
remember her name. You have too many sisters. Whichever one it is, put
her and Eleanor both to work."

"I can't put Eleanor to work. She's coming here to rest up and to
attend the wedding. She got rundown and fell ill after her husband
passed away. And I don't know exactly when Marni is arriving. She's on
her own version of a bookshop tour in Scotland. Trying to pin down
that particular sister of mine is impossible." Way back when I'd invited

Marni, I had no idea we'd already have a wedding in the works by the time she arrived. I wished she could be uninvited. If my new business venture was going to flop, I didn't want witnesses who knew me to witness it go down. That would be mortifying.

"Okay, so we can solve this problem, one way or the other. Really. Take some deep breaths," Emmaline said. "I'm serious, though, about me coming down to help. Let me know which day and I'll be there. Oh, one more thing. You've told Marni and Eleanor the wedding is absolutely hush hush until it's over, right? Raine will be very upset if the press finds out about it."

"I told Marni. I assume Raine told Eleanor, though I can mention it too." Raine and Eleanor were stepsisters, even though they barely knew each other, but their relationship was the reason we'd been able to book the wedding. Eleanor had told Raine about the place and shown her the pictures I'd sent. "Don't worry about secrecy." We had far more problems to face. "I guess we don't have a choice. But it's not going to be my fault if someone complains to you that the place is shabby. Remember that."

"It will be fine, really. And shabby chic is a thing. Raine has seen the video I sent, so she knows what to expect. Look, I have to go but I'll call back later."

I stared at the phone after she ended the call. Three weeks! My whole carefully planned out schedule had just become obsolete.

My phone pinged again. A text from Emmaline popped up. *One more thing. Raine would like some photos taken outside as well as inside. Can you find a good spot for that? I told her the garden was a little wild at the moment and she says she likes that because it fits her personality.* Emmaline added an eyeroll emoji. *But she means wildly photogenic, not wildly weedy. And someplace where she won't be standing in water if it has rained.*

Emmaline had come out to visit the weekend we had a deluge. She'd seen all the flooded areas. I glanced out the window. I thought we weren't going to have to worry about the outside with so much to do inside. Wrong.

I saw Davin hadn't left yet. He was back talking to the gardener.

I ran outside, not bothering to slip on shoes, which made me realize running across gravel in socks was not the most brilliant of choices. I ended up hobbling the last few feet as I called Davin's name and yelled, "Wait!"

The smile dropped from his face as soon as he saw me. What was it about me to cause him to go all cold? I didn't remember being mean to him as a child. I never said a word back then about the size of his ears or his nose, at least not in his hearing, though I might have called him a clodhopper a few times when we'd had some childish disagreement about a game. But insulting someone's big feet should not be held against a person forever.

"I <u>would</u> like to set up a time to meet," I said. "You're right. I do need to have something done about the drainage. I can read your survey tonight. What would be a good time to talk? You couldn't come by again tomorrow by any chance?"

"I could only do tomorrow if you could meet midmorning."

"That's fine. I'm here all the time."

We settled on a time. As he drove away, I said to Mr. Mackenzie, "I didn't remember Robin at first. You must be pleased he's still in the area."

"Aye, yes, I was very fond of the boy, though I did get into a fair amount of trouble letting him muck about the garden here. His grandfather was furious when he found out, but your grandmother smoothed it over. Quite a tyrant is Master Robin's grandfather, even still."

I remembered Mr. Mackenzie had always referred to him as Master Robin, which I'd thought a little strange, because he'd just called the other boys by their last names. I suppose it was because Robin was clearly the leader of the group.

"He'll do a good job fixing the place up. He knows his business, he does," Mr. Mackenzie said.

"We'll have to have him work around the wedding that's coming up. We can't have everything all torn up the day of. I hope it's all right if I take a look around and let you know which areas need to be worked on beforehand. They want wedding pictures outside as well as inside."

"Lots of places for pretty pictures, Miss Libby," Mr. Mackenzie said. "The whole grounds."

I didn't want to point out how many weeds were growing everywhere because I knew Mr. Mackenzie was doing his best.

"Yes," I said, deciding to have a better idea in my head of what areas could be cleaned up before bringing specific projects to him. "Well, I'll leave you to it," I said. "Don't overdo it."

I went back to the plastering, trying to figure out when it would have to be done to dry in time to paint. I'd have to stick with it, instead of my usual desire to skip from project to project, doing a little bit of one and then moving on to another. I knew it would be better to finish one completely, but sometimes when there was so much to do, I couldn't manage that.

Betsey reappeared, bringing me one of Kiki's socks, a cute one that had flamingos on it. I looked down at the thong still on the floor, trying not to remember Davin's look when he'd seen the underwear.

"Maybe we can change out Palmer the swan for flamingos," I said to her. "I've never heard of a vicious flamingo."

I put on some music, hoping my renovation playlist of my favorite Irish musicians and my grandmother's favorite swing music would inspire me to finish the job. The music kept me moving as usual, but it didn't help my concentration after Davin's appearance. Now that I knew who he was, I couldn't believe I hadn't recognized him. I'd spent so many hours with him and the rest of them. Long days outside playing our pretend games, minotaur in the maze, a pirate hideout on the island in the pond, an elf kingdom in the woods. Even though I had loved that time, all the children blurred together in my memory. I had pushed all those memories down when we'd left the last time and refused to think of them since. Some people delight in their childhood memories. I envy those people. Others, like me, find them mixed in with other memories that are too painful, so it's easier just to forget them all.

"The past is the past," I said. "Time to concentrate on making something new." Something all for myself that didn't involve William or anything from the past, not even Davin de Bourgh. He was just one of the professionals I'd have to work with to get the project to succeed. It had to succeed, not only for me but for Kiki too.

"Concentrate, Libby," I scolded myself. Sometime much later I heard more skittering in the walls. Betsey, who had come back to keep me company, ignored the noise. "I'll make something new that doesn't include rodents!" I yelled, thinking maybe I'd scare them away. I wanted to kick at the wall but was afraid I'd leave a dent I'd have to repair. Even one extra small repair would throw off my timetable all the more, and I absolutely wasn't going to allow that. Not me, the new and improved Libby Darcy, capable entrepreneur, list maker, and queen of renovations, or at least capable watcher of how-to videos.

Chapter 3

Countdown to the Raine Randolph/Stefan Andris
Wedding
~~30~~ 23 days

To Do List:

Finish fixing damaged plaster in the dining room

~~Choose paint color for it— either Fredericka's Blushes pink or Lyme Sea blue-gray~~

~~Negotiate with the mice to vacate their hideout behind the wall.~~

Break off negotiations with mice. Declare war.

Fix the front door lock so door will stay shut and random handsome strangers can't walk in and find me a mess

Tell Kiki to keep her underwear locked up

"I HEARD YOU yelling earlier but I was right in the middle of something, and then you stopped so I figured you weren't being chased around by the ghost," Kiki said from the doorway. "Did you at least see her?" Her tone was hopeful.

"No, but I'd rather see a ghost than hear the mice." I climbed down from the ladder, realizing my arm was tired from holding it up for so long. "We really need those live traps. It may not be as comfortable in the woods for the mice as it is in here, but they'll survive just fine." Her expression darkened. I'd need to be more convincing. "It will be like a wilderness vacation for them. They can build little bonfires and roast bits of marshmallows stolen from us. Just get some marshmallows and sprinkle them on the terrace to make it easy for them. Okay? What kind of live traps have you found that we can order?" A few weeks before she'd claimed she'd look for some, saying she wanted to make sure they were humane enough.

Kiki didn't look at me. "I've got a few possibilities. I'm still narrowing it down." That meant she was avoiding it, but I was too tired to press her on it right then. "Dinner will be ready soon," she added as if trying to distract me.

It worked. I hadn't realized it was getting dark, and at the thought of food, my stomach rumbled.

"Good, I'm really hungry," I said. "What's for dinner?"

"Just pasta with broccoli. Nothing elaborate."

"Great!" I meant it. Some days I just wanted basic food, instead of one of Kiki's experimental concoctions. "Oh, and could you take your underwear and your sock away? Betsey dragged them in here."

"Betsey!" Kiki scolded. "I put the clean laundry basket up on the dresser so she couldn't get at it, but she must have found a way."

"She'll always find a way. You may have to start locking your door to keep it closed." Many of the doors at Pemberley were warped or the hinges had sagged, so they either didn't shut properly or didn't stay shut.

"I will. You may have to get that cat a therapist though. She's not getting any better."

"I know," I said. "Poor baby." I'd need to buy her a few more cat toys. Eventually I'd find one she liked. "I'll clean up and come help you finish dinner."

Once everything was put away, I went back to survey my work. I'd finished the plastering repair, which meant at least one item could be crossed off my list.

I grabbed my bracelet on the windowsill, where I'd left it so it wouldn't get dirty, and put it back on, feeling better the minute it was in place. I didn't like not wearing it. Even after I'd sworn I hadn't wanted to come back to Pemberley, it had been a link to my grandmother. She'd had it made for me, after I had discovered the small amber gemstone in a crack in the floorboards of the bedroom I'd slept in.

She'd thought it must have been broken off a larger piece of jewelry. I was sure it was a magic stone, one that would grant wishes. I quickly learned that wasn't the case, but I still loved the stone, and had it put on new bracelets as my arm grew. My grandmother liked amber better than traditional precious and semi-precious stones. *It had to change to survive,* she'd said. *That's something we should all remember.*

Over the years I had taken to fidgeting with the bracelet when I was nervous or anxious, something that made me feel better when I couldn't indulge in my other stress reliever, which was doodling pictures of rabbits. I'd added some silver beads to the current bracelet which I'd count to myself as I twisted the bracelet around my wrist. It had driven William up a wall, because he thought I should have been able to control myself, especially when we'd have to sit on stage while his father was preaching, in front of hundreds of people and the cameras that recorded every sermon. I'd never grown accustomed to that. "But no more," I said to Betsey. "I'll never have to sit up there again."

After cleaning off the plaster tools, I went into the kitchen, Kiki wouldn't let me help finish dinner, so I sank into a chair, grateful I didn't have to do any cooking. She knew I disliked it and she also knew I usually made a mess when I tried, one she'd have to help clean up.

"So tell me more about the visit with Davin de Bourgh. He's quite a vision," she said as she stirred the pasta.

I took a sip of wine, settling back and flexing my hand, trying to get the muscles to relax after holding the plaster tools for so long. "He may be quite a vision but he's too old for you. Besides, vision or not, he's going to be getting money we really could have used for other things. You know, like furniture and such. It would be nice to have a few more chairs, don't you think?"

We ate in the kitchen because it was the only place with both table and chairs. We'd arrived at Pemberley to find it nearly empty of the smaller furniture and paintings and knickknacks. Mr. Mackenzie had told us the former estate manager had taken things away to sell, which the gardener presumed was because my grandmother had ordered it. She'd been in the U.S. at the time, so he didn't think to check with her. She hadn't ordered the estate manager to do any such thing, and whatever money the man had raised had gone with him to his rumored relocation in South Africa. I'd filed a police report when we finally realized what had happened, but because we had no documentation of what furnishings had actually been in the house, there was not much they could do. My crying over all that had finished weeks ago, faded mainly to an irritated regret.

Kiki added various pinches of spices to the pasta to finish it and then brought the bowl over to the table, serving me a large portion. "Well, the grounds are very shabby," she said, "and you keep saying there is too much work for Mr. Mackenzie, so isn't it a good thing that someone with experience can make things right? We need the outside to look good too."

I knew she was being logical but I wanted sympathy instead. "Yes, I suppose so. But if the house falls down, a beautiful landscape won't do us much good. And I don't like the fact that Davin gets to decide in the end how the money will be spent. I can just imagine him being all patronizing and 'I know best, blah, blah, blah.'" I took a bite of pasta. Whatever Kiki had done to it, it was delicious.

"You're imitating William when you say that," Kiki said. "Not every man is like William."

I scoffed. "As if you have known so many men in all of your twenty-one years on this Earth. And there are more men like William than you think." I could still hear his voice in my head pontificating on all the things 'he knew best.' I pushed the thought of him away so he wouldn't spoil dinner. "What kind of cheese did you use in this?" I asked.

"Two kinds. The cheddar is Cornish Cove and then I added a little Twineham Grange instead of parmesan."

"Definitely a keeper recipe," I took another bite. Good food, decent wine, and no mother around to monitor how much Kiki and I were eating. That was enough to take a little of the edge off.

"Did you go through the mail?" Kiki asked. "There is a fancy envelope in the stack from someplace called the Bingley Hotel Group. It looked important."

"It's probably just a brochure. I'll look at the mail tomorrow." I'd come to despise the mail, because I could imagine each bill blabbering at me to pay it. After I'd inhaled about half the pasta, I put down my fork. "Now tell me about this ghost," I said.

"I know you don't believe me, but I really did see something."

"Describe it again. I wasn't concentrating on your description earlier." I picked my fork back up and took another bite. It really was delicious.

Kiki leaned forward like she didn't want the ghost to hear her. "Okay, so the ghost was an older woman in an old-fashioned nightgown. She drifted through the hall between the ballroom and the side door to the conservatory. She called out asking if anyone had seen Peg or pig or something like that. It's very faint but I swear I heard it and I saw her. I swear."

I had hoped Kiki would just tell me she had glimpsed a shape or something out of the corner of her eye, but this was too detailed for that. Kiki got up and took a few gliding steps, her hands held out in front of her.

I burst out laughing. "I don't know if I'd call that drifting. You look like you're pretending to skate."

She sat back down. "Well, excuse me if I can't drift like a ghost, but that's definitely what she was doing."

"That is very weird but you don't seem too upset now," I said. "You, the girl who can't go into Halloween haunted houses." I knew I would have been upset. Even though I didn't believe in ghosts, I wasn't ashamed to admit I'd managed to scare myself a number of times in dark, empty places, though for some reason I'd never been scared at Pemberley.

"It mostly startled me. She didn't seem to see me, so I guess that's why I'm not scared. If it was a ghost dragging a clanking chain around or carrying its head under an arm chasing after me, I'd be a little more upset. And she's kind of pathetic. I felt bad for her."

Leave it to Kiki to have sympathy for a ghost.

"If there is a ghost, I don't suppose we can do much about it," I said. "It's not like we could afford an exorcism or anything like that, though

I have no idea what the going rate is for an exorcist. Whatever it would cost, it's not in the budget." I was just joking, because I couldn't deal with the idea of a ghost. It was too absurd. Until I saw it myself, I was not going to be convinced.

"Didn't you ever see anything spooky when you visited?" Kiki asked. "Or didn't your grandmother ever mention anything about a ghost?"

"Nope, and nope." I hadn't been one of those kids who liked spooky things. As an older sister, it had been my job to tell the younger ones there were no monsters in the closet or ghosts haunting the basement.

The pasta on my plate had disappeared so I picked up the last piece of bread and slathered plenty of butter on it, which distracted me from thoughts of ghosts. The butter was so much better in the U.K than the U.S., and I couldn't get enough of it. We joked that it must come from extremely happy cows.

"Well, whoever she is, she's certainly looking for something or someone," Kiki said. "Maybe she wasn't really calling for a pig. Her clothes were too fancy and her voice was very 'la la' upper class English. A woman like that wouldn't have anything to do with pigs. She probably said 'Peg.' Maybe that was her daughter and the child got kidnapped and the woman died before the girl could be found and that's why she haunts the place." Kiki sat back so she could take a breath after that string of words.

I was about to comment on her elaborate flight of fancy when the refrigerator shrieked. I dropped the butter knife, almost afraid the refrigerator door would blast open and a ghost roar out of it, but then the thing gave a loud clunk. Then nothing.

It had hummed before, loudly enough to be annoying, so the silence was obvious.

"Uh oh." Kiki got up. "I was afraid of that." She went over and put her hand on it.

"Afraid of what?" I asked, though I already knew.

"The motor has definitely quit. It hasn't seemed to be cooling enough the last few days. And it is ancient."

I got up and kicked it, which only resulted in a painful foot, not a return to the humming.

"Great, just great," I said, hopping back to the chair. "And when a refrigerator is dead, it's really dead. No hope of its ghost coming back to haunt it by keeping it cool."

"I'm sorry," Kiki said.

I sighed. "Don't apologize. It's not your fault." Blasted thing. "We obviously can't live without a regular refrigerator." We had another small one that had been in the housekeeper's rooms but it was not even close to large enough to cater a wedding. "I suppose we'll have to go refrigerator shopping. Like soon." I had no idea what they cost or how long it would take to get one. And we'd have to scrounge up some coolers and ice to keep things cold in the meantime.

"I can take care of refrigerator shopping. I know just want we need!" Kiki said. "I've been shopping online already, because I knew we'd have to have a new one at some point soon. The one I picked is a beauty."

I had a sinking feeling. "How much does it cost?"

"Well, it's expensive, but it will make it easier to pass the health inspection." We'd already registered as a catering business but we'd yet to be visited for the inspection.

She went over to her laptop on the counter and pulled up a page. "See, here it is. I've already measured and it will fit if we take out the one cabinet."

The price was depressing, but she was right. We needed a bigger one better suited to supplying food for weddings.

"Okay, but only if we can get that model right away. Can you figure out how to arrange for one and how to get it delivered?" I didn't want to waste hours and hours on refrigerator shopping.

"Yes, I can do it." Kiki looked pleased I was giving her that responsibility. Since she was the baby of the family, my siblings and our mother never seemed to realize she had actually grown up.

"What if we tried unplugging it and plugging it back in?" I asked, though I knew it was a silly suggestion. Kiki didn't bother to reply.

I finished off my piece of bread and then slumped back in my chair, working up the energy to get up and get back to work. The next thing I knew Kiki had her hand on my shoulder.

"Wake up! You're going to fall out of your chair."

I rubbed my eyes which felt like they had bits of plaster in them. "Did I really just fall asleep sitting up?"

"You did. Your head was nodding back and forth."

"I haven't been sleeping very well."

"I can tell. Have you seen yourself in the mirror lately? You look like you came from a family of raccoons with those dark circles under your eyes."

Maybe that was why Davin didn't recognize me. He'd mistaken me for a raccoon.

"You should go to bed. I'll clean up." Kiki pointed at the ceiling.

I had planned to read Davin's report but I just couldn't face it. "Okay, but I'll be up early."

"Fine. Now go."

Betsey followed me upstairs and meowed worriedly all while I was taking a shower as if fearing I'd be washed down the drain and disappear on her.

"Okay, okay," I said when I finished. "Everything is okay. I'm right here."

As I dried off my hair, I looked at myself in the mirror. I did see the resemblance to a raccoon. Not good. Not that it mattered how I looked though. Nobody cared what I looked like at the moment. *Except you don't want to look terrible when Davin shows up,* a little voice in my head whispered. Betsey meowed at me again. "I'm not interested in Davin," I told her. "I'm not interested in anyone. I have too much else to worry about. And Davin is probably still bossy and way too much like William and he doesn't like me at all."

I felt like I was six years old again, the first summer I'd come to Pemberley, and was faced with a gang of boys running around the garden. At first they'd only grudgingly let me play, but when I'd taken the blame for crushing some special lilies that Mr. Mackenzie had planted, they'd accepted me. The lily crushing had been Will's fault when he'd fallen on them, and he'd nearly cried at the damage he'd done. I stepped up, somehow already aware that as Mrs. Darcy's granddaughter, I wouldn't get in as much trouble.

Once I had climbed into bed, Betsey darted over to the door, picked something up and brought it to me. It was a crumpled up piece of paper. When I smoothed it out, I saw Kiki's handwriting and the words *You can do this.* While I talked to myself, Kiki wrote herself little notes of affirmation, which her therapist had taught her after the breakdown. It seemed to help.

I was very glad I hadn't received another underwear present. The cat began to purr, convinced I was happy with her gift. I picked up my drawing notebook and started drawing my rabbit of the day, my other coping mechanism. I thought I'd draw a rabbit with a butterfly net chasing a herd of mice, but as my pencil moved it morphed into a rabbit with extra large ears and feet who wore a hat very similar to the one Robin/Davin had worn when we were children. It was kind of a silly hat, Indiana Jones in style and much too big for him, obviously pinched from an older relative. He'd worn it all the time, even if it didn't fit the game we were playing. The rabbit in the drawing had his paw up in the air, as if he was about to say, "I have the best idea!" I could almost hear the boy Robin's voice saying that.

When I finished the drawing, I shut the notebook and let the cat jump up on top of me, so she could knead my stomach as if to hold me in place all night. Not that I wanted to move anyway. It would be nice to spend all of one day in bed. All my big plans for working on the renovation during the day and doing my own painting in my makeshift studio in the tower at night weren't working out at all. So far, I'd only managed parts of three different canvases. All of them needed hours more work, but I'd felt too guilty devoting any time to them when there was so much real work to be done.

I petted Betsey. "Protect us from ghosts tonight, okay, Betsey?" If she wouldn't chase mice, maybe she'd be our ghost detector.

I listened for the sounds of rain, hoping we'd be spared so I wouldn't have to get up in the night to deal with buckets. I'd started to have nightmares about the dreaded "Damp" I'd heard about over and over from the contractors who'd come to view the house. The Damp was a problem throughout the place, creeping in silently where I least expected it and then taking over a floor or a wall or an entire room, like some Stephen King horror novel.

The roof was the worst of the problems. If only the money Grandmother had set aside for the landscaping could be used for something else, it would have paid for an entire new roof. "Drat Davin de Bourgh and whatever spell he'd cast on my grandmother," I murmured to Betsey. "Right sort! I am the right sort! We'll show him. We'll show everyone."

Chapter 4

Countdown to the Raine Randolph/Stefan Andris
Wedding
22 days

<u>To Do List</u>:
Clean the East Room
Make sure Kiki orders live traps for the mice
Tell Kiki about the additional guests!!!!
~~Pay one bill.~~ Look at bills and estimates, add new ones to the spreadsheet
Read Davin's report
Find lipstick
Meet with Davin...

I WOKE UP way too early from a dream where I was chasing the ghost about the house, begging it to take a vacation until the wedding was over. For some reason I was trying to send it on a Caribbean cruise. Except I could never quite catch it. Each time I got close, it would turn a corner and speed up. I woke up in the middle of it to find Betsey sitting at the end of the bed glaring at me like I'd disturbed her slumber.

It hadn't occurred to me until the dream that the ghost might be an actual concern. What if it did show up at the ceremony? Which was worse at a wedding? Mice, falling plaster, or ghosts? With that important question to ponder, I knew I'd never go back to sleep.

As I got out of bed, I felt my jaw crack. I'd been clenching it in my sleep again. The headache was there too, the one I always got when my body decided that holding itself rigid for hours was the right response to a little anxiety.

I tried to stretch out the tightness while I searched for clean clothes. Laundry had dropped way down the to-do list quite a while ago. I didn't want to appear like I'd dressed up for Davin, but I also wanted to look serious, like someone who could handle the renovation of a large estate even if I didn't look like I belonged. In the end, I picked out some black jeans and a red top, both much nicer than I usually wore to work around the house, not because I'd be seeing Davin, but because I didn't have anything else clean, or so I told Betsey as she watched me get dressed. I found a lipstick and put it in my pocket, knowing if I put it on too early, it would all have vanished by the meeting.

Downstairs and in the kitchen, I sidestepped around the cat as she tried to sit on my feet, made myself a quick pod coffee and took it to the study, which still had a giant carved wooden desk, though little else. I settled into the moth-eaten brocaded wingback chair I'd brought in to use as a desk chair and shook the lamp a few times to get it to turn on. It was vintage, along with the outlets, so it was a tossup if it would turn on and stay on. Betsey jumped up on the desk and plopped down on the pillow I'd put there for her. I settled down to read.

Davin's proposal was several pages long and very thorough, as he'd said. The first part was all about the need to stay within the guidelines of Pemberley being a listed historic garden. I wanted to stop reading right there. I knew the building itself was considered of historic significance, which really limited how we did the restorations, and meant we needed the approval of various organizations to carry them out. I hadn't realized the gardens were affected by that too. The weight of that realization made me dread to see what that would add in terms of cost and time.

There were multiple pages describing a drainage survey he'd had done along with the recommendation to clear out debris that had built up in the stream which kept overflowing, and then to repair the French drains, of which we apparently had many. I was so tired that the phrase "French drain" struck me as particularly funny. Why did the French have a drain named after them anyway? I had no idea even what they were and I didn't really want to become an expert on drains. Trying to become an expert on plastering and other house repairs was about all my brain could handle.

The next part was shorter.

Prune the maze. Replace hedge plants as needed. Add crushed stone as needed to the pathways.

The maze had been designed to view from the morning room, but it was so overgrown the pathways were no longer distinct looking down on it from above. The only part Mr. Mackenzie had managed to keep up were the large rabbit topiaries on either side of the entrance. They were still nearly perfect, and I didn't have the heart to tell him his time might be better spent on other projects rather than snipping away at tiny leaf shoots for hours on end. It's not that I wanted to get rid of the topiaries. My grandmother had loved them and they were the start of my own rabbit doodling habit, but we could have lived with shaggier leaf bunnies.

When I'd first arrived back at Pemberley, I'd tried to force my way through the overgrowth in the maze, but had given up about ten feet in. I'd need to talk to Davin about how many hours it would take to accomplish what was in his three short sentences in the report.

I heard Mr. Mackenzie whistling outside. Betsey heard him too and leapt from the desk to the window ledge. He went by with the wheelbarrow again, this time filled with mulch. He moved slowly, as always, and I felt a pang of guilt that I hadn't hired anyone to help him. The grounds were far too much for him. He'd claimed he didn't need any help when we'd first arrived, but the state of the grounds was evidence that wasn't true. I hadn't wanted to be seen as too bossy right away, since he'd been at Pemberley for so many years, but we'd have to make some changes before long.

The next bits in the report were more about specific planting areas, and I had a hard time focusing. I decided that when Davin and I talked, I'd tell him my first goal was to get the place ready for the wedding. I couldn't have sections of the property dug up and mounds of dirt for the wedding guests to view. We had to look like a successful venue right from the start.

As much as I hated to give William and his family credit for anything, their mantra had always been that success breeds success. If you look and act like things are going well, people are more willing to trust you, which in their world meant "give you money." I wasn't greedy like they had been. I just wanted enough to keep the place from falling down and to have a place Kiki and I could live.

"Fresh scones!" Kiki came into the room carrying a tray. "And good coffee." Kiki didn't approve of my coffee pod machine. She had insisted we acquire an actual coffee maker with all sorts of bells and whistles.

"Thank you," I said. "Just what I needed." I glanced at the plate of scones, thinking if I ate something, my stomach might calm down. No bits of green were showing on the scones so that meant no pickles or peas or anything else non-sconeish. They were an odd brownish color, which was a bit concerning. Cocoa, maybe? Hopefully not pureed lentils. Kiki was very fond of lentils.

"Did you look through the mail yet?" Kiki asked. "It's really building up."

"No, I can't face more mail at the moment." I hadn't looked through it all week. "Once the pile is big enough, I'll sort through it." If there were any bills in it, they'd wait their full thirty days to be paid or even longer, depending on how large they were.

"Okay," she said. I thought she'd go back to the kitchen then but instead she wandered around the room, running her finger through the dust on the shelf.

"Everything all right?" I asked. Kiki was never aimless.

"I got a letter from Mom," She glanced out the window as if she feared our mother was right outside peering in the window, and then she stuck her little finger in her mouth and chewed on it, something Kiki always did when she was trying to control her anxiety.

"She wrote you an actual letter?"

Kiki sighed. "Yes. I haven't been opening her emails. She's apparently enabled a tracker thing to see if people read her emails and I haven't opened them for weeks."

I didn't open her emails either. That probably meant a letter was on its way to me too. Our mother didn't like to call because she couldn't list all her grievances as easily over the phone when we could find excuses to cut her off.

"I'm sorry," I said. "Was it the usual?" I knew I didn't even have to ask. It would be the usual.

"Yes, the same bit about how she doesn't understand why I came all this way. How I don't appreciate all she's done for me and have I lost any weight and have I met any men and how I'm ruining my life."

"Ruining your life to help with a project that will fail," I added, because I knew that's what my mother would have said.

"Yes," Kiki said. "And I should be doing something that will actually help me in the future, not following some ridiculous dream."

"My ridiculous dream." I added that in, because it was all I'd heard since I inherited the property and decided to keep it, instead of selling it and dividing up the money between all my younger half-siblings who weren't related to my grandmother at all. Our mother was the only one who wanted me to do that. The rest of the family understood why I'd hesitated, knowing the property had been in my father's family for generations.

Our mother's reaction shouldn't have been surprising. She was never happy with our choices, no matter what they were, and she had always been quick to criticize anything that wasn't her idea, and sometimes even things that were her idea. She'd hated that I'd received an inheritance and then broken off my engagement to William. The engagement had been her greatest triumph since she'd pushed so hard for it for years. I still heard the words she'd yelled at me when I told her I broke up with him. *You'll never find another man who will want to marry you. What do you have to offer anyone? Nothing special. You can't even bring in an income since you failed the bar exam. Nobody will care about your weird poetry and your weird paintings and certainly no one will ever pay you anything for them. You'll regret not trying to get him back.*

"What did you do with the letter?"

Kiki pulled a folded up piece of paper out of her pocket.

"Here, let me see." I held out my hand and Kiki gave me the letter, which I promptly crumpled up and threw away. Kiki gave a little gasp.

"Don't worry," I said. "There's not some hidden camera broadcasting our every move to her. You're here to see if you want to do this. It's a good thing. I wish I hadn't let her try to manage my life for so many years." I didn't want Kiki to waste the years I'd wasted trying to please someone who couldn't be pleased. "You're doing good," I added. "You managed to stand up to her and you're here. I'm proud of you. And it's not like your life is going to be over if this business idea doesn't work out."

"Of course it's going to work out!" she said. I could tell her mood was lightening.

"Yes." I forced another smile.

"I should get back to the kitchen," she said. "Don't leave the mail too long. I don't think all of it is junk mail. I know what you are doing. Avoiding things doesn't make them go away."

"Yes, oh, wise little sister." She knew me too well. I was the champion avoider of problems, conflicts, doctor's visits, you name it.

"That fancy envelope does look important," she said. "You know what, I'll just get it for you."

I took a nibble of the scone when she left the room. It had some spice flavor, maybe cardamom. It was good.

"What's the flavor in these?" I asked when she came back.

"Oh, they have chai in them. Do you like?"

"I do," I said. "The recipe is a keeper."

She handed the envelope to me.

It was fancy, the paper thick and creamy. The return address read *The Bingley Group*. There was a boutique hotel nearby called Bingley Dower

House, which had originally been a part of the massive estate in the neighborhood, Bingley Manor, and I assumed there was a connection. Emmaline had shown me the section on the Dower House website about hosting weddings there, which she thought would inspire me but had actually overwhelmed me. We needed to get way more of the renovations done before I could even consider a glitzy website with images of brides floating about the place and fancy appetizers on beautiful china. All we had as a website was a holding page with a picture of the house from better days and a few words about 'more to come.'

"I hope they aren't writing to complain about something." I knew our property bordered theirs, but it was just a stretch of woodland, and a pasture that we rented out to a local farmer to graze cows. At least we rented it out on paper. He'd gone through hard times recently and hadn't paid rent for a couple of years. I was steeling myself to get tough and demand he pay up, though I didn't really want to kick him and his cows out if I could help it. The cows added a nice pastoral touch on the drive from the village to the entrance off the road.

"Aren't you going to open it?" Kiki asked.

"Yes, I suppose so." I had a bad feeling about it.

The letter inside was on some sort of paper that felt almost like silk. I'm sure it cost almost as much too.

Dear Ms. Darcy:

The Bingley Group is well-known for its collection of boutique hotels around the world. We specialize in restoring historic properties to preserve them for the enjoyment of our guests now and for future generations. We would like to set up a meeting with you to discuss the possible sale of Pemberley to our group.

We are prepared to offer a generous price for the property even in its current condition. Please contact us at to discuss this. If you prefer, I can meet with you at the site if that is more convenient.

Sincerely,

Caro Bingley

Contact information was included below the signature.

My first impulse was to crumple the letter up and throw it away as well, but instead I folded it up and put it back in the envelope, my mother's voice still in my head. What if she was right about our plans and we were doomed to failure? I had an easy way out in front of me.

"Libby. Libby! Earth to Libby. Anything important?" Kiki made a motion to take the letter from me but I moved away from her.

I put the letter under the stack of bills. "No, nothing important. How's the reception menu coming? I want to run it by Emmaline when you've finished."

"Great! I just want to try a few more things. I've got a great idea for another appetizer."

"What? Tell me!"

"You'll see. Dinner is a sampler of appetizers so I can get your opinion."

"Okay. I'm looking forward to tasting them." I wanted to cross my fingers behind my back that they didn't include any really odd combination. She'd been so disappointed I hadn't liked her mustard dill strawberries.

"The spreadsheet for the time management is coming along too," she said. "And the one of what supplies we need and when to get them. Oh Libby, it's going to be fantastic! I just know it. And it will be so successful, everyone who comes will recommend us to all their friends and relatives and we'll have lots of weddings scheduled. I know we can do this!"

I pasted on a smile. With her hair in pigtails, Kiki looked so much like the little girl who used to follow me around, willing to do whatever I wanted just so she could spend time with me. "Yes, well, if we pull it off, your food will be what makes it a success. Now I've got to get back to this."

After she left, I set aside Davin's proposal. I needed to look at the house repair estimates and bills to try to make a few decisions, especially since we needed the new refrigerator. I shuffled the various pieces of paper around, as if that would change the amounts and then opened a few estimates I hadn't been able to face earlier.

The first one was bad, very bad.

The solar tower is not structurally sound. It appears that at some point in the past the bolts holding the walls together were cut off. To repair the problem, we would replace the rods. As the mortar joints between the stones are in poor shape, the entire structure needs to be tuckpointed as well.

My grandmother hadn't used the tower room at all. Back when I visited, it had a few bits of old furniture in it. As a child I'd taken it over as an art room and museum instead, setting up a small display of treasures in one corner, nice rocks, feathers and dried flowers. This time when I'd come back, I'd set up a painting studio, intending to paint when I had free time. That, of course, hadn't really happened yet except for a few hours stolen here and there, and now according to the estimate, the whole thing could fall down at any moment.

I looked at the letter again and wanted to cry. There was absolutely no money for both the tower and the roof, and it would take years of weddings to pay for it, even if there was nothing else to repair. I could feel my jaw clenching again and my stomach churning. The only solution was to try again to get a bank loan, though I'd already been turned down by three banks. The last loan officer had looked over the top of his reading glasses and said, *You expect to begin holding weddings this year? There is still quite a bit of work that needs to be done from what I can see of your proposal. And you have no experience in this field nor any other source of income?*

I'd crept out of the bank in a state of extreme mortification, sure if I'd only been able to sound more confident, instead of being a stuttering mess of nerves, I might have convinced him I was a good bet. Each time I got turned down, it took an extra nick out of my confidence.

The roof. The tower. The wiring. The heating. I'd been a fool to think it could be done without a massive amount of cash on hand. Unless some miracle happened, we weren't going to be able to carry out all our plans after all.

Chapter 5

Countdown to the Raine Randolph/Stefan Andris
Wedding
22 days

To Do List:

Clean the East Room

Get Kiki to order live traps for the mice

Tell Kiki about the additional guests!!!!

~~Look at bills and estimates~~, add new ones to the spreadsheet

~~Read Davin's report~~

~~Find lipstick~~

Meet with Davin

Get a machete for the conservatory

I COULDN'T BEAR to sit at the desk for one more minute, especially since shuffling papers wasn't accomplishing anything. Whatever happened in the long run, we had to get through the wedding already scheduled. I couldn't let Emmaline down, even if it was our one and only wedding. That meant I had to deal with the problem of the conservatory repairs. If Davin's company wouldn't work on it, I needed to figure out what could be done before the wedding and who could do it. Raine, the bride, wanted the guests to mingle there before the ceremony, with a small bar set up in one corner to serve drinks. Emmaline was arranging all the alcohol and bringing people who knew what they were doing to serve it. I just had to make sure the space was ready for them.

I wrenched the glass doors to the conservatory open and went in, pushing a vine away that seemed to have grown a few feet overnight. The smell inside was always fabulous, that rich earth scent like after a rain. Vines climbed up all the larger plants, and smaller plants meandered about far from where they'd originally been placed, spreading into every crack and cranny. Some plants had creamy white flowers which smelled like the ripest of peaches, though even I knew enough to know they weren't peach plants.

The space had once been a courtyard between two wings of the house, but my great grandmother wanted to be able to use it all year long. She had convinced a builder to put a glass roof on it, not realizing how much upkeep it would take, forcing all her descendants afterwards to spend and spend and spend, barely keeping ahead of the necessary repairs. When my grandmother had been forced to leave due to her declining health, it had been left to go wild.

The conservatory had always been the best part of the house. Once I was inside it, I felt hidden away, in a whole other world, where parents and problems didn't exist. I had drawn up childish plans for a whole conservatory house I wanted to build some day, with a bed tucked in one corner, a canopy of vines over it, and a shower enclosed by tall ferns.

But since I'd grown up and lived in the real world, the first step after our arrival had been to notice the leaks. Getting the glass cut for the roof wasn't the hard part, it was finding someone who could put the panes in without breaking other glass panels. The man who had come to look at it told me the glass was so old and thin, it was incredibly fragile, but I couldn't afford to replace every single small pane of glass.

One of the vines had dropped several flowers on the floor so I picked them up and stuck them in my hair, thinking of how Kiki and I had done that back home, with the wildflowers that grew behind my stepfather's diner. A rustling noise came from behind me. I knew it wasn't Betsey with a gift because she didn't rustle. She was too good at creeping around silently. Ghosts don't rustle, at least as far as I knew. And it couldn't be mice. They didn't get big enough to rustle like that, or at least I hoped they didn't. The sound grew louder.

I turned around and caught a flash of purple and a rattle of beads as someone leaped forward. "Surprise!"

Not a ghost, but Marni, the smartest and quirkiest of all my siblings. She grabbed me and hugged me, her face beaming,

"Oh, it's so good to see you! I'm so sorry I didn't come to your grandmother's funeral," she said. I noticed she had a few more freckles than usual and her brown hair had the red highlights she got when she'd spent time in the sun. She looked so fabulous and so Marni. As a child, she's been awkward and afraid to express herself, but at some point she'd come into herself. Her current outfit consisted of a purple scarf to keep her hair back, which somehow went perfectly with dangly copper earrings, three turquoise necklaces and some bracelets made of beachy colored beads. She had another scarf tied around her waist, one I knew she had knitted herself, in a rainbow of colors. Only she could carry off that much jewelry, probably because her clothes were in such sharp contrast. She almost always wore jeans and hiking boots, just in case a hike presented itself to her. She always claimed her own grandmother had been one of the original hippies, and Marni was determined to carry on a little of that tradition when she wasn't in her academic mode.

"I didn't expect you to make it to the funeral," I said. "My grandmother would have wanted you to concentrate on your thesis defense instead of flying across the country for a funeral of someone you never met." Even though it had been a year ago, my voice got a little shaky at the thought of the funeral. I gulped back tears. "I'm so glad you are here, <u>Dr</u>. Smith! I don't think I've said it enough. Congratulations! And congrats on the job. What classes will you be teaching?"

"A section of intro to sociology, a gender and sociology course, and the course of my heart, a senior seminar on social stratification and mobility in the 21st century." Her expression changed. Her mouth turned down and the happiness fell away, but a second later she was back to smiling.

I didn't know what that was about. She'd worked at her studies for so many years, I thought she'd be ecstatic, but I hadn't talked to her, really talked to her, in a long time.

"You're happy, right? And that sounds very distinguished! I'm humbled in your presence." I took a step back so I could bow at her.

She didn't answer the happy question. Instead, she laughed. "No, you're not humbled by me, but thank you. What a place this is! It's unreal. When you told me you inherited a house, I thought you meant, like, a house, not a mansion from a BBC miniseries. I hope you don't mind that I let myself in. No butler around as far as I could tell," she teased.

"I wish I'd inherited all the servants in those shows. You're looking at the butler, the housemaid, the scullery maid, and the parlor maid, as well as the general fixit man, whatever they called that person." It all came out a little more harshly than I intended.

She put her hands on my shoulders. "You're okay, right? This hasn't been too much for you? You look tired and you have big dark circles under your eyes."

"Thanks," I said. "Love you too."

"I'm pointing it out because I do love you. This is a huge project you've taken on. I didn't know you even liked house renovation and fixing things."

"I like some parts of the renovation," I said. "Way back when, before I started taking everyone else's advice about my life, I thought about studying interior design. You should see some of the fabulous wallpaper samples I'm looking at for the drawing room and the morning room. It may seem weird but looking at paint chips and wallpaper samples is the best part of this project." I had collected enough samples to make some sort of large scale collage with them if I wanted.

"That makes sense. Why didn't you ever tell me that? I thought you always wanted to be a painter. The great part of this is the place is big enough for you to finally have a painting studio at least. You do have a painting studio, right?" Marni had always been great at encouraging me to paint, practically the only one. I had finally realized I was never going to take the art world by storm but it was something to keep me sane.

"Yes, except I can't spend too much time there." I decided not to mention that it might fall down at any moment. "I need to concentrate on getting the house in shape. I'm good besides that. But what are you doing here this soon? I thought you weren't coming until you had hiked all over Scotland and gone to every bookstore you could find."

"That was the plan, but then I twisted my ankle and wasn't making much progress and then I met up with a couple of hikers heading back to London. They offered me a ride."

"Is your ankle okay?" She didn't seem to be favoring it. "We can sit down..." I looked around. "Somewhere else."

"It's fine now but after five miles or so, it really starts to ache."

"Five miles? Is that all?" It was my turn to tease. We all liked to hike but Marni could walk an amazing number of miles in a day compared to the rest of us.

Marni took me seriously. "Yes, I know. Pathetic, isn't it? But forget about me. I want a tour!" She let go of me and looked around. "This place! I love it. Ooooh, is that a tibouchina I see?" She went over to a small tree blocking another door that led into the nearly empty sculpture gallery. I'd been meaning to cut the plant back but since the sculpture gallery contained only one sculpture, I hadn't gotten around to it. It was a pretty plant with purple flowers that had gotten much too big for its space.

"What did you call it?" I asked.

"A tibouchina. It's also called a princess flower. Perfect for a place like this."

"How do you know what it's called?" Marni had all sorts of obscure knowledge from her various part time jobs over the years when she was in school, but I didn't know she knew plants.

"Don't you remember? I told you I worked at a garden store on weekends last year."

"Oh, right." I was a little ashamed I'd completely forgotten. I'd been so taken up with my own problems that I hadn't paid much attention to my sisters' lives. And William had always complained I cared more about them than him.

Marni wandered around checking out different plants, stopping to weave an escapee vine tendril back around the main stem. When she noticed the statue at the far end of the room, she gave a little squeal of delight. "Oh, I love this! Who is it supposed to be? Some muse or something?"

The statue was of a woman in flowing robes with flower vines draped over her head like a veil, holding a pitcher in her hands. "My grandmother always said she thought it was of Chloris, who I guess was a wood nymph in Greek or Roman mythology. I can never remember which."

"Greek," Marni murmured. Of course she would know this. The statue stood on a plinth at the back of a semi-circular raised bed full of some sort of plant with foamy white flowers. Marni knelt down to look at them. "Did this used to be a pool?"

"Yes, the water poured out the pitcher, but even when it was a pool it didn't work very well. My grandmother always complained about how it just trickled out. I haven't even begun to think about getting it fixed."

"It would be spectacular if you could. You could have koi in the pool."

Marni's enthusiasm was nice to see. I tried to smile but the thought of adding fish and fish food to a to-do list would take me over the edge. With my luck, the fish would develop some exotic disease requiring the services of a fish veterinarian, or they'd only eat shrimp flakes from some rare species of Antarctic shrimp which I'd have to import.

"Maybe," I said. "At least our first bride likes it the way it is, so that is one thing that doesn't have to be fixed. I just need to get the place a little less 'Land of the Lost with possible dinosaurs hiding in the ferns' and more like 'lovely old-fashioned conservatory.'"

"Who else is coming to help?" she asked. "I know you said someone named Eleanor would be here, that accountant from William's megachurch."

"Yes, Eleanor, but I didn't invite either one of you here to help! I want you to have fun and relax. I wanted Eleanor to have a break. Her husband died last year and she's worn down from taking care of him during his illness and then dealing with the funeral and all that. She has an eight-year-old son, and he's having a hard time too." I motioned around me. "I thought a change of scene would be good for both of them. She's quit her job and she'd be coming for the wedding anyway. In fact, she's the whole reason we got the wedding booking. The bride is her stepsister."

"I'm sure it will be good for them," Marni said. "This place would be amazing for kids to run around in. You have your own little island on that pond! I saw it when I came up the drive. I can't wait to get a closer look at everything."

"How did you get past the swan?" I asked. Marni didn't look disheveled or out of breath like she'd survived a Palmer death greeting. "I inherited an attack bird along with a mansion."

"I didn't see any swan."

"Oh, good. Though it's probably just on a break from its guard duties. I'm sure it hasn't suddenly had a change of heart and now loves humans. Be on the lookout any time you go outside."

She moved over to look at a large ferny plant trying to consume a rusting bistro table and chair in one corner. "It really won't take all that much work to get the plants in shape. This vine just needs to be trained up around this African Linden, instead of trailing on the floor."

She took one end of the vine and climbed up on the rickety chair.

"Marni, your ankle...that chair is probably not...."

She and the chair toppled over before I finished my sentence.

I darted toward her, knowing I wouldn't reach her before she hit the floor, but she didn't hit after all. Davin de Bourgh caught her as he came into the conservatory. Or rather she fell at him and somehow she ended up in his arms. If it had been me walking in, I probably would have thought I was being attacked by some large flying pterodactyl and put my arms up over my face. He didn't seem to have had that fear and held onto her like it was nothing.

"Whoa!" he said, looking down at her. "Hello. This is a surprise. I don't usually have women falling into my arms."

I doubted that. I could imagine him walking into a bar and having women mysteriously fall off bar stools at him.

He set her down but kept holding onto her until she took a step back from him. "Are you all right?" he asked.

"Yes. Sorry! I don't usually need to be rescued, but thanks for catching me," she said.

"Not a problem. Any time." Now that I knew who he was, I could see the boy Robin better than I had been able to the day before. Davin wasn't dressed as formally as he had been then. Instead of a suit, he wore a button-down shirt and chinos and well-worn boots. I could also see a silver chain around his neck, though I couldn't see what it held, because it was inside his shirt. A gift from a girlfriend? That thought jumped into my head out of nowhere, as if it mattered to me where a piece of jewelry had come from.

He looked over at me. "Your sister let me in but then ran back to the kitchen because something might have been burning. I hope you have some fire extinguishers around."

"Of course we do!" I said a little more sharply than I intended. Did we have one that worked? I actually didn't know.

"Kiki is still trying to figure out the oven," I said to Marni. "It's a monster of a thing called an AGA. I'm scared to go near it." They were both looking at me and I realized I hadn't done any introductions.

"Marni, this is Robin...I mean, Davin De Bourgh. He's a landscape architect who is going to be working on the property. Davin, this is another one of my sisters, Marni Smith." I usually had to explain to people that Marni and Kiki had different last names from me because we were half-sisters with the same mother but different fathers. Looking at Davin I decided not to bother this time. He didn't need to know every detail of our lives.

"Oh hi," Marni said. "I only saw a little of the grounds when I came in, but I could see how fantastic it is. How great you get to work on it."

"It is great," he said. "I'm looking forward to getting started."

"Libby, as I was walking up the drive I had a terrific idea," Marni said. "You have so much land, you could raise llamas here! Wouldn't that be great? Llama wool is very valuable, great for knitting, and you could sell it in local shops. That would give you some extra income."

"Oh, well, we'd have to see about that," I said, though I couldn't imagine dealing with llamas, no matter how much their wool could sell for. Ever since she was a child, Marni had wanted to raise animals that produced wool. Marni had her share of quirky ideas.

"Llamas? I'm not sure the climate is right for them here," Davin said. He looked shocked for some reason, as if Marni had suggested raising hippopotamuses or some equally ridiculous creature. It irritated me, because it really wasn't his business what we raised here.

"Oh, it's perfect. They'd love it here," Marni said. "I know all about them."

"Maybe that wouldn't be such a bad idea." I only said it to annoy him, but he didn't need to know that. "Davin, I've got your proposal in the study, or what used to be the study, if you want to talk in there."

"Why don't we walk around the grounds while we talk? It's easier to visualize the problems and the solutions that way," he said, still glancing at Marni from time to time as if expecting her to go on about the llamas.

I wanted to tell him I could already imagine the problems but he was right, probably better to face them down than try to ignore them.

"Marni, do you want to come with us?" I asked.

"If you don't mind, I want to see Kiki and then I need to check emails and let some people know I haven't fallen off the face of the earth, before someone sends out a missing persons alert on me. I'm kind of behind in all that."

"Oh, right!" I said. "You're probably hungry too. The kitchen is at the back of the house. Kiki will feed you, and then show you to your room. Explore all you want, except don't go up to the third floor. Too many rotten floorboards up there. I'll come find you when I'm done."

"Sounds good. Very nice to meet you," she said to Davin. He smiled at her, though it wasn't exactly full of warmth.

The bit of a smile dropped away when he turned to me. "Shall we?" he asked.

"Yes, of course," I said, thinking I sounded very business-like. As we went out the doors, I saw myself reflected in the glass and realized my hair was still full of flowers, and then I looked down at my feet. No shoes either. *Great, just great. Wonderful way to start off a business meeting, Libby.*

Chapter 6

Countdown to the Raine Randolph/Stefan Andris
Wedding
22 days

<u>To Do List</u>:
Clean the East Room
Get Kiki to order live traps for the mice
Tell Kiki about the additional guests!!!!
~~Look at bills and estimates~~, add new ones to the spreadsheet
~~Read Davin's report~~
~~Find lipstick~~
Meeting with Davin
~~Get a machete for the conservatory~~
Learn to appreciate newts

A PAIR OF Kiki's shoes sat by the door, so I slipped into them, even though they were too big. I pretended they fit just fine as we went outside, squeezing my toes to hold the shoes on my feet. As we walked, I plucked the flowers from my hair and dropped them to the ground in as casual of a way as I could manage, though it looked like I was leaving markers so we could find our way back to the house.

Too late, I also realized I hadn't put on any lipstick, not that Davin would notice anyway. But lipstick wasn't necessary to sound business-like so I led with what I hoped would start a professional conversation. "As I understand it, repairing the course of the stream will help with the soggy ground," I said, to prove I'd read his report.

"Yes, the stream has so much debris in it, it can't handle any excess rain. It will certainly help on the west side of the property." He pointed to the west as if I didn't know my directions. "The other drainage issues will take a bit more work and repair."

"Can the stream problem be fixed before the wedding?" I asked.

"When is it?'

"Um...three weeks."

I could hear a sharp intake of breath from him. "That's not very far away."

As if I didn't know that. I wasn't going to explain all the circumstances. "I'm aware of that, but my sisters are here to help."

He didn't look as if that convinced him of anything, but just because my sisters could seem a little flighty on first meeting them, it didn't meant they couldn't put their minds to something and work hard at it. I wasn't going to try to convince him of that. It had nothing to do with him.

"So can it be fixed in time?" I pressed.

"Yes, at least the part where we clear it out. We may need to bring in some extra stones to stabilize the banks. They'll have to be placed in a way that looks natural, which can take some time but that part can be

done later. I assume the wedding guests won't be wading in the stream."
He did actually smile at me then and I relaxed a tiny bit.

"No, that's not on the schedule," I said. "Though maybe when we're totally operational, we'll offer it as one of the options."

That kept the smile on his face. "You never know who might take you up on that. I've been to some interesting weddings myself."

I wanted to ask if he'd been married, but there was no good way to bring that up, and then I realized he might be currently married and just not wear a wedding ring. Maybe landscape architects didn't. I had no idea.

He interrupted my thoughts on his marital status. "At least we won't need permission to do any of it since we aren't changing anything."

It took me a moment to remember we were talking about the stream.

One bit of good news. "I wanted to ask you about this," I said as I led the way to a garden area on the east side of the house. There was an overgrown pathway through an abandoned cutting garden that led to another water feature, a rectangular one with an ornamental bridge over it. The bridge needed to be painted at some point in the future but was still in fairly good condition, as far as I could tell, or at least not in danger of imminent collapse.

"I thought this might be a good spot for photographs if the water feature could be restored or at least cleaned up. Wasn't this called the Dutch Garden?" I remembered it hadn't been as interesting to us as the stream or the large pond because the area was shallow and full of water lilies, which we weren't supposed to disturb. Its current state gave no hint to its former days of glory. The lilies had disappeared and algae choked most of it.

"Could we fill it in and plant it with lots of showy flowers?" I asked. "It seems like it's going to be a lot of work to maintain it and to get lilies to grow in it again."

He shook his head. "No, it can't be filled in. It's a protected habitat for a colony of crested newts. We can't do anything but manage it."

It took me a moment to process what he'd just said. "Seriously? Crested Newts?" I had a vague idea that newts were sort of like lizards. I scanned the area. "I don't see any newts. Are you sure they are still here? Maybe they moved on." Surely there were other and better more upscale newt colonies.

He bent down and lifted up a rock on the edge of the murky water. A shiny lizard-like creature scurried away and disappeared in the undergrowth. "They're here," he said. "Didn't you read that part of the report? I discussed them. This is an almost perfect habitat for them."

"Um, I was tired when I read it. I guess that part didn't sink in." Great. Just great. "So what do you mean by manage? I don't need to get a newt survey done by a newt specialist, do I? I had to do that for the bats roosting in the roof." Bat specialists didn't come cheap. Newt specialists were probably even more expensive.

"No, you don't need to call experts in since we already know they are here. We can reintroduce the lilies and clean up the edges a little. It was called a Dutch garden because it's supposed to look like a Dutch canal. I suspect that many years ago there were tulips planted all along the edges, but it would be hard to recreate the original look without disturbing the newts."

Must not disturb the newts. At least some creatures on the property had a place to live that didn't need extensive renovations. I didn't want to be told they needed special little newt houses built for them. My jaw tension, which had been easing slightly, came back with a jolt. I tried to move my mouth a bit and heard a crack, but it didn't help much.

"The amount of work you say that needs to be done overall is a bit overwhelming," I said, staring down into the murky water.

"I assure you, I'm not making up work." From the coldness in his voice, I realized I hadn't worded my sentence right. He thought I was accusing him of adding on work that didn't need to be done.

Before I could explain what I meant, he added, "In fact, the value of the work is more than double the funds your grandmother set aside for it. I'm willing to do it all because I have a fondness for the place. I'd hate to see it fall into even more disrepair."

"I don't want you to do work you can't be paid for," I snapped. "Do what you can with the money set aside, and then later I'll pay you for what else needs to be done." I was certainly not going to accept charity.

"We didn't know everything was so bad." He really did think it was my fault for the current state of the place. If he was trying to make me feel guilty, it was working. "My grandmother had an estate manager and a housekeeper while she was in the nursing home in the U.S.. They never told us about any problems and then we found out the estate manager was not doing his job and he was ripping us off too, by selling off things in the house."

"But the housekeeper did write to your grandmother," Davin said. "She told me so."

"You're still in touch with Mrs. Ellis?"

"Yes, she's in a care home near here. I saw her shortly before she moved there."

"I didn't know where she'd gone." When Kiki and I first arrived, Mr. Mackenzie told us the housekeeper had nothing to do with the theft of the furniture, but I'd been so angry the woman hadn't informed my grandmother about it, I didn't bother to try to contact her. It's not like the housekeeper and I had ever been close. I had mostly stayed out of her way when I'd visited.

"I never saw the letters," I said. "My grandmother never mentioned anything about this." I'd assumed since my grandmother hadn't known the estate manager was stealing the furniture, he hadn't told her things were being left to ruin either. As I said that, I realized if there had been letters, my stepmother would have seen them. After my father's death, my stepmother supposedly took over dealing with everything. When my father died without a will, it left a huge mess. I had offered to help my stepmother with paperwork, but she'd turned me down.

"I didn't want to bring it up in my letters to your grandmother because I thought she was aware of the situation and there were money issues," Davin said. "I wish I would have now."

"She wrote to you?" My grandmother had never mentioned Davin de Bourgh and she had never asked me to help with any estate details. I would have gladly done so.

"Yes, she didn't write often because she said she didn't have much to say. She wrote about you, though. She was very proud of you. Especially when you graduated from law school and then passed the bar exam." There was something in his voice, like he almost wanted to make it a question, and I feared that meant he somehow knew I hadn't actually passed the bar. But he'd have no way of knowing that. I was just letting my own shame make me paranoid. It had been the worst lie I'd ever told.

I almost blurted out the truth, that I lied about passing the bar exam to make my grandmother happy. She was so worried for me because she knew how stressed I was about it. I didn't think it would help her to know when I got the results. She had been fading fast at that point.

Before I could decide how much else to say, my phone buzzed. It was a number I didn't recognize, but I did recognize the area code, Charlotte, North Carolina. I declined the call and put my phone on silent mode. I was afraid William was using a different number so I'd answer. He'd tried that already.

I sighed. "Look, I'll admit I'm overwhelmed by the problems with the grounds. Do what you think needs to be done. I don't care." I kicked at one of the taller weeds. I'd care if I had more time, but the garden had to remain low on my list. It was just one more burden.

"Fine," Davin said. "I'll have a crew here tomorrow. We'll start on the drainage issue and I'll have someone help Mr. Mackenzie spruce up the front of the house. I assume you want it to look good for the wedding guests."

"Yes, fine." We seemed to be saying fine a lot, but I didn't feel fine.

He hesitated and then said, "You know, if you ever decide to sell the place, I know someone who would be interested."

"I'm not selling the place! Where did you get that idea?"

"It is quite a commitment of time and money. Not something most people would want to take on. You said you were overwhelmed. I'm not sure raising llamas is going to help you either. I'm just saying I hope you let me know if you decide you want to do something else. It's a fantastic place and I'd hate to see it fall into the wrong hands."

He'd only talked to me twice for a few minutes total and he'd apparently already decided I couldn't complete the renovation. Was I really projecting that much incompetence? I took hold of my bracelet and twisted it around, giving myself time so that when I spoke, my voice would be steady.

"It's going to stay in my hands," I said, deciding a few words were all I needed to say on that subject. I made the mistake of taking a step backwards to move farther away from him. It was distracting me to be so close to him. But in doing so, I put my foot down too close to the bank and it slipped in the mud. He caught me just as I was about to crash down on Newtville, which would have been like some horror movie out of the 1950s involving a giant woman destroying a peaceful town.

He smelled good, very outdoorsy, which I reminded myself is exactly how he should have smelled, being outdoors so much of the time. It would have been weird if I caught the scent of something like attorney office leather or attorney expensive cologne or church flowers or any other scent I'd come to avoid. Whatever he smelled like, it was distracting me and I couldn't think straight.

Trying to get ahold of myself, I moved to more solid ground, and he let go of my arm. "Thanks," I said. "I should be more careful. Perhaps we can schedule a time next week to go over where we are at, and how everything is progressing."

"Fine," he said. "Would it be possible to get your phone number so I can text you to schedule something?" Very business-like of him.

"Of course," We exchanged phone numbers and then there didn't seem to be anything left to say. I had been planning on asking what had happened to the rest of our gang of children but the time didn't seem right. He seemed so far away from the boy he had been, he really was a stranger. "I should get back to work," I said.

"I'll let you get on with it then," he said.

Mr. Mackenzie appeared and launched into a discussion with Davin about the shrubbery at the end of the drive, so I said goodbye and went back inside, not feeling great about how the whole meeting had gone. It was as if we'd never met before, had never laughed ourselves silly over our attempts at pirate talk or had shared in the excitement of finding a broken bit of pottery when we'd dug for treasure.

It was better that way. The past was done. He was a different person. So was I. He probably didn't even remember most of it.

Feeling bad I'd left Marni to fend for herself, I went in search of her but found only Kiki in the kitchen.

"I got her something to eat and then showed her to her room," Kiki said, "and she's sending emails right now. She said not to worry about her and that she doesn't want to get in the way."

"Okay, thanks," I said. "I'm off to clean the East Room."

She went back to her laptop. "Better you than me."

Emmaline had told me we needed a room for brides to dress in and the East Room seemed the best place for that. The room was a pretty little space with faded floral wallpaper and a white marble fireplace adorned with carved foliage. One of the pieces of furniture I most regretted losing was a small antique writing desk that had been placed in one corner with a view out of the windows of the gardens. There had also been an old worktable pushed against the east wall where my grandmother had kept pots of geraniums. The pots had been there when she'd first come to Pemberley and even though at the time she wasn't a fan of geraniums, she'd come to enjoy them, and kept up the tradition of placing them there. I had a plan to replace the table and get new geraniums someday, but neither of those were important enough to go on a list.

The only furniture remaining when we'd arrived had been an ancient footstool with a shredded top and a few bits of stuffing scattered about the floor. Most of the stuffing was gone, no doubt carried off by thieving mice to what must have been their well-padded apartments in the walls. I had a chaise lounge and a dressing table and chair on order which absolutely had to arrive before the wedding. Emmaline had insisted on them.

Earlier, I had cleared away the worst of the cobwebs, but the whole room still needed to be dusted and scrubbed down. Betsey followed me as I wheeled the cart of cleaning supplies in. The cart had originally been a drink cart, probably from the 1920s or 1930s, but it had rusted badly and one of the wheels wobbled so much, it lurched as it moved. I could imagine the piece in its heyday, being wheeled into the library by a butler, so guests could enjoy an aperitif. Now it held floor cleaner, a mop, wood polish, a dustpan, a pail of water and assorted sponges.

Betsey walked around gingerly, lifting up the one paw she had put down and giving it a quick bath. "There's too much dust in here still," I said to her. She apparently agreed and backed away, somewhere out of my sight. I was thankful she hadn't meowed to demand I clean a path for her.

More spiderwebs had appeared since I'd last done a bit of cleaning. I didn't see any actual spiders but I knew they had to be somewhere. The webs didn't generate themselves out of the ether. Spiders weren't as bad as mice, but they were not high on my list of creatures I wanted to befriend. I took the broom off the cart to get the worst of the spider webs and to provide myself a weapon in case a ninja spider leapt on me.

I hoped to find a big mirror in the attic we could put in the room once it was clean. The attic at Pemberley was vast, and some of it was undamaged from the roof leaks. Given the amount of undisturbed dust, our estate manager thief hadn't been absolutely thorough in looting there. Much of it was broken furniture and old books my grandmother hadn't gotten around to restoring, but there were also some pieces that had been placed there mainly because they'd gone out of fashion.

When I'd been up in the attic as a child, I had been much more interested in the trunks of old clothes, because my grandmother had let me play dress up with them. I still wondered what had happened to my favorite, a dark red beaded velvet cape that my grandmother had said was called an opera cape. By the time I had discovered it, half the beading had fallen off and there were little moth holes throughout it, but I had loved it, feeling like it made me brave and invincible. I didn't know what had happened to it, though I assumed the housekeeper had just thrown it away at some point.

I wished I had a bravery cape as I tackled the cobwebs, trying to keep from shrieking as some fell on me and stuck to my hair. Once that was done, I sponged down the walls, finishing just as the doorbell rang. I hadn't heard Palmer the swan squawking at anyone's approach so the sudden noise made me drop the sponge into the bucket, splashing some of the water up on me. I realized I should have changed my clothes before I started. My nicest clean outfit was now my grubbiest outfit.

The doorbell rang again. No time to change. I went to the hall and opened the door to find a woman in a gray business suit and impossibly high heels. Her dark hair was pulled back in a sleek bun and her makeup was perfect. I tried to keep up a confident face but she was the type of woman who made me want to curl up in a ball. I'd seen plenty like her in law school and at the law firm where I'd interned. Some women manage to keep their hair and their nails and their makeup and their business attire perfect for hours on end, whereas I can manage maybe one or two of those things but not all of them no matter how hard I tried.

"Hello," she said. "I'm looking for Libby Darcy."

"Um...that's me," I said. I couldn't think why a woman like her would be at the house. Emmaline would have told me if any wedding-related people were supposed to appear.

"Do you think I could come in?" the woman asked.

I realized I'd been staring at her as if she were some sort of image on television.

"Oh, yes, of course." I moved backwards and she came in, her pointy heals making clicking noises on the tiles.

I felt a bit of cobweb tickle my face and I brushed my hair back, wondering how bad I looked. I knew I probably had dirt on my face.

She took in the hallway, her gaze moving around the entire space and then she turned to me. "I'm Caro Bingley, of the Bingley Hotel Group. We sent you a letter, but since I hadn't heard from you and I was in the area, I thought I'd stop in and we could discuss the contents of the letter without all the back and forth and go-betweens."

"Oh," I said, trying to focus on her words. I'd never expected a real person to appear as a follow up to the letter.

"And I admit I wanted to see the inside of the place," she added. "I haven't been here since I was a child. It's gotten quite rundown, hasn't it?"

"You've been here before?" I didn't think she was the adult version of any child I'd met here, but since I had been mistaken about Davin, I couldn't be sure. I'd been the only girl in our little gang of playmates but it was possible I'd met her at some village event.

"Yes," she replied. "I have relatives at Bingley Manor right down the road. Surely you know it?"

"Yes." My grandmother had liked old Mr. Bingley but hadn't been fond of one of his daughters who had run the place. Supposedly the Bingleys and the Darcys were related somehow far back in time, but I'd never inquired as to the connection. I hadn't ever met any of them as far as I remembered and we'd never had an occasion to go there.

"I'm sorry you've wasted your time coming here but I am not interested in selling. I haven't had time to respond to your letter."

She didn't reply to this. Instead, she said, "I hear you are trying to turn it into a wedding venue."

How had she heard that? Only a few people knew and they weren't people this woman would know. The upcoming wedding had fallen into our laps, and I wanted to get through one to make sure it wasn't a disaster before committing to anything else with a lot of publicity.

"Yes," I said. "That's the plan."

"Hmmm...Renovation work is so costly and time consuming, especially with listed buildings. I suppose you know all about the rules and regulations."

I could hear the questioning note in her comment.

"Yes, I know. We're getting everything approved as we move along." I didn't add what a headache it all was. I didn't want to sound like I wasn't all in on the project.

"That's good, because if the commission finds out you aren't renovating correctly, they can force you to redo it all, no matter what the cost."

She looked around as if trying to find evidence of some error to report.

"I'm not really interested in selling," I repeated.

"You're American, right?"

I knew she knew I was American, because my accent was obvious. "Well, I have dual citizenship because my father was British, but yes, technically I'm American if you consider where I grew up."

"I'm only asking because most Americans don't fully understand how difficult it is to renovate these monstrosities."

"Oh, I'm aware of that. Yes, it is difficult but I like a challenge."

She raised an eyebrow and I knew she didn't believe me.

At that moment Betsey appeared with something in her mouth. I could only hope it wasn't more underwear. When I got a better look, I thought it might actually be one of the many cat toys I'd bought for her to convince her she was in a happy place. Up until that moment, she'd mostly ignored them.

It seemed to be one of the toy catnip mice. I could see a tail sticking out of Betsey's mouth. She brought it over and laid it at my feet. I stared down at it, slowly realizing it wasn't a toy mouse at all. It was very much real and very much alive and very mouse-like. Before I could react, it wiggled and then staggered to its feet. Betsey put a paw on its very real tail but then the mouse darted away into the East Room. Betsey ran after it. I stopped breathing.

When I started breathing again, I glanced up at Ms. Bingley. She didn't look as horrified as I felt. In fact, she let out a little laugh. "You poor dear," she said. "Let's talk money. I'll offer you a more than fair price and you won't have to deal with years of work here." She named a sum and it was all I could do not to gasp. It was far more than the estate had been valued at.

"What do you think?" she asked. "Shall I have the papers drawn up?"

The amount she offered would be enough to buy a small house and send Kiki to culinary school and have enough left for me to live on for several years. I immediately thought of a long ago dream of mine, to have a cottage with one room set aside for painting, and of seeing my work for sell. It had always been just a dream, because I knew how hard it was to get a painting or a show in a gallery. Could that actually become a reality? I hadn't wanted the legal career I'd tried for. Did I want this? My head was so muddled with everything, I didn't know what I wanted.

A breeze blew threw from the windows I'd opened in the East Room, and the scent of the roses came with it. I'd considered selling Pemberley when I'd first learned about the inheritance. Both my mother and William had pushed me to do so. Was I only holding onto it to do the opposite of what they wanted? Was I only holding onto it because of the memories of a few happy summers?

And then I remembered my grandmother could have sold Pemberley herself, but she'd chosen to keep it and to leave it to me. That meant she thought I could manage it, though her belief in me was based on thinking I could accomplish things, like passing the bar. I wanted to accomplish something even if I hadn't managed that.

I heard myself saying, "No, I'm sorry, I'm not interested."

She gave a tiny shrug. "All right. I'll be curious if you still feel the same way a month from now. My offer stands, though I don't know for how long. If another similar property becomes available, we'll use our expansion funds on that instead of Pemberley, but I do expect to hear from you. Trust me. This project is too much for one person. The sooner you get away from this, the better."

She didn't wait for a reply, which was good, because I didn't have one. The door closed behind her before I could move.

Chapter 7

Countdown to the Raine Randolph/Stefan Andris

Wedding

22 days

To Do List:

~~Clean the East Room~~

Get Kiki to order live traps for the mice

Tell Kiki about the additional guests!!!!

~~Look at bills and estimates~~, add new ones to the spreadsheet

~~Read Davin's report~~

~~Find lipstick~~

~~Meeting with Davin~~ ☻

~~Get a machete for the conservatory~~

Learn to appreciate newts

I WAS STILL standing there when Marni came down the stairs.

"Now I remember why I hate emails and why I needed a vacation," she said. "And why I was serious about working on the conservatory. I need something active after sitting in front of my laptop."

"Except you should probably rest your ankle," I said, trying to focus on Marni. I still didn't understand why Ms. Bingley had shown up in person. It made me think they really did want the place, which seemed a poor negotiating strategy. But then I'd never been good at strategy, so what did I know?

"The ankle is fine as long as I don't go on long hikes," Marni said. "I'll take plenty of breaks. Have you got garden tools, like pruners and loppers?"

I'd think about the Bingley offer later. "Mr. Mackenzie does." Better to concentrate on what could be done that day. "If you're sure you want to do it. The bride wants to have drinks served in the conservatory as the guests arrive before the ceremony, except I don't know how we are going to manage that if it rains."

I rubbed my eyes, feeling so tired I was afraid I'd burst into tears at any moment. I never used to be weepy so it was annoying that the slightest thing wrong at Pemberley made me want to cry. I grabbed hold of my bracelet, reminding myself to hold it together. I'd told Davin de Bourgh I could manage, and I would, at least for that day. Random weeping was not going to help at all.

"We'll think of something. Hey, I'm curious. You said the stuff on the top floor was damaged, but what happened down here? Where is all the furniture and everything else? I'd have expected this place to be full of paintings and knickknacks and mirrors and vases and everything that people accumulate when they've lived in a place for a long time."

I explained about the estate manager and what Davin had told me about the letters. "That's why there are no mirrors in the place, not because we are afraid we're vampires, and why the sculpture gallery has only one sculpture in it." I was still angry enough about it all to want to kick something. "I wish I had known what the man was doing because I could have been able to stop it."

"Well, that really sucks," Marni said. "Curses on him. May he be eaten by fire ants or leopards or something equally painful."

That actually made me laugh. "Yes, curses on him! Oh, but you should see the one remaining sculpture. It's got a plaque on it that says 'Fitzwilliam Darcy.' It must be a long-ago relative!" A sudden drumming of rain on the glass drowned out her response. "Uh oh. I need to make sure we've got enough buckets in the conservatory." I went back in, this time nearly wrenching the door off its hinges to get it open. A splash of water hit me on the forehead and ran down my face.

I glanced around to find only two buckets next to the door where I'd put them after emptying them out last time it rained. "Can you put those buckets under the worst drips?" I said to Marni who had followed me in. "I need to get some pans from the kitchen to catch the leaks so the whole place doesn't flood. I told Kiki to leave them but she's nabbed them again." The majority of our buckets were strategically placed on the third floor to catch drips. We'd resorted to pans for the conservatory.

"No problem," Marni said. "Go!"

"Kiki! We need those big pans," I called as I barreled through the kitchen door. There were two people in the kitchen. At first I thought the extra might be a delivery person, but then I recognized her. Katie, Kiki's ex-friend. Drama girl, as I nicknamed her because every small thing became worthy of a stage production for her.

"Katie, what are you doing here?" I blurted out. I looked over at Kiki. She avoided my eyes. I'm sure she hadn't mentioned Katie was coming to visit. If she had, I would not have encouraged it.

"Libby! Great to see you! Kiki told me all about the place and since I'm taking another gap year to finish the draft of my novel, I thought I'd pop in when Kiki invited me," Katie said. She paused and glanced back and forth between Kiki and me. "You look surprised. I hope Kiki told you I was coming and it's all right?"

Kiki continued to avoid my gaze. I noticed the luggage piled on the floor. I had a sinking feeling Katie wouldn't be popping out soon after popping in. It's not that I didn't like the girl but Kiki had taken their friendship breakup hard. My sister was all confidence and sunshine on the outside, but inside she spent every day worrying she wasn't good enough, thanks to our darling mother. Katie had stolen Kiki's first and only boyfriend, which had really brought her confidence down.

"Um...we've been so busy, it slipped my mind," Kiki said. "I knew Libby wouldn't mind, right? And Katie can help me with the food for the wedding. Right, Katie?"

"Right!" Katie flung her arm around Kiki's shoulders. "I'm not too bad in the kitchen. I can make great pancakes."

I wasn't sure pancake making was top of the list of skills we needed. They were both looking at me and I realized Kiki was wanting me to agree I wouldn't mind about Katie.

"I don't mind," I said, though it was a little like suddenly getting an extra sister I'd have to worry about. When Eleanor and her son arrived, I'd have them to fret about as well. My worry basket was already nearly overflowing.

"Kiki said there is an amazing library in the house. And she was just telling me about the ghost! That is freaking awesome!" Katie was so excited she was rocking back and forth on her feet as if she were about to do a ghost hunting sprint. "Maybe there are even secret passages and hidden stairways that have never been found. I can't wait to look."

I didn't mind her childlike enthusiasm. It was the sort of place to inspire that. "I think I'd know if there were any secret passages," I said, "but you can look."

"And it's so exciting that Raine Randolph is actually getting married here!" Katie's eyes got very big. "I can't wait to see her in person. I loved her in Ice Planet Earth when I was little! I must have watched that movie a hundred times."

"It is exciting," I said, "but it also needs to be a secret, so don't post about it on social media anywhere, okay? She doesn't want any paparazzi, and our reputation as a wedding venue will be hurt if we can't do what she wants."

"Okay." Katie made a zipping motion across her mouth. "I can keep a secret."

I hoped that was true. "We have a lot of work to do to get ready." I knew I was sounding like a mood killer, but the girl had to know what she'd walked into. "Did Kiki tell you the house is not in great shape? We're kind of camping out on the second floor. The roof and windows leaked so much we had to throw out mattresses and curtains and rugs. They got all moldy."

"It won't bother me," Katie said. "I stayed in a youth hostel in London for a couple of days and I didn't mind."

"Great, but the upper floors are about at the level of a youth hostel, so I hope you are serious that it won't bother you," I said, trying to think of another way to discourage a lengthy visit. I glanced at Kiki again. She was beaming at Katie. I hoped Kiki stayed that happy. She had been doing so much better since we came to England. I didn't want her to go backwards.

A burst of thunder reminded me why I'd gone to the kitchen in the first place. Ever since I'd started on the renovation, my mind couldn't focus on any one thing for long. It's as if once I had too much to juggle, I couldn't juggle anything.

"We need those big saucepans again," I said to Kiki. "Why don't you just leave them in the conservatory?"

"I hate to see them sitting on the floor," Kiki said, giving a little shudder. "You're going to have to get real buckets. If the food inspector shows up, I don't want her to see the good pans sitting on the floor in another room."

Kiki was right, unfortunately. "Okay, move buying more buckets to the top of the 'to buy' list, but today we need the saucepans," I said. "It's hard to get the water up off the floor if too much rain falls."

I grabbed as many as I could carry. Marni and I placed them around in strategic spots. As soon as they were all in place, the rain stopped.

"It's usually this way," I said, surveying the wet floor. "I'll get a mop."

After we finished cleaning up the water, Marni said, "I'd really love to get started on some real work in here. You said there were tools I could use?"

"I don't want you to think you need to jump right in and get to work after you just got here."

"I was serious. I really, really need to do something that doesn't involve my own work. Please!"

She did sound serious, and a little desperate, which was weird. "Okay then, since you are sure. Let's go find Mr. Mackenzie. He has a garden shed/office where he goes when it rains. Maybe he's still there."

As we made our way to his shed, I told Marni about Katie's arrival. "I just hope she doesn't upset Kiki, not now, not when Kiki is doing so well here."

"At least she's an extra pair of hands to help, that's good, right? She can be Kiki's kitchen minion in payment for room and board, just like I'm going to be your garden minion for the same reason."

"That's not why I invited you!"

"It really will be fun for me to help, I promise. I know you are sometimes too proud to ask for help, but I'm helping whether you like it or not. You don't always have to prove yourself, not to me."

Marni had talked me through many tough times when I was ready to quit college, when I was sure I was going to fail, encouraging me to find study partners, and telling me to break down the work into small bits instead of just floundering around at the enormity of it all. She had been sort of my own personal life coach, which was a little embarrassing considering she was the younger sister. I'd hoped I'd outgrown needing her as a coach but here she was again propping me up.

"Okay," I said. "But I want you to relax here too."

"Working with plants is relaxing so let me get started."

"Mr. Mackenzie is a man of few words," I warned her as we drew close to the shed. He'd seemed old back when I was a child so I'd been shocked to learn he still worked at Pemberley. He'd been devoted to my grandmother, which meant I hadn't the heart to ask him to leave, even though it would have been practical to hire someone with more energy. So far, I'd let him do whatever he thought needed doing, because I certainly didn't know anything about gardening.

"He is actually really kind in his own way though," I added, "so if he acts like he doesn't want to talk to you, it's more bluster than anything else."

When I first came to visit my grandmother, I'd been scared of her, having heard stories from my own mother about how terrible she was.

How my grandmother was a recluse who hated people, who hated Americans, and who hated children.

None of that was true of course. My grandmother didn't like my mother, but she was neither a recluse nor a witch, and she actually was quite fond of children, as I came to learn. But that first summer, I'd spent as much time as possible in Samuel's and Mr. Mackenzie's cottage, where the snug spaces and plain furniture were less intimidating than the halls of Pemberley, and less intimidating than the plain-spoken woman who oversaw it all. Samuel and I ran in and out of the cottage, taking biscuits from a tin that seemed to magically refill. Mr. Mackenzie was gruff with both of us, but I knew behind his manner he was glad to have Samuel about, and me as Samuel's friend.

Mr. Mackenzie was just coming out of the shed when Marni and I reached it. I introduced them. He nodded at Marni but didn't speak.

"Is that a Golden Rain tree that's been newly planted along the drive?" Marni asked him. "I didn't know they did well here."

She said the right thing. His expression brightened. "Aye." He began talking about how he'd always wanted to plant one, and then they got into a discussion about water needs and amounts of sunlight.

After several minutes, Marni looked over at me. "Libby, don't worry about me. You can go do what you need to do. I'd like to ask Mr. Mackenzie more about some of the plants here if he has a few minutes."

I walked back to the house, thinking how well Marni could get along with Davin, since she knew about plants and all. That is, if he was willing to find out more about her and not just judge her for her llama idea. The two would have something in common, which I'd come to realize was far more important than I'd imagined when I was younger.

When I'd foolishly agreed to become engaged to William, he'd been happy to talk about his interests with me, and I'd listened, thinking I too would get interested in golf and Bible study. But I'd been unable to care about golf, especially William's version which meant spending hours at a country club fawning over wealthy donors. And William's Bible study groups were just him pontificating and being sanctimonious. He got bored when I talked about art or movies or music, so we'd ended up just talking about the people we knew, which was not all that interesting. I was much better off without him.

Back inside the house, Betsey was waiting for me. "Hey, Sweetie, you and I will stick together, right? We don't need any distractions of the male variety."

Betsey flicked her tail in agreement. I took out my to-do list. I finished off a few items and did remember to tell Kiki about the extra guests. She jumped immediately to her spreadsheet to recalculate amounts of ingredients like it was the most fun task imaginable.

Later at dinner, I had to admit the extra people made the meal more fun. I'd been thinking guests would be a drain because I'd have to entertain them, but Marni and Katie ended up doing the entertaining. It was nice not to be just Kiki and myself, constantly talking about things that needed to be done.

When Kiki brought out the first plate, I held my breath, a little afraid of what she'd unveil.

She set it down and grinned, revealing a plate of gorgeous rice paper rolls in a rainbow of colors. "Chopped shrimp with purple cabbage, carrots, red peppers, lettuce, yellow beets and a bit of hoisin sauce," she explained. "Jump in."

"These are almost too pretty to eat," Marni said. "Almost. I'm way too hungry not to eat them."

We were quiet for a minute while we devoured them.

"Yes?" Kiki asked. "What do you think?"

"Yes," I said. "Amazing."

"You get to decide the food?" Katie asked her. "I thought brides wanted to taste everything and they decided."

"Luckily not this bride," I explained. "Raine wants the table full of different bites of food. She said she wants it to look like 'a table set for magical creatures in the woods' as she described it, so as long as it's beautiful and colorful and there are enough vegan and vegetarian choices, she doesn't care. We'll have a lot more work to do before we can have other weddings though. Emmaline says we need to come up with a whole list of possibilities and then be prepared to do samples when people come to look over the place."

That part seemed like a tremendous amount of work to me, but Kiki had assured me it wouldn't be too bad. She'd never been frazzled by working in her dad's diner back home, no matter how busy it had gotten. The few times I'd helped out, I'd been totally wiped out at the end of the day.

William and I hadn't gotten to the food stage of our wedding planning before I broke it off. Planning my own wedding was something I had avoided, which probably should have been a clue to me that the relationship wasn't going to work out.

"I've been texting Raine with my ideas and she's been happy with all of them," Kiki said. "Emmaline told me Raine is used to delegating work, so she doesn't micro manage unless it's something she wants to be very involved in."

"You've been texting her?" I asked. I was glad Emmaline hadn't asked me to text the bride. I was sure to send some wrong message.

"Yes, Emmaline gave her my number and said we should stay in touch. I'm so excited. It really will be beautiful. The florist is going to decorate the table with ferns and flowers among the food trays.

Raine had all these wooden trays made for the food itself, and she's also providing the china, something she's going to keep for future entertaining."

We would have struggled to buy the serving trays and china ourselves on such short notice. We'd have to invest in all that for the future but I thanked my stars not for this wedding. I was still seething that all my grandmother's china and silver were gone. There had been many pieces collected over the generations we could have used.

"Next course!" Kiki announced. "Silver dollar cornmeal pancakes topped with muhammara. Katie made them."

Those too were delicious, as were the other things Kiki and Katie brought out. I decided not only that I should be glad Katie showed up, I could at least stop worrying that the food wouldn't taste good. Whether or not it could all get done at the right time and be unburnt on the day of the wedding was still a question though.

I relaxed a little. We might be able to do this. At least for one wedding.

My phone pinged. A text from Emmaline. *You like dogs, right? Neither you nor Kiki are allergic to them, right?*

Right, I texted back. *Why?*

I waited but the reply didn't come immediately. When it did, it just said *We'll talk tomorrow.* I promptly forgot all about it.

Chapter 8

Countdown to the Raine Randolph/Stefan Andris

Wedding

22 days

To Do List:

~~Clean the East Room~~

Get Kiki to order live traps for the mice

~~Tell Kiki about the additional guests!!!!~~

~~Pay one bill. Look at bills and estimates~~, add new ones to the spreadsheet

~~Read Davin's report~~

~~Find lipstick~~

~~Meeting with Davin~~ ☻

~~Get a machete for the conservatory~~

Learn to appreciate newts

AFTER DINNER, Kiki and Katie shooed Marni and I out of the

kitchen. "Take a bottle of wine somewhere and catch up," Kiki said. "Marni, don't let her work anymore tonight. She needs a break."

"I can make sure of that," Marni said. "Hand over the wine and we'll get out of here."

My phone buzzed with the same unfamiliar number and North Carolina area code. I declined it, thankful an ocean stood between William and myself.

I was about to protest that I had more cleaning to do but Marni already had the bottle in hand. "Bring the glasses and show me a room that has furniture in it," she said. "Preferably somewhere we won't be dripped on if it rains again."

I gave in. "The library, as long as the mice haven't gotten together in the past few day to unstuff the old sofas." I hadn't spent much time in the room since we'd arrived, though I loved it. It was too easy to get distracted by taking a book off the shelf and getting lost in it. I couldn't afford distractions.

Marni walked in and gave a little gasp. "This is awesome! I would have lived in this room as a child."

"It is amazing," I said. I turned on the lamp and settled on one of the lumpy sofas in the middle of the room next to the fireplace. I hadn't noticed Betsey following us until she jumped up beside me.

As I watched Marni explore, I realized it was good to see someone else appreciating the place, because I usually just saw things to be dusted or repaired. The room had been designed as a serious library, not just to display books with fancy covers. There had been desks or reading chairs at each of the large windows, but the walls themselves were completely covered with bookshelves. The two remaining sofas stood in the middle of the room and two refectory table took up space, one at each end. One of the tables held some ancestor's display cases of his bird egg collection, and the other held books too large for the shelves, mainly atlases. One giant rug covered the center of the room and smaller rugs were laid on each end.

Marni wandered around. "Some of these books look really old. Are any of these valuable? You're lucky your villainous estate manager didn't take off with them."

"Yes, some of them are valuable though it would take an expert to know which ones. I think that's why they were saved. The estate manager didn't want to bring someone in who might ask too many questions about why the books were being sold. When I first got here, the library doors were locked and I couldn't find any keys. I guess the housekeeper locked up the room when she left, though it wasn't before most of the smaller pieces of furniture must have been moved out. I had to have a locksmith come out to open up the room."

I had nearly made myself sick waiting for the man to get in the door, afraid all I'd find were rows of empty shelves. Seeing the rows of books once the door had been opened almost made up for everything else that had been stolen.

"Didn't you tell me a long time ago your grandfather was a bookbinder?" she asked as she flipped open one of the atlases.

"No, it was my grandmother. That's how she met my grandfather. She was hired to repair some of the books. I always thought it was kind of a romantic way to meet. After they were married, she made sure every book in here was in as good a condition as possible. You should have a better look tomorrow in more daylight. The lighting in here isn't great."

"I will definitely do that."

"My house is your house," I said. I meant it. I couldn't believe I'd wanted to disinvite Marni. Now that she was here, she lightened the dread that had been hanging over me ever since we booked the wedding on such short notice.

Marni took a seat on the sofa across from me. I poured us both some wine. "Tell me where you'll be living and all that when you start teaching," I said.

"I don't know yet." She stared at her glass instead of looking at me. "I need to get back online and do some looking." Her tone was unenthusiastic.

I was a little shocked since she only had a couple of months before classes began. "You are happy about the job, aren't you?" If anyone could recognize avoidance and what it meant, it was me.

"Yes, I mean, I should be." She sighed. "I don't know. It's all getting real now. You work for something for a long time that's in the distance, and the working for it becomes your life. You're used to that, and it's comfortable. Now that I'm there, it will be a major switch. I'll have to convince other people I'm good enough at what I claim I can do. It's way more pressure than I expected and I haven't even started yet." She swirled the wine in her glass and then took a drink. "I don't want to sound like I'm complaining. So many people would give anything to be where I'm at, but it's hard to believe I can actually do what I'm supposed to do."

I understood that. We were often our worst enemies, always listening to the voices telling us we couldn't do things. It wasn't usually like Marni to have doubts though.

"You know why I know you can do it?" I said. "Because when you talk about social stratification and private school education in the twentieth century, you can actually make other people excited about it too, people who wouldn't normally care about anything except how to...how to do something silly like take a picture with a penguin so they can trend on social media. You have a tremendous skill. You are going to be a tremendous teacher."

"Maybe," she said. "At least I know I can always call you for a pep talk."

"Any time!" I said. "I owe you several hundred pep talks."

She leaned forward. "Enough about me. Now tell me exactly what happened with William. You didn't give me a lot of details in your message about the breakup and I know enough not to believe Mom's version."

William had been so far from my thoughts for the last several hours that I hated to bring him back into my head. But I couldn't avoid her question. It was better to explain once and be done with it, rather than brushing her off and having her question me again at another time. I shifted around, trying to find the most comfortable spot among the lumps on the sofa while I figured out how to make the explanation as brief as possible. "I finally realized he was never going to stop treating me like a child, a child to be told what to do, what to think, and how to behave. I can't believe now I said yes in the first place, but he wore me down asking me to marry him all the time, and Mom was pushing for it. I think if my dad had still been alive, I never would have said yes."

Betsey got up and bumped my hand. I nearly spilled my wine. "Hey, clumsy! What are you doing?" I moved my hand away so she jumped down in a huff and skulked away. I went back to the rest of my explanation. "The whole thing with his father's church was the last straw. William lied to me. I knew he was religious, but he never once said in all the years I knew him that he was going to take over his father's church. The time I asked him what he planned for the future, he just told me he was going to work in the organization and write his books. I should have realized what it meant. I should have asked him for more details. It's partly my fault."

"It's not your fault. A lie of omission is still a lie," Marni said. "I'm sorry." She seemed to be struggling to find something else to add, so I held up my hand to stop her.

"I know you never liked him, and I know this is all for the best. You don't have to say anything else." I leaned over to clink my glass against hers. "I'm just so glad you are here. Let's not talk about him anymore. I don't even want to think about him."

Marni poured more wine for herself but I waved away her offer to top off mine. Morning was going to come soon enough.

"I won't bring him up anymore," she said. "You've come to a great place to forget about him."

"Yes, though it makes me remember lots of other things. Now that I'm here, I feel bad that my grandmother spent so many years living away from Pemberley. She loved it so much."

"But I thought you told me she couldn't live here on her own, not once her MS got bad."

"Yes, though when she moved to the states so my father could help her out, he only lived two years after that. I never even asked if she wanted to come back to England once he was gone. I should have asked." All the guilt I'd been holding in poured out and I came very close to letting some tears out until I saw the stricken look on Marni's face. "I'm sorry," I said. "I shouldn't dump all that on you."

"Don't be silly! Say anything you want. At least she got to be near you in the states. I'm sure she wanted that more than she wanted to come back to England. You were close, right? She would have told you if she wanted something different."

"I suppose." I knew she never wanted to be a burden on anyone. She was too proud for that. I had to find something else to talk about because the tears were still threatening and I'd just dumped too much on Marni.

"All right, I can tell you don't want to talk about this anymore." Marni knew me too well. She especially knew I didn't like to cry. "Let's talk about the wedding. I guess it didn't register with me that you have two famous actors coming here. Worries about paparazzi! That's big time wedding issues, not just something like the groom getting drunk and not showing up. What else can I do besides help with the conservatory?"

Talking about the wedding was actually a relief compared to talking about family or William. "Well, Raine wants some photographs outside, so we need to find some scenic spots and get those cleaned up. You could look about and tell me which sites wouldn't take too much work to get into shape and would make good photographs." I'd always been impressed by Marni's photography skills. She'd taken one class in college and blown me away with the portfolio she'd made from it. "I'm having a hard time focusing on anything outside with so much to do inside," I added.

"What did your landscape architect say about all this? Can his crew do some of the work?"

"His crew is going to work with Mr. Mackenzie on the front that the guests will see when they arrive, and on the drainage problems so if it rains the house isn't surrounded by a moat."

"I liked him," Marni said. "It's nice he'll be around. And he is a bit of a dish, as they used to say in the olden days."

"I suppose," I said. "He's really good-looking, but he doesn't seem to like me very much. I think he's more your type."

She raised an eyebrow. "I have a type? Do tell."

"Okay, so I can't think of any particular type." Marni had always been a casual dater, and I realized she didn't actually have a type. "But he likes plants and you like plants."

"Are you actually trying to set us up?" she said, laughing.

"You could be a dream couple. It's better than having nothing in common!"

"What do you mean, he doesn't seem to like you?"

I explained his coolness toward me.

"Maybe he's just trying to stay professional, since you're technically the client."

"Maybe." I told her about how we'd known each other as children.

She laughed again. "Robin Hood? That's super cute! Though I have a hard time picturing him as a child. Was he one of those boys you just knew were going to be really good looking?"

"No. I don't know. He was just one of the gang. I was just a child, remember?" And Samuel had been cuter to my childish tastes back then, though I couldn't pinpoint why.

"Okay. That makes sense. Mr. Mackenzie is certainly in his fan club. Your gardener is a man of few words unless it comes to plants or Davin."

"Yes, Mr. Mackenzie always seemed to like him. Me, he just tolerated and a few of the other boys regularly got scolded, but never Robin...Davin. Mr. Mackenzie is hard to please but somehow Robin managed."

She poured herself some more wine. "Did you know Mr. Mackenzie wants to move to Australia?"

"What?" That staggered me. "No, why? To live with Samuel?"

"Sort of. He wants to live nearby. You don't know, do you?"

"What?"

"His grandson has cancer."

I felt like I'd been punched. Not Samuel, he was the same age as me. "I had no idea. What kind of cancer?"

"Some sort of leukemia. Samuel's wife spends time getting him to and from doctors. Mr. Mackenzie thinks he could help out on their farm, but he wants to sell his cottage here so he'll have enough to buy a place of his own. He says they don't have enough room for him with all their children too, and he'd like a little peace and quiet anyway."

I was stunned. I had no inkling of any of that. "He's never said a word. I asked him how Samuel was doing and he just said 'fine.'"

"I think it's because he sees you as the lady of the manor now. He called you 'Miss Libby' the whole time I was talking to him."

That explained his behavior to me since I'd come back, which had been very standoffish. I had thought he saw me as an annoying American who really didn't have a right to be at Pemberley, since I'd spent so many years away.

"Well, Mr. Mackenzie should go then," I said. "I mean, I've thought he was too old to be doing so much work around here and I suppose we can find someone else..." Could we? I had no idea, and I had no idea what the going rate for a gardener was. My grandmother had left a little money for him in the will, and I'd been paying him the rate he'd been getting the year before, but I realized I never even questioned if that was fair, or if he'd been given a raise at all since my grandmother had gone to the U.S..

"You'll have to talk to him. I don't think he's going to bring it up himself until he actually lists his cottage for sale. He said he'd talked to the real estate agent in town but doesn't want her to put up a sign yet. He doesn't want to worry you with 'all the bother and goings on' with the wedding, as he says. Your grandmother was really lucky to have him." Marni yawned. "I'm sorry. The day is catching up with me."

"Yes, me too." I needed some sleep and then maybe I could think about Mr. Mackenzie's situation more clearly. I took a last drink of wine and was about ready to get up when the lamp flickered. An electrician had finally come in to repair the wiring to the one outlet in the room, though he had shaken his head at the state of it. "This could be part of a museum exhibit," he'd said. "You're lucky it hasn't started a fire."

I already had nightmares about fires, so I'd moved electrical repairs up high on my list. Many of the bills piling up in the study were for that work. We'd had to have the ballroom rewired first, because Emmaline had told me that some wedding bands would need plenty of electricity for their equipment and we couldn't have the fuses blowing during the wedding dance.

The light flickered again so I put my hand on the lamp base and shook it. I hadn't realized it had gotten so late. The sun was close to setting and most of the room had darkened outside the pool of light from the lamp.

I saw Marni take another swallow of wine and then she froze, the glass still at her lips. She put it down slowly as she looked over my shoulder.

"Kiki?" she said.

Chapter 9

Countdown to the Raine Randolph/Stefan Andris
Wedding
22 – 21 days

To Do List:
Clean the East Room
Gilding touch up
Get Kiki to order live traps for the mice
Tell Kiki about the additional guests!!!!
Pay one bill. Look at bills and estimates, add new ones to the spreadsheet
Read Davin's report
Find lipstick
Meeting with Davin ☻
Get a machete for the conservatory
Learn to appreciate newts
Research ghost detector devices

I HEARD Betsey hiss and looked down to see her creep around the edge of the sofa, belly low to the ground, staring in the same direction as Marni. I turned around. The other end of the room was in gloom, the only light coming in from one window. I didn't see Kiki. I didn't see anyone.

There was a door at that end of the room leading out into another passage, and it always squeaked badly when it opened. I hadn't heard any squeaking.

Marni set her wine glass down on the edge of the table, too close to the edge. It fell off and hit the carpet. She didn't notice. She stood up and I saw her fists were clenched.

That made me stand up too. I looked again. "I don't see Kiki. What's wrong?"

"A woman..." Marni's hand shook as she pointed toward the door. "A woman in a long white nightgown or...or...a long dress just walked out of the room....but...but she didn't open the door. Did you see her? Did you hear her? She was calling out for something."

"I didn't see or hear anything. You've been talking to Kiki, right?" I asked. "She set this up, didn't she? To tease me?"

"What do you mean?" Marni gave me a quick look and then went back to staring into the gloom. "Didn't you see that woman? Or...or whatever it was. What was it?" Marni's eyes were open so wide, I could see the whites all around them.

A low growl came from Betsey. I realized Marni wasn't teasing. I made myself walk down toward the end of the room. There was nothing there. I looked out the window. The moon was up and there were clouds in the sky. As soon as one passed over it, the library grew darker.

"See," I said. "Maybe when the clouds moved away from the moon, you saw a moonbeam." Please let it be a moonbeam.

"A moonbeam wearing a lacy nightgown with ruffles and long graying hair," Marni said. "And calling for something. I don't think so. That would be some trick for the moon to carry out."

I closed my eyes, as if I was a child wanting a problem to go away. "Okay," I said when I opened them again. "I don't know what you saw but I believe you. Don't say anything about it to anyone, okay? Kiki thinks she saw a ghost too, but if you tell her, she'll start seeing it everywhere. It makes me jumpy when Kiki shrieks, so I'd like to keep the shrieking down, if possible." It wasn't much of a mood lightener but it was the best I could do.

Marni put her hand on the top of the sofa as if to steady herself. "You mean, there is actually a ghost here? I'm not just hallucinating or something?"

"I don't know." I came back to the sofas. "I've never seen it and I've never heard of one, but Kiki thought she saw a woman in a long nightgown too."

Marni sat back down and picked up her wine glass off the floor. "Okay, then. I did not expect this. Seriously. I was not expecting to stumble into a gothic novel. There's not a mad woman imprisoned the attic, is there?"

"No, though Katie would love something like that, so don't suggest that in front of her." I sat down too. "Do you...do you...believe in ghosts?"

"Not until three minutes ago," Marni said. "But when one floats through the room and then disappears through a closed door, yes, I absolutely believe in ghosts." She poured herself the last of the wine and drank it down. "I can't believe you didn't hear her. It was faint, but definitely a voice." She smiled at me, all tension gone.

"You don't seem really scared by it. Are you? If I have to become a ghostbuster, I don't want to do it alone. I need a trusty band of brave souls to help me." I was still joking because I had no idea what else to do. None of the renovation books I'd read contained chapters on dealing with resident ghosts.

"I guess I'm not," Marni said. "That's weird, isn't it? But the woman wasn't rattling chains or beckoning me to follow her into the beyond or anything like that.. She just seemed confused. Like she was looking for something. She reminds me of Great Aunt Joan who could never find her glasses even when they were on the top of her head. Remember? That's not exactly frightening, especially since it sounded like this ghost was calling for a pig. That's what I think I heard her say, "Pig! Where's my little pig?" Marni covered her mouth and giggled. "If you had asked me what kind of ghost I thought I might see, it wouldn't be her. How much wine have I had?" She picked up the bottle and looked at it. "Oh, it's empty, isn't it? We did a good job on the wine, well, I did a good job on the wine, but I swear it wasn't the alcohol. I swear I saw something."

"I believe you. Tell me if you see it again." As if I could actually do anything about a ghost. It's not like I could have a conversation with it and ask it to leave off the haunting during the wedding. A wild thought passed through my head that if the ghost wanted a pig, I could get a pig for her, or at least a piglet. Put a piglet in the front yard and hope the ghost drifted out there after it? Probably a bad idea. With my luck, the ghost wouldn't budge out of the house, Palmer the swan would attack the piglet, Mr. Mackenzie would break his leg trying to separate them, I'd have a meltdown and Davin de Bourgh would show up right at that moment and be forever convinced I was incapable of anything, much less taking care of Pemberley.

You're catastrophizing again, a little voice in my head whispered. "Well, I'm good at that, aren't I?" I muttered.

"What?" Marni asked.

"Nothing. Let's go to bed. Hopefully the ghost doesn't climb stairs. Kiki saw her on this floor too but hasn't seen anything upstairs." Though if a ghost could go through a closed door, it would probably be able to float up a staircase, according to whatever super special ghost laws of physics applied.

My rabbit drawing that night was of a ghostly elderly bunny who floated about the ground in a nightgown with its tail sticking out. Elderly rabbits were tricky to draw and I added in too many wrinkles to its ears, so it looked like they'd been held underwater too long. Not one of my more successful attempts. I put the notebook away and fretted about the ghost until I fell asleep.

When I woke up, the fretting came right back. Marni was not the kind of person to let her imagination run wild. If she said she'd seen a ghost, I had to believe her though I didn't have a clue what to do about it.

My phone rang. It was Emmaline.

"Just checking in," She was very bubbly, probably having consumed several expressos already. "We're getting close! It's so exciting! How is it going there?"

Should I tell her about the ghost? I was still debating when she said, "Libby, are you there?"

I decided not to tell her. After all, what would I say? *Oh, by the way, we might have a ghost who might appear at the ceremony wandering about in a nightgown looking for a pig.*

"Everything is fine, or fineish, I should say. We're working hard to get ready. You're not calling to add more guests, are you?" She didn't usually call so early in the morning.

"No, nothing like that. The dress designer wanted to make sure you knew the room Raine is going to use to get dressed shouldn't have too much furniture in it, and it has to be spotless. They're bringing a stand to hang the dress on to steam out any wrinkles and some drop cloths for the floor so the dress doesn't get grubby. There needs to be room for all that. I know we talked about a chaise lounge and a dressing table and chair and some extra chairs and a table. Now I'm not sure we'll have room for a table unless it's a small one."

"Who are all these people that will be crowding in there?" The room wasn't that big.

"The makeup artist and the hairdresser and the dress designer and they'll have assistants with them too."

Why hadn't I realized there would be staff? One of many things I'd been worrying about was that Raine would be a nightmare to deal with. Wouldn't actors be the bridezillas of all bridezillas? "Are you sure Raine isn't going to have a meltdown when she gets here if everything isn't perfect?" I asked.

"No, no, she's a lovely person, really. I was surprised by how nice she is. You'll love her. She's a diva, but in a sweet way."

Somehow 'diva' and 'sweet' didn't fit together.

"Ask your friend Eleanor," Emmaline said. "I'm sure she'll tell you Raine won't be a bridezilla."

Except Eleanor and Raine barely knew each other, even though they were stepsisters. Raine's mother married Eleanor's father only a couple of years earlier, long after Eleanor had left home.

"Instead of a bridezilla, we might have a mother-of-the bridezilla though. I'm a bit worried about that," Emmaline said. "Raine has mentioned that the woman is difficult, which is why Raine isn't even telling her about the wedding until a few days in advance. She absolutely does not want her mother involved in the planning. I think that's why it's all so secret. I thought it was to keep the press away, but it's also about keeping the mother out of her hair. Her mum is the ultimate stage mother and has apparently been that way Raine's whole career."

I felt a ping of sympathy for Raine. I understood not wanting an overbearing mother trying to control things.

"All right, I'll make sure the room is extra clean," I said. "We have to feed all those people too, right?"

"Yes, at least to provide them with water and snacks. I've been in touch with Kiki about it. We're having platters of food delivered for them and a small tent with a serving table, some small tables and chairs set up off the kitchen door. All Kiki has to do is direct the delivery people where to put things. She's got that on her list. She's a calm one, that girl."

I suppose that was true when it came to food and cooking. In any other part of her life, no one would call Kiki calm.

"Yes, she's doing a good job," I said. I was proud of her. My mother had done everything she could to convince Kiki that her dyslexia and poor grades meant her only future was to stay and help at the diner. Being here was finally giving her the confidence she could do far more than that.

"One more thing," Emmaline said. "We'll have a security guard at the gate checking who is allowed in. Marni won't be coming and going, will she? If you think she might, I can put her name on the list."

I hadn't thought about that at all. So many details were escaping me, and I'd thought I would be good at all this. "I don't think so, but put her name on the list. And Kiki has a friend here too. She should be added as well." I explained about Katie. Even though Kiki was so organized, I could envision her needing one more ingredient and sending someone zipping off to the village to get it.

"All right. That's all I have for now," Emmaline said. "Text me if you need anything."

I was fully awake by then so I got dressed and made it downstairs. Everyone else was already in the kitchen munching on bacon sandwiches Kiki had set out.

"Lunch is egg salad and asparagus tartines," Kiki said as she put eggs on to boil. "I need to get the size of the tartines right so they aren't too messy to eat. You can be my testers."

While we ate, I looked over my list. Eleanor and Mark were due to arrive and I realized both Marni and Katie needed to know some details about Eleanor's situation so they wouldn't say something to make her uncomfortable. I explained about Eleanor's husband and then added, "Don't ask Eleanor about the job at the church. Something murky happened and she doesn't want to talk about it." There were a number of possible scenarios. William's father had a whole team of accountants and Eleanor was the most junior of them. The group gave new meaning to the term "creative" accounting.

I hoped Eleanor hadn't been drawn into any kind of mess there. She didn't deserve that. She was also the first person who had seen me after I found out I'd failed the bar exam, and had put up with me crying on her shoulder, even though I had barely known her at the time.

"When will she be here?" Katie asked.

"Soon," I said. "Their flight should have landed this morning and she's hired a driver to bring them here. Kiki, did you order the live traps for the mice?"

"I did," she said. "But you are going to have to be the one to carry them in the woods to release them. They're going to be so frightened, I can't do it."

"I'll find a good place," I said. "Maybe they'll like the woods better anyway. Fresh air and all that. I read you a bunch of books when you were little about how the English woodland creatures make little snug homes in the woods and frolic about at night in the light of the moon. Keep that vision in your head."

"Very funny," she said. "But I'm not six years old anymore. I'm not going to fall for that."

After breakfast Marni went back to work in the conservatory and I needed to start on the gilding repair in the music room where the ceremony was going to be held. Much of the decorative gilding over the years had flaked off, and even though Raine liked the faded look, that room needed a lift. Touching up the gilding would make the photographs look better, I had reasoned. Mainly, I liked to work with gold paint, and delicate painting work was something I could actually do well. The other repair work was all hit or miss and learning on the fly, so way more stress than I wanted.

First, though, I remembered to tie up a string across the stairs leading to the third floor, the former servants' quarters, on both the front and back stairs. I didn't want Mark wandering up there and falling through some rotting floorboards. I hoped he was the kind of child who would listen to rules, because if not, Eleanor and I would have to come up with some other way to keep him out of there. As an eldest child, I was of course a rule follower, but I knew from my blended family of half siblings and step siblings, rule following was not a given.

When Eleanor and Mark did arrive, Eleanor looked so worn down, I might not have recognized her if I had passed her on the street. She'd also cut her hair very short and the brown color was threaded with gray, which I had not noticed before. She wore an oversized gray cardigan and gray slacks and I could tell she didn't have on any makeup, which she usually wore, because her eyelashes and her eyebrows were so pale, they were barely there. It was as if she was trying to be invisible. I gave her a hug and she sagged down like she couldn't hold up her own weight.

"I'm so glad you are here, both of you!" I said. Her son Mark stood solemnly by the luggage as if he was guarding it. He clutched a little stuffed animal, a dolphin from what I could see of it.

"We are too," Eleanor said. "It was a long trip."

"Hi, Mark," I said. "Welcome to Pemberley." I introduced Marni, who had come out of the conservatory to meet them. The boy was small for his age and reminded me of a little pixie child with his delicate features, big brown eyes and a triangular face. He also had a cute cowlick, though not as pronounced as the child formerly known as Robin.

"Hi," he mumbled. "I didn't know we were coming to a fancy house with a mean swan."

"Oh, I'm so sorry. Did the swan charge at you?" I was going to have to do something with that bird.

"Yes, but an old man working outside shooed him away," Eleanor said.

"The house may look fancy but it isn't really and there are lots of places to play," I told the boy. "Both inside and out. I played here when I was your age."

"Hey there," Katie said as she and Kiki came in. I introduced them as well but the boy didn't speak. He clutched the dolphin even tighter and his lower lip trembled.

Before I could think of what to say to help the situation, Katie spoke up. "You look like the kind of kid who might be willing to help us make cookies. Do you like cookies?"

He nodded and I could see some of the tension drain away from him.

"How about a snack first before we start baking?" Kiki said. She was like an old grandmother, with her instinct to feed a guest the moment they walked through the door. "I just made some shortbread and it's pretty good if I do say so for myself. It will give us energy to bake something amazing."

I hoped it was plain shortbread. Her jalapeno variety would probably not appeal to an eight-year-old.

Mark looked at Eleanor and she nodded. "Go on."

Kiki grabbed hold of one of Mark's hands and pulled him toward the kitchen, the girls giggling like they were Mark's age.

"They'll keep him busy," I said to Eleanor. "I've put you and Mark in the housekeeper's suite. It's on this floor. Is that okay? There is a bedroom and a little extra room that was her sitting room. We moved a cot into that room for Mark. If you don't want him to have his own room, we can move the cot in with you."

"It's perfect," Eleanor said. "We'll see about the cot. He hasn't wanted to sleep by himself since...since..." Her voice trailed off. She glanced over at Marni.

"I told Marni," I said. "I hope you don't mind."

"I'm very sorry for your loss," Marni said. "Please don't feel like you can't speak in front of me."

Eleanor nodded. "Thank you." Her shoulders slumped again and she swayed a little.

I picked up two of the suitcases. "Let's get your luggage in there and then you can take a nap if you want. We'll all keep track of Mark." I explained about the third floor and she told me not to worry, that he was good about following rules.

"I don't think he'll go anywhere on his own," she said. "He hasn't liked to be in any room by himself and I don't think he'll start now. Thank you for all this," she said again. Her voice was so trembly I could tell she was trying to hold back tears of exhaustion. It made me realize I shouldn't have been moaning and complaining so much. Eleanor was the one who had the reasons to cry. My problems paled in comparison.

Once she was settled in her room, we left her to rest.

"I feel really bad for her," Marni said. "It's great she is here though. Maybe the change in atmosphere will help."

"I hope so. She looks so worn down." I felt guilty I hadn't been there for her. I'd bolted from North Carolina with only the thought of how many miles I could put between myself and William, not thinking of anyone else.

"Libby!" Marni waved her hand in front of my face. "Listen to yourself. You look almost as worn down. I'm worried about you too. Have you seen a doctor lately?"

Ever since Marni found out I had inherited a form of anemia from my father, she fretted like an old mother hen about my health. Since she was so overwhelmingly healthy herself, she viewed it as a tragedy when someone didn't feel well.

"I thought my paleness fit in with the décor of the house," I joked. "Faded and worn down. Maybe we can start ghost tours and I'll play one of the ghosts. I'll float around in long dresses to add to the atmosphere."

"Seriously, you are very pale."

"I know. I'll find a doctor here as soon as the wedding is over. I just hope neither Eleanor nor Mark spot the ghost," I said. "That's the last thing they need. I want to check on Mark before I get back to work."

Kiki and Katie had put the boy to work helping to make dough. "I want to time the whole process so I can put it on the schedule for the wedding," Kiki said. The boy seemed perfectly content, wrapped in a big apron and standing on a step stool. They had music blasting and as we left the kitchen Katie burst into song.

Marni went back to the conservatory and I went back to gilding touch up until I ran out of paint. Eleanor slept through lunch but found me in the study as I was sorting through bills before dinner.

"Thanks for letting me sleep," she said. "I'm sorry to leave Mark to you for so many hours."

"He's been no trouble," I said, though I wasn't the one who had been looking out for him. Katie had taken him to explore the house after lunch, and I hadn't seen them at all, except I'd occasionally heard sounds of her laughter floating down the stairs. I hoped he was laughing too.

"Are you busy?" she asked.

"No," I said. I flipped through a stack. "Just admiring my collection of bills. Shuffling them around, you know, in case I've become a magician and one magically disappears."

My spreadsheet of bills and estimates was supposed to help me figure out how to decide on which repairs to tackle first, but no matter how I shuffled the numbers, they always came up short of what was in the bank account.

I picked up the roof estimate. "It would be great if I could turn this one into a paper airplane, send it out the window and then the problem that goes with it would disappear as well." I laid it back down.

She glanced at it and then took a second look. "Ouch! Why is this so high? I mean, I know the place is huge, but this is the cost of buying a new house in some places."

"I know. It's because there is an organization in Britain that keeps track of what are designated as historic buildings, and the classifications limit how you can fix up a place. It's sort of like having something on the National Historic Register in the States. Pemberley has been given a grade II star listing, which means all the repairs have to keep the integrity of the original time period in which it was built."

When I'd read the requirements, I hadn't fully realized what they meant in practical terms. "It's got a slate roof, so it has to be repaired with slate too. The good news is the slate tiles are in mostly good shape, but some of the rafters have to be replaced because they are rotted." I explained some extra details and then realized it was all very boring if it wasn't your roof and your house. "There, now you know more about slate roofs than you probably ever wanted to know," I said.

"I don't mind. I always thought I'd like to buy a fixer upper someday. I get tired of sitting in front of my computer all day. Though not this size, of course! Is there any chance of you getting a loan? Surely this place could be collateral."

"I tried that route. I should have done it differently and applied first thing but I was so anxious to make the house livable when we first arrived. To do that we had to get the plumbing fixed right away, and of course that cost twice the original estimate. I used up too much of the money. And since I don't have another source of income and no way to get one, at least not while I'm living here, I got turned down. The fact that it's a listed building makes it even more difficult, because of the extra cost for any repairs using historic materials."

I leaned back in the chair, trying to ease the tension in my muscles. It was a relief to talk money problems with Eleanor. She understood money and budgets. "I could go back to the states and work for a couple of years to save up some money. There are places that would hire me even if I didn't pass the bar, or I could try again to pass it." I tensed up again even at the thought of that. "But there's Kiki. She needs to be here, or at least far away from my mother."

Eleanor motioned to the stack of bills. "You know, I could at least help you out with keeping track of things, if you like. I mean, I know you can do it but for the time being you have a resident accountant without enough to do. It would free up your time to do other things."

I sat up. "No! I didn't mean to make it sound like I was begging for help. I'm sorry I dumped that all on you. You're here to have a vacation."

"I like organizing things. You know me. It gives me a feeling of accomplishment."

"I'm not going to burden you." I was absolutely not going to be so weak as to make her take over some of my work.

"All right, but I'm going to keep offering. I really came in to talk about something important."

She sounded so serious, I began to get worried. "Of course."

Eleanor went over and closed the door and then came back. "I wanted to talk to you alone. Have you heard from William?"

"He's tried to call me but I haven't taken his calls." I hadn't thought of William all day. At some point people would stop mentioning his name and I could forget all about him.

"Good. I don't want to interfere, but I'm relieved you seem to have moved on. You have moved on, haven't you?"

"If you mean, do I want to meet someone else, absolutely not! If you mean, am I never going back to William, yes, absolutely!"

"Good. Stay as far away from him as you can." She looked back over her shoulder as if checking to make sure the door was still closed. "Not just because you broke up, but because the church finances are a terrible mess. They're worried they may be audited by the IRS, and that is a big deal. It takes major red flags for the IRS to audit a church. I knew there was something fishy happening, though not in what I was asked to do, but I quit anyway. I don't want to be peripheral damage. And William is of course in the middle of it all. His signature is on many, many documents."

"I didn't know that." I didn't feel surprised by the information. William had been very vague about his role at the church. He acted as if he just used his office at the church headquarters to write his books, but I should have realized he'd be involved in all of it. Another example of gullible, stupid little Libby. "It explains why he wanted me to sign a nondisclosure agreement when we broke up. I thought he was being extra paranoid."

"He wasn't."

My phone rang. William's name came up on the screen. "Speak of the devil," I said. "It's William." He'd found my new number . He'd probably just called my mother and asked for it, even though I'd told her I didn't want him to have it. I thought about declining the call but I knew he'd just try again later and keep trying. "I'm going to shut him down once and for all."

"Good," Eleanor said. "You can do it." She motioned toward the door and I nodded my head so she left the room and closed the door behind her. It would be better talking to him without anyone listening.

I took a deep breath and answered the call.

Chapter 10

Countdown to the Raine Randolph/Stefan Andris
Wedding
21 days

To Do List:
Gilding touch up – order more paint!
Pray the ghost doesn't reappear
Change phone number
Remember you are not the old Libby

"WILLIAM, WE have nothing left to discuss. I wish you'd stop calling me." My first words came out firm and confident. I could do this. Maybe.

"Hello Libby," he said. "I wanted to check in and see how you were doing."

"I'm fine," I gripped my fingers more tightly around the phone because they had begun to shake.

"I'm worried about you."

"You don't need to be. I'm fine. There, see. Goodbye."

"Wait! Wait! Don't hang up. I'm not calling just to check on you. There's something else. And I thought last time we spoke, we agreed to be civil."

"I didn't agree to anything. And it's difficult to be civil when you sent your father's attorneys after me. I told you I wouldn't say anything about the goings on at the church. You don't need to keep insisting I sign a nondisclosure about it. You can trust me." I actually didn't really know anything about the workings of the church, though I had vague suspicions.

"<u>Can</u> I trust you?" he asked. "And it wasn't me who involved the lawyers. It was my father. When I told him you left in the middle of the night without a word beforehand, he got concerned. There are so many people who are looking for a way to take him down."

If William's father had been an ordinary minister, he wouldn't have had enemies trying to take him down. "If he's running a legitimate church, he has nothing to worry about," I said. "He's the one who decided to spend millions of dollars on houses and jets and cars. He must have realized a lavish lifestyle would draw attention to him." The megachurch William's father ran raked in an incredible amount of donations, though very little of it actually went to helping parishioners or other needy people.

"Now Libby." I recognized that tone. It was William's patient 'let me explain it to you, you ignorant child.' It had taken me far too long to notice it. When I'd been a teenager and he a twenty-something, I'd thought he was so worldly and I needed to learn all the things he told me.

A trickle of sweat ran down my back. The room felt hot. I got up and opened the door and then went over to the window to get some air.

"You know the muckraker journalists will make up stories if they can, or twist the truth so it sounds bad," he said. "You were going to sign a nondisclosure as part of the prenup, so why not still sign just the nondisclosure?" He paused. "And to show there are no hard feelings, my father would like to give you a gift, something to help you with your renovations. It's very generous of him given that he's so hurt you don't want to be part of our family. He'd like you to have $100,000."

I thought at first I hadn't heard him right.

"Libby, are you still there?"

"I'm here." A hundred thousand dollars would be manna from heaven. Or, as I quickly reminded myself, manna from the devil.

"How is the renovation going?" he asked, as if he had any real interest in it, beyond hoping it would fail. When I'd first learned I'd inherited the property and brought up the idea of fixing it up, he'd told me I'd never be able to do it, that I didn't have the skill or knowledge or ability to oversee such a massive project.

"The renovation is going fine. We have our first wedding in three weeks." He didn't need to know how far we had to go in those three weeks.

There was a long silence. "William, are you still there?" I asked.

"Yes, I'm sad it's not our own wedding you're getting ready for. Look, I know I threw too many expectations at you and I understand why that scared you off. I've talked to my father and we've decided you wouldn't really have to play such a role in the church when I take over. I'm sure we could work out something that would make you happy. I can get a flight tomorrow so we could talk about it. You could come to London and meet me."

We've decided. Of course they had. They decided everything for the assortment of people who kept the church running. Where a person should live, how they should dress, what they did in their free time and how to think. I should have realized William's mother only seemed to play an important role, when actually she always agreed with what had already been worked out. Her only role was to make 'suggestions' to people. Things like, *Oh, Libby dear. That dress is a little too revealing. You don't want to appear too flashy, do you?* or *You're looking a little pale, dear. A bit more makeup would help, and it would show off your pretty eyes much better.*

"So what about it?" William asked. "Can you meet me in London tomorrow? Or I can come to you."

Betsey dashed into the room and leapt up on the desk, knocking the stack of bills off the desk. I jumped up to catch them, knocking over a container of pens, which scattered everywhere. I let out a few choice swear words.

"Libby, really! You don't need to swear at me. That is very unlike you."

"No, I wasn't swearing at you. And also, no, I'm not meeting you anywhere. I'm far too busy with this wedding and there's nothing to talk about. It's really over, William. I'm not the right person for you. You need to move on."

Betsey jumped into my chair and began to clean her paw. At least she hadn't brought me a mouse.

Another long silence from William. "I hope you'll change your mind," he said. "But in the meantime, it would mean so much to my father for you to sign the nondisclosure. Once you did, he'd transfer the money to you immediately."

A hundred thousand dollars would repair the tower with a little money left over for the rest of the renovations. But it would be something William could hold over me, that I really hadn't been able to renovate the house by myself as he had predicted. That I'd needed him and his family to help because I was just little helpless Libby Darcy, who'd managed to fail the bar exam and couldn't follow through on anything.

"Libby?" he said.

I shooed Betsey off the chair and sat back down. She ran back out the door. "I'll think about it. But don't call me, I'll call you. And we really are done. We will never be a couple again."

I ended the call and then looked up to see Davin in the doorway. I don't know how much he'd heard or what he'd make of any of it.

"Hello, your sister answered the door and said I could find you here," he said. "She was worried about something burning in the kitchen so she pointed me here."

Why did it seem as if the burning of things took place just when Davin showed up? "Oh," I said. I tried to push William out of my head. "Did you need something from me?" I was not in the mood to talk to anyone, not even Davin.

He walked in and glanced. I realized the place looked as if I had trashed it. Papers and pens were everywhere. I jumped up and picked up a few bills. "Sorry. The cat knocked everything off the desk."

He didn't say anything to that. I wished Betsey had still been in the room so I could point to her to make my explanation sound more plausible.

"Kiki told me there weren't going to be any large tents outdoors for the wedding," he said, "and not many cars, is that right? I didn't want any of our projects to get in the way of a company erecting tents or blocking off parking areas."

"Right," I said. "It's just a small wedding."

"Someone in the future might want tents, though," he said. "We should adjust the landscape renovation plan to account for that, and to set aside a grassy area or put in a graveled area that could be used for parking."

If there were more weddings. I could feel a headache tightening its grip on me. "Yes, maybe," I said. "Can we talk about that later, maybe after this wedding? It's not going to interfere with any of the immediate work, is it?"

"No," he said. "Did you notice that I said in the report we'd put down new gravel on the existing graveled areas where it needs to be replenished?"

"Yes," I said, though I actually couldn't remember that part.

"It should help in case it rains in the days before the wedding. There won't be so many puddles for guests to navigate around."

A scene from a movie flashed in my head, where a group of people on a quest were picking their way through a swamp. The laughter threatened to bubble up as I imagined people in all their wedding finery jumping from dry spot to dry spot. It wasn't even that funny, but I was so tired my brain was misfiring.

"Yes, good," I said, looking down at the bill I'd picked up off the floor, the roof estimate. I couldn't stop thinking about what William had offered.

After a moment, I realized Davin was still standing there.

"Sorry," I said, pointing to the papers. "I'm just distracted."

"We need to set a date when the gravel can be delivered and put down so it won't interfere with anything else, like deliveries." He said this very patiently as if explaining it to a child. I hated when people talked to me like that, even when I hadn't been paying attention just like a child. I forced myself to look at him and to look alert.

"A car could go around the equipment on the grass if it's not raining, but there shouldn't be any delivery vans or trucks doing that," he said. "They are too hard on the turf."

"Oh, right." He did sound like he knew what he was doing. I had a big paper calendar sheet on my desk with the days leading up to the wedding so I'd be sure not to miss anything. I pointed at it. "What day works for you?" He came around to my side of the desk and leaned over to look at the calendar. I noticed he smelled like outside, like freshly cut grass or herbs or something, though he wasn't dressed as if he'd been doing work. It was distracting and I almost had to pinch myself to concentrate on his words.

We settled on a date, and then he acted as if he wanted to say something else.

My phone pinged with a text message.

He said, "All right then. We're set. Thank you. I'll let you get on with it."

I wanted to tell him to wait, but the message was from Emmaline. He was out the door before I could explain why I needed to respond to the text.

The groom wants to come down in a few days with the jewelry designer. He wants to give Raine a bracelet that will remind her of the house and the ceremony. Okay?

Another flash of panic. The groom hadn't seen the place. What if he hated it? *Will he mind that we aren't ready yet?*

No, I warned him

Okay, I suppose. Very romantic gesture. What do I need to do?

Just be there to show them around. I'll text you time and day

I took a moment to realize my new normal. Stefan Andris, soon-to-be groom, major celebrity, was coming here for me to show him around, though I probably shouldn't be excited because he was sure to be really annoying and stuck up. Good looking men or men with money usually were since they got used to women falling all over them. William was not good looking but he certainly had plenty of little church groupies who clung to his every pronouncement. Everyone had been assuring me Raine was lovely, but no one had said a word about Stefan. Were there groomzillas?

As I was worrying about that, another worry struck me. With the wedding moved up, painting the dining room couldn't happen when I'd planned. The plaster needed at least three weeks to dry, or otherwise the paint might fall off. That put us to painting the day before the wedding. I hated the idea of a last minute scramble to get things done. It felt like every day was a rush to get things done since we'd booked the wedding. I didn't work well under such pressure, because I was much more likely to screw up.

One hundred thousand dollars. Such a lot of money. It was so tempting and then I reminded myself of the source. "Don't cave, Libby. Think of your pride." Taking that money would be a last resort. "Get through the wedding before you do anything." Yes, I was talking to myself again, but I needed the pep talk.

At dinner that night, Kiki burbled away about the renovation plans for the kitchen garden. "Davin and I went over all sorts of possibilities and it's going to be fantastic! He has it all planned out and he was so enthusiastic about it, like it was going to be his own garden."

It was not going to be his own garden. It was ours. "I didn't know Davin talked to you," I said. "He told me you took off for the kitchen after you answered the door."

"I did, but he came to see me after he talked to you. I asked how you seemed after talking to William. Eleanor mentioned William called."

"You asked Davin?" He really didn't need to know about my disastrous love life.

"I hope you don't mind I said something about it." Eleanor said.

"No, I don't mind." Though I did mind.

"Yes, I was worried you'd be upset," Kiki said. "I explained all about William and how you broke off the engagement because he's such a pompous...." She looked over at Mark and cut off what she had been going to say. "A pompous doofus," she said instead.

Mark giggled.

"You're too kind, Kiki," Marni said. "That's not quite how I'd describe him."

"You told Davin all that?" I was mortified. He already had doubts about my ability to carry off the project. I didn't want him to think I was falling apart over something personal.

"Yes, he was very interested. He wanted to know all about it. I told him how you'd called me in the middle of the night and said you'd broken it off with William and I was to get on a plane right away so we could go to England together." Kiki stopped to take a breath. "And how you'd cried when we arrived because the place was in such terrible shape and how you used to love it here, but it was all so different now. Then he told me all about the games you used to play here. You never told me any of that!"

I was still trying to absorb how she'd spilled my life to Davin. "It never came up," I said.

"Oh, and I started to tell him about your study abroad year here but he knew all about that."

"He did?" I said faintly. Another time in my life I'd like to forget. I'd spent too much time enjoying myself and not enough time studying. Learning how to open champagne bottles without spilling any and how to pull together wild outfits for fancy dress parties were not skills I'd used much since then.

"Yes, he's friends with someone who knew you."

"Who? Not Emmaline because she would have mentioned that. Though I wasn't sure I'd ever told Emmaline his name.

Kiki got up and took a plate off the counter. "Dessert! Carrot cupcakes with blackberry goat cheese frosting. Tell me if the carrot flavor is coming through enough."

I had to repeat my question to her.

"Someone named Henry Crawford." Kiki said. "Is that the guy who kept calling you the summer after you came back?"

Henry Crawford. Another disaster. I'd thought we were madly in love with each other, and he'd talked about us getting married. I'd already had doubts about William. Then as soon as I agreed Henry and I should get engaged, Henry lost interest, as if the pursuit had been the real purpose. Worse than that, I found out he had been cheating on me right and left. I fled back to the U.S. as fast as I could, refusing all his calls for months after that.

"That's the guy," I said. "But not a good guy." He was such a smooth talker and nothing was ever his fault. It made me wonder what version of our romance and breakup he'd told Davin.

I realized everyone else was taking in all of Kiki's talk about me, and I could feel my face get hot. "Let's talk about something else," I said. "Guess what? Stefan Andris is coming to look at the place before the wedding."

Chapter 11

Countdown to the Raine Randolph/Stefan Andris
Wedding
20 – 14 days

To Do List:

Gilding touch up – order more paint!

Pray the ghost doesn't reappear

Better strategy - Act like the ghost is not a problem.

Change phone number

Remember you are not the old Libby

Convince Betsey dogs are not evil

THE NEXT DAYS were full of flat-out work as the clock ticked down. One more ghost sighting by Marni, though I hoped it was a trick of the sunlight. Marni said she spotted an older woman in one of the third floor windows looking down on her while she was weeding one of the perennial beds. I decided I wouldn't worry about it. My days were scheduled hour by hour until the wedding so I couldn't waste any hours figuring out how to deal with a ghost, unless it started shrieking or chasing us about.

Marni spent most of the time outside working on the garden areas we'd decided would be good for pictures. I'd catch occasional glimpses of her from the windows, often in conversation with Davin or members of his crew. I was happy she seemed happy, though she definitely didn't want to talk about her upcoming job and she made no mention of when she'd be leaving. The pangs I felt seeing her and Davin talking together weren't pangs of jealousy. They were stomach pains from worry, or at least that's what I told myself. I was not going to develop an interest in him even when random thoughts about him snuck into my head. At least he was getting to know her, and he'd realize she was someone to be taken seriously. He seemed to be avoiding me, which was fine by me.

The new refrigerator arrived and even better, the box of mouse traps appeared as well. I opened the package to find several plastic tube-like contraptions which reminded me of Kiki's marble run toy she'd had as a child, except these had little air holes in them.

Marni pulled out the instructions. "Easy," she said. "We put a bit of soft cheese in the end here and then the mouse runs in and it closes on them."

I examined one to make sure the mouse couldn't spring out of the trap without warning. "I wish the tubes weren't clear. The mice will be able to stare at us with their furious little beady eyes, plotting revenge while they are being transported away."

"Relax," Marni said. "I'll do it. I'll be the mouse transporter."

"You are a dream houseguest," I said. With any luck, at least the downstairs mouse squatters would be relocated by the wedding. I thought about making a list of all possible disasters that could occur during the wedding but restrained myself, talking to Betsey about how I should be more optimistic that things would turn out just fine.

"And no dragging underwear about!" I said to her. She looked at me as if such a thought never came into her little fluffy head.

Katie helped Kiki in the kitchen and the two of them found ways to keep Mark entertained when he wasn't outside. I was still worried about Eleanor. She had a bit more color to her but she spent most of her time in the library on her laptop. I peeked in one day to find her dozing so I tiptoed away to let her sleep.

We would all meet up at dinner, still mainly testing Kiki's food as she tweaked her recipes and timing. Katie found a book on the history of the Darcys and entertained us while we ate by filling us in on my ancestors.

"It was written by a woman who descended from a family named Bertram, so there is a lot about that family as well. A Darcy son married the daughter of a couple named Edmund and Fanny Bertram. The daughter was named Susannah and she wrote the book. She must have liked scandal because she included a bit about an aunt of hers named Maria who ran off with someone who wasn't her husband."

"Tell us more." I served myself another few cherry tomatoes. Kiki had stuffed them with smoked salmon, cream cheese and dill. I couldn't get enough of them.

"Where did they run to?" Mark asked. "Were they in a marathon?"

"Um...no," Katie said. "Um...they ran because there weren't any cars back then."

Eleanor jumped in and changed the subject. "Marni, have you ever run a marathon?"

Mark didn't ask any more questions about the ancestor, though I would have liked to hear what else Katie knew. My grandmother had never been terribly interested in things like ancestors, only the books the ancestors possessed. I hadn't been interested in family history either until I'd come back to Pemberley. I wished I knew more. It might explain the presence of a ghost because it surely had lived here, or at least died here. My ghost knowledge may have been limited but I knew enough to realize they didn't just pop up in random places. I thought about asking Katie to research it and then decided against that, because it wasn't as if we could sit down with the thing and have a discussion about the conditions of haunting.

The next day Eleanor practically wrestled a paint brush from me. "I need to do something," she said. "I'm used to being useful. It's weird for me to just sit around and not even have to cook. Please! Let me help."

I agreed she could help me paint the bathrooms on the first floor that we'd had redone and expanded.

"This is pretty," she said when I opened the tin of the shade I'd picked, a light color called Folklore Green.

"I'm glad you like it." I stirred it, still admiring the choice. "I looked at hundreds of shades of green to pick this one. I think I liked the name as much as the color."

Eleanor adjusted one of the drop cloths we'd put down "You know if you had told me two years ago, I'd be in England painting a bathroom of a fantastic house you'd inherited, without a solid plan for the rest of my life, I never would have believed it."

"I wouldn't either. I think back to those days when school guidance counselors had us make five year plans and ten year plans and twenty year plans, they had to have known life could go absolutely sideways for some of us. They should have mentioned that little fact." I knew I'd taken my life sideways on purpose, but I still hadn't been prepared when I'd done so, because I'd let too many other people make decisions for me in all the years before.

"Exactly," Eleanor said. "I don't know why I assumed my life would follow the path I wanted as long as I was sensible about things. I never wanted too much or things that were too hard to get, so I thought I'd be fine. I didn't plan on a giant sinkhole appearing in the middle of the path." She took the painters' tape and began to tape around the window frame. "At least it's a luxury for me to be in a completely different and beautiful setting with some time to figure things out."

"Ah yes, the luxury to paint a bathroom in a beautiful setting," I said as I poured the paint into a tray. "After this, I'm going to push you out the door so you go for a walk or something. You should explore the village since you've come all this way. It's cute, just like one of those pictures you see of traditional English villages."

When we finished the bathrooms, Eleanor did agree to leave the house. I knew I had to get back to the gilding work I hadn't finished. I'd only been at it an hour or so when Mark dashed into the room nearly knocking over the paint can. He was carrying an umbrella, though it wasn't raining, but before I could ask about the accessory, he burst out, "Help! There's a strange noise! Something is out there on that little castle on the island!"

My first thought was that Palmer the swan had decided to torture someone he'd chased over to the island. My second thought was that our ghost had moved there but I quickly realized that was wishful thinking.

"You have to come see. I can't find my mom," Mark said.

"She walked down to the village. What kind of a noise?" I put down the brush.

"Like there is a hurt animal over there." He twisted his hands together. "I don't like the sound."

"I don't think an animal would swim over to the island if it was hurt."
I said this as if I were an expert on animal behavior, which I absolutely
wasn't, except for cats. I knew Betsey wouldn't swim over to strand
herself on an island, hurt or healthy. She'd have no desire to visit an island
for any reason, especially if she had to swim there.

"Then what is it?" His eyes got very wide. "Maybe it's the ghost."

I should have been more insistent that no one mention the ghost
to Mark. "It's not a ghost. I think our ghost doesn't like to go outside.
Maybe it's scared of the swan," I said. "Where were you when you heard
it? Maybe the noise is coming from somewhere else."

"I was messing around the edge of the pond with a stick. The noise
really is coming from the island."

Investigating strange island noises was not on my to do list for the
day, but I didn't see any way out of it. "Okay, let's go look."

The pond was near the front of the property bordering the lawn on
one side and woodland on the other. Supposedly it was originally a mill
pond back before the house was built when a small but now lost village
depended on it for milling grain. Nothing remained of any of that except
the pond itself.

At some point a Darcy ancestor had decided to turn it into a scenic
part of the garden, making use of the small island in the center as a place
to build something to show off their wealth, a small stone folly that
looked like the remains of a castle tower.

Back in my childhood days, we'd had a rowboat to use to get there.
The rowboat had really been for the gardener to go over and maintain the
island but we'd requisitioned it for our own use whenever we wanted.
That rowboat was long gone, probably decayed into nothing. A new
rowboat had been on an early list of things to acquire for the wedding
after Emmaline had explored the grounds and thought it might be great

in pictures. I hoped she had forgotten about that idea for the moment. I didn't have time to shop for a rowboat before the wedding.

"Who built that little castle?" Mark asked as we walked to the pond. "And why is it so small?"

"It's called a folly," I explained. "It was built to look like a ruined bit of a castle, but it was never used for anything. It's just to look at."

He shook his head. "That's really silly."

"Yes, I suppose it is." He'd change his mind if he had a boat to get over there and some friends to play with. The folly had been the best clubhouse ever.

"I don't hear anything," I said when we reached the edge.

"I know I heard something," Mark insisted. "Really."

Just then a strange sound came from the island, like a mix between a small lion roaring and a whining sort of howl.

"That's it!" Mark cried. "That's the sound I heard! What's making it?"

It was a weird noise. "I suppose it could be a dog or a fox." Maybe it was echoing through the folly, making it sound so strange. The acoustics in the place amplified noises, which we'd discovered early on when playing pirates, delighting in how our "arghs" sounded particularly fierce.

I looked around for Palmer. I didn't think a swan made that kind of noise but I hadn't spent much time with the cantankerous creature to know. There was no sign of him.

"Have you seen the swan?" I asked Mark.

"He was here earlier but he left when I opened the umbrella and twirled it around like Mr. Mackenzie said."

"Mr. Mackenzie showed you that?" He'd never mentioned a word about an umbrella to me. It was embarrassing to think of how many times he'd seen me jumping around and making hooting noises at the brute to keep it from attacking me.

"Yes, Mr. Mackenzie said it makes me look like a big bird and Palmer would go away. It works too."

A thought flashed through my mind that we could hand out colorful umbrellas as wedding favors when the guests got out of the cars.

I was busy imagining how that would go over when Mark said, "It could be a badger on the island. Mom says they have these black and white ones here like you see in picture books. We don't have those kind at home."

"Are badgers dangerous?" I asked, trying to refocus on the immediate problem. I didn't know one single fact about badgers, though relying on an eight-year-old for scientific information was probably not the best choice.

"I don't know. They look cute in the pictures I've seen."

"Cute animals usually aren't dangerous," I said, more for myself than for Mark.

"We can't just leave it there," Mark said. "Whatever it is, it needs help."

He was right about that, though that meant somebody had to do something. It would have been great to have another somebody to take action, but I really couldn't ask elderly Mr. Mackenzie to investigate. I'd have to be the somebody.

"Okay, I'll go across and see what it is." Just as I began to imagine getting bitten by a rabid fox or something, I remembered the country didn't have any animals with rabies. That still left another problem. I didn't know how I could rescue a hurt fox. A wild animal would surely try to bite if a person got too close. The noise came again, this time a little fainter, but definitely coming from the folly.

I knew if I put off the rescue mission any longer, I would just imagine more and more impossible scenarios which would morph into dangerous and possibly fatal ones. Catastrophizing was one of my more annoying habits. Better just to do something, anything. I debated about taking off my clothes, and then decided against that. I'd have to rinse off the pond water and change anyway.

I did take off my shoes and socks and remembered to take my phone out of my pocket. The pond had been too deep for me to stand as a child. I hoped I'd grown tall enough to be able to walk across. As I walked in and it grew deeper and deeper, I should have realized I hadn't grown all that much since I was ten, and five foot three was not enough. The squishy feeling of the mud in my toes reminded me why I hadn't liked going in the pond when I was young. By the time I got a third of the way across, my chin was level with the surface of the water and I resorted to swimming, happy to be free of the mud.

When I reached the shore of the island, I walked up the bank, parting the weeds in front of me. The sight of the weeds made me remember Mr. Mackenzie taking a reel mower over there in the boat once every few weeks to mow. I suppose he had given that up when the boat fell apart.

Much more moss covered the folly than I remembered, as if it were slowly becoming part of the island itself. I walked around to the opening and found myself trying to be extra quiet. Once there I peeked around the corner in case something dark and scary jumped out at me. I had to remind myself I wasn't starring in a horror movie. At first I couldn't hear anything, and then a faint whimper came from the far side.

I went in, wishing I had my phone so I could have a light. My eyes adjusted and then I spotted it. A scrawny little dog huddled in the corner. When I saw the small size of it, I was amazed the loud sound we'd heard could come from it, even with the folly amplifying it. I wasn't great at identifying dog breeds but at least knew enough to see it was a pug. The poor thing whimpered again when it saw me.

"Hey there, little guy." I held out my hand to it. It stood up but was shaking so badly, it quickly went back down. I got closer and petted it. It gave a little moan but did not seem the least bit aggressive so I reached down and picked it up. The dog turned his head toward me and licked my chin. I could feel its ribs. It was shivering badly.

"Come on, let's get you out of here." I held it against me, though since I was soaked, I was no warmer than it.

"It's a little dog!" I called out to Mark when I came around the folly.

He jumped up and down in excitement and nearly fell into the pond. "Is he okay?"

"He's very thin," I called back.

It wasn't until I reached the edge of the pond that I realized I had a problem. I couldn't carry the animal back across and swim at the same time. The animal seemed so weak, I wasn't sure it could swim by itself. If it had been able to do that, it wouldn't still be on the island. I had no idea why or how it got on the island in the first place.

"Mark, I'm going to need some help," I called. "Can you go find Kiki? Explain what's happening and tell her to bring me one of the old cushions or pillows in the attic." I could float the animal across on a pillow. It couldn't have weighed more than fifteen pounds or so.

Mark came back faster than I thought, and not with a pillow but with Davin.

"I told Mr. de Bourgh what was happening so he came to help," Mark yelled.

"I'll come over and carry the dog back," Davin said as he pulled off his boots and socks and began unbuttoning his shirt.

Once he had his shirt off, he dropped it down on top of his boots. He looked down at his jeans and then over at Mark and then me. Instead of taking them off, he took out his phone and put it next to his boots. As he stood up, all his muscles apparent, it was hard to imagine he'd ever been the scrawny boy with the big ears.

Of course Davin was tall enough to just walk across the pond, the water coming up to just under his chin. I had a burst of short girl anger at that. So annoying when tall people could easily do things I couldn't.

"I miss the old boat," he said as he came up on the bank. I noticed he was wearing the necklace I'd seen under his shirt the day before. It wasn't just a chain. An antique coin hung on it. It reminded me of all the times we'd gone treasure hunting, hoping to find a hoard of ancient Roman antiquities.

"A boat would have made things easier," I said, shifting my gaze back to the dog. I didn't want Davin to think I was staring at his chest.

"Here, let me look at the poor fellow," he said.

I handed the dog over. It whimpered again but didn't struggle.

"You've had a rough time," he said to it. "It's okay." He rubbed the dog's ears and it closed its eyes. He studied it and then said, "I think this is the housekeeper's dog. As I remember it was a pug and it got lost several months ago. I wonder where it's been? It can't have been on the island the whole time."

"It's Mrs. Ellis's dog?"

"Yes. I saw signs about it in the village." The dog gave another little whimper. "A vet should look him over."

"I'll take him right away." Now that I had a better view of the dog, I was getting worried we wouldn't even make it to the vet. The shivers that rippled across its body were the only signs it was alive.

"Let's get him to the other side," Davin said. He walked back into the pond lifting the dog over his head as he carried him across.

I swam after them, again cursing my own shortness.

Mark got very upset when he took a close look at the dog.

"Is it going to live?" Mark asked. "It looks really awful." His voice choked.

"We just need to get him to a vet," Davin said. "Here, hand me my shirt and I'll wrap him up in it. He's shivering because he's so thin. He can't keep his body temperature up."

Once the dog was wrapped up, Davin said, "Can you hold him, Mark? I need to get my boots back on. Hold him close and he'll be warmer."

Mark took him, murmuring something to the dog I couldn't make out.

"Can I come with you to the vet?" Mark asked me. "I'll hold onto him in the car. Please?"

"Sure. Let me tell someone where we are going so your mom won't worry when she gets back."

"I know a vet," Davin said. "I'll drive you both and bring you back."

"We all aren't going to fit in your car," I said.

"Oh, I've got a work vehicle today. It's got plenty of room."

"But you're soaked. You must want to change." I didn't want to feel obligated to him.

"I've got some spare clothes in my car. I always carry them in case I get mucky on a job, which I often do."

"All right." He clearly wasn't going to take no for an answer. "I'll get you a towel then and show you where you can change."

"No need. I've got a towel and I can change in the garden shed. I don't want to drip all over the floor of the house. You could get a towel or an old blanket for the dog though."

I should have thought of that. I needed to change as well. Mark and the dog went off with Davin after I said I'd meet them at Davin's car.

When we were underway to the vet's office, I said, "Thank you for driving." It was still stressful for me to drive in England, worrying about turning into the right lanes and maneuvering through the roundabouts. The thought of a boy and an injured dog in my car would add to the stress.

"No problem," Davin said. "I'm glad you found that dog when you did." He didn't add any more to the sentence but I knew he meant the dog wouldn't have lasted much longer.

I looked over at Davin, still thinking about the necklace he wore. "I noticed your necklace," I blurted. "Is that a Roman coin? Did you actually find a treasure hoard?"

"So you remember that." His voice lightened a little. "I did, though not here. Believe it or not, I found it in my family's own back garden one day when I was bored and had been told to stay out of the house. I'm not sure they realized I decided that meant I could dig up part of the lavender bed. Besides destroying some of the lavender, I found twenty-three silver denarii in a small bronze vessel. Up to that point, the finding of it was the most exciting day of my life. Most of what we found was donated to the local museum but I begged to keep this and...well, a few other pieces."

"That must have been thrilling." It had been such a dream of all of us to find treasure, making big plans about what we'd do with the money.

"Yes, it was." He glanced over at me and started to say something else, but then Mark said, "Can you drive faster? I'm really worried."

Luckily we didn't have to wait long to see the vet. He and Davin knew each other, and they made a bit of small talk where I learned Davin's dog had passed away the year before.

"I'll get another one at some point but I've just been traveling for work too much lately," Davin said in response to the vet questioning him about a new one. I could see Davin with a dog, maybe a Border Collie, one that would go with him on jobs.

I didn't realize I was deep in this vision until I heard the vet ask if I knew how long the dog had been missing.

"I don't know," I said. "I've been here about eight months, but the place had been empty for a while before that." I looked over at Davin.

"I'd say about nine months. I remember Mrs. Ellis put up missing signs when she was still there." Davin's phone rang. "Sorry, I have to take this," he said as he left the room.

"Too bad the dog can't talk," the vet said. "I'd like to know where he's been all these months. I suspect he showed up on someone's farm and they've been feeding him. He couldn't have lasted all that time without someone feeding him. Pugs aren't very good hunters or scavengers."

"Wouldn't they know he was lost and try to find the owner?" Mark asked. He was squeezing his hands together like he was trying not to pet the animal.

The vet placed his stethoscope on the dog's chest and listened, then took it away. "He's a little wheezy but not too bad. Whoever has had him may frequent a different town which is why they didn't see the missing posters, or else they just wanted to keep him."

Mark frowned. "That wouldn't be nice of them. Do you know his name?"

"It's Mr. Puggums," the vet replied. At that, the dog gave a wag of its stump of a tail.

"Mr. Puggums?" Mark sounded indignant. "That's a very silly name. Poor dog."

The vet laughed. "I've heard worse. Much worse."

"Well, I'm going to call him just Mr. Pug, or Pug," Mark declared. "Mr. Puggums! That's so silly!"

"At least he seems to know his name." I was impressed that the dog remembered his name after all that time. I'd never been able to tell if Betsey understood any words, or if she did and just ignored being called.

After the vet finished examining the dog, the man said, "No obvious issues, besides the touch of a wheeze and being seriously underweight. I'll give him an antibiotic shot though none of the scratches are serious. He's in a weakened state so the shot will help him fight off any infections. I'll give you some cans of dog food that will be good for him for a few days. Only feed him a bit at a time, because his stomach isn't in any state to have too much food in it. I'll write down the amounts to feed him and the intervals and how to start to introduce regular dog food."

Davin came back in and the vet repeated the same information. "Put it on my bill," Davin said after the dog had gotten his shot and we were given the food.

"I can pay!" I protested.

"No, let me," Davin said. "It will be quicker. They've already got my information and I need to get you back to the house. I just had a call about something I need to take care of."

I couldn't argue with that. Davin had gone into all business mode like the first day he'd been at the house.

The ride back was mostly Mark talking to the dog, though at one point he spoke up and said, "Do dogs see ghosts? Maybe Mr. Pug will be able to see ours."

It was cute that Mark had laid ownership to the Pemberley ghost, but I had no idea how to answer his question.

"I believe your sister mentioned a ghost," Davin said, glancing over at me. I saw one side of his mouth turned up in a smile. "Just how old is your sister?"

"It doesn't have anything to do with her age. If Kiki says she saw a ghost, she did." Once again I felt like I had to defend my sister.

"Yes, Kiki has seen her," Mark said. "And Marni too. I haven't yet. She's an old lady that floats around the house."

Davin raised an eyebrow. "I suppose a story like that might be good for the place's reputation," he said. "Especially if you want to attract Americans. Nothing like a haunted mansion for tourist interest."

"It's not a story!" All of the sudden I wanted the ghost to be real, so he wouldn't think I was trying to make the place into a tourist trap.

We were almost at the house. "Who am I to say you don't have a ghost?" Davin said as the car came to a stop at the front entrance. "Are you all right dealing with the dog?"

I bristled even more. I knew he thought I was too incompetent to renovate the house, but I hoped he would believe I could take care of a dog. "Of course!"

"Good. I'll see you later."

"What's going to happen to him?" Mark asked me as we carried the dog and supplies inside.

I hadn't thought about that. "His owner might want him to go live with someone she knows. I'll go visit her and ask." I set the dog down.

Mark's face fell. "I thought he might be able to stay at your house. I'd help take care of him. Don't you need a dog? Everybody needs a dog. Mom says we can get one soon since I'm eight now. She says that's the best age to get a dog."

I absolutely did not need a dog but how did I tell him that? How did parents resist woebegone little faces? If I'd been Eleanor, I'd be tempted to get him a whole pack of dogs.

"We'll see," I said, meaning no without saying it. "But I really do have to let the owner know we found him. Imagine how worried she must have been about him." If the housekeeper didn't have a place for him to go, I'd find the dog a good home after Eleanor and Mark left.

"I suppose," Mark said. "But maybe she doesn't like him all that much and she'd be glad for you to keep him. She did name him Mr. Puggums after all."

I couldn't argue with that logic.

Betsey came running but skidded to a halt when she realized there was an actual dog creature in the house. She arched her back and hissed. Pug didn't take this seriously. He just wiggled his little butt like he'd met his new best friend. Betsey was not charmed. After an additional hiss with a snarl added on for emphasis, she backed away and then ran back up the stairs.

"She'll get used to him," Mark assured me. "I bet they'll be best friends."

I very much doubted that. I held back a sigh. Here was yet another being I'd have to worry about. Pug rescue had not been on the to-do list. The wedding loomed ever closer and there were no more hours being magically added to the days. The dog wobbled toward the kitchen, which is probably where Mrs. Ellis had fed him. We followed after him.

"Let's go feed him," I said. "I'm sure he's very hungry." I was too, even to the point of eating Kiki's jalapeno shortbread, though I'd have to eat quickly. I had to get back on track with the to-do list after that. I could not afford anything else that might pop up to distract me.

Chapter 12

Countdown to the Raine Randolph/Stefan Andris
Wedding
13-11 days

To Do List:
Dust and vacuum the library
Find the dog a new home
File a restraining order?

I THOUGHT DAVIN might stop by in the next few days to see if I was keeping the dog alive but there was no sign of the man, though his crew continued the work outside. Not that I was really interested in his whereabouts, I told myself, but I did bring up his name at dinner in a casual sort of way. Marni told me he'd gone out of town for a few days but was due back the next day.

Things were moving smoothly and I actually began to hope we'd just roll right up to the wedding day with no problem. Silly me. I learned about the first hitch from Katie when she found me as I was about to dust and vacuum the library. Emmaline had told me we needed a place for the string quartet to hang out before the ceremony and a place to store their instrument cases. The library was large enough for both, but I needed to get it clean enough so they wouldn't think they were being stuck in an abandoned part of the house. I also wanted to see if the ghost would appear with me in there. Did ghosts wander about when no one was around? Or did they just appear when a living person was present? Questions to ponder as I dusted. I did not want to be distracted by Katie.

"I just wanted to thank you for letting me stay," she said. "It's such a great place and I'm having a wonderful time."

"I'm glad," I said. "Thanks for helping. You're doing so much work helping Kiki, I want to pay you."

"No! Just getting to stay here is fantastic. Look, I know you don't like me much." I started to protest but she held up her hand and kept talking. "I was really stupid when I broke up Kiki and her boyfriend. But I was young then." (She had been all of two years younger.) "I should have realized how much she cared about him."

"As long as you realize how much it did hurt her. There are lots of people who wouldn't forgive you for what you did." Like me, I wanted to add. I wasn't nearly as generous or forgiving as my littlest sister. As the elder sister, I felt it was my right to point this out, though Kiki would be furious if she knew what I was doing.

"Oh, I know! Kiki is special! And beyond that, you letting me stay here means a lot. It's helping me figure out things. I can't think at home, not with my dad always on my back."

"Some parents are like that," I said. I didn't remember Kiki ever telling me about Katie's home situation, though she may have and I just didn't listen. I picked up the dust cloth, wanting to cross the dusting off my to-do list.

"Yes, he keeps telling me to grow up and live in the real world. But I don't want to live in his idea of real world." Katie gestured toward the window as if the real world was right outside pressing against it. "There isn't only one, right? My real world will be full of fun and possibilities, where you can't be being dragged down by people who want you to be as miserable as they are."

Obviously not a good home situation. "Keep that idea," I said. "Definitely don't let other people get you down." I thought our conversation had ended, and I wasn't in the mood for more life philosophy talk when I had what felt like acres of books and bookshelves to dust, but she didn't make any motion to leave. "You don't mind if I dust while we talk, do you?" I asked, swishing the cloth across the tops of a section on history.

She didn't respond to my question. "So there is something you should know," she said. "Kiki is better here than she was at home that year, but she still thinks way too much about your mother. Did you know about the letters?"

I stopped dusting. "I knew she'd gotten one. There have been others?"

"I don't know how many, but Kiki got one this morning. She wouldn't let me read it. It must have been bad because she barely ate anything for breakfast and she cried when she broke a glass. Kiki never cries."

A volcanic rage rose within me so fast I could feel my heart speed up. "Okay," I said. My voice was shaky. "I'll take care of it. Thanks for telling me." I set down my dusting cloth. "I'll take care of it right now."

I found Kiki outside the kitchen door, sitting on the steps with her arms wrapped around her knees. She had flour on her cheek and looked about ten years old.

"Hey," I said, sitting down beside her. "How is it going?"

"Good," she said. "I needed to rest my feet for a bit."

"Can I see the letter?"

She pulled it out of her pocket. It looked like she had crumpled it up and then smoothed it out again and refolded it. I opened it up. The handwriting sprawled more than usual and there was no greeting or signature.

This is the gratitude I get for bringing you into this world and raising you? Your father needs help in the diner. He's not getting any younger.

How many times do I have to tell you that your sister will never make her crazy scheme work? And for you to think you can cater weddings is just ridiculous. Going from cooking in a diner to fancy wedding caterer just doesn't happen. That property should be sold and the money should go to help our family. Your smarter brothers and sisters deserve to go to college. I know Libby is selfish but I didn't expect you to be that way too.

And I can only imagine how much weight you've gained without me there to remind you not to eat so much. Don't think you can come crawling back here when it fails and expect that I will have forgotten you ran off without a thought for your family.

I ripped the letter into tiny bits and threw them up into the air, wishing I had a match to light them on fire instead. "This is the last one," I said. "I promise. I'm sorry we got stuck with such a bad witch for a mother. But we're the good witches, right?" When we were younger, I'd told her we didn't have to grow up like our mother, that we'd be the good witches to her bad and learn counter spells to put good magic in the world. It had made her smile then. Not anymore. She nodded but wouldn't look at me.

"She's right, you know." Kiki whispered.

"She's not right about anything!"

"I can't do it," Kiki said. "I can't cater this wedding. It was stupid of me to think I could. We're going to have to hire someone more professional than me."

I put my arm around her shoulder. "If we don't try, she wins. I know you can do it. You're a brilliant cook and the guests are going to be blown away by your food. In fact, I predict some day you will be famous for your chai scones and all the other great things you make. I mean it, that was the last letter," I said as I got up. She didn't even nod or look at me. I hoped that once I told her I'd spoken to our mother, she'd be able to pull herself out of the spiral down. If not, I'd have to keep a close eye on her to figure out if she needed to go back to her therapy zoom visits. She'd said she didn't need to continue them because they were too expensive even on her father's health insurance, but we'd find a way.

I went into the study and shut the door. I didn't want to hear my mother's voice, except she'd left me no choice. I'd long ago given up trying to understand why she behaved the way she did. Something was missing in her, that part of a person that allowed them to find happiness in small ways. I think she recognized she didn't have it and couldn't stand that other people did.

When she answered, I launched right in before she could stop me. "From now on, I'm opening any letter you send Kiki. Don't think you can get around me. She's going to decline your calls and not open your emails either. We're going to put a block on the emails. She's happy here and she's going to stay that way, which means she doesn't need to be in contact with you."

There was a long silence. "Nice to hear from you," my mother said. "I wondered if you'd forgotten you had a mother. I have no idea what you are ranting about. We're all fine here. Thank you for asking."

She was just going to pretend everything was fine.

"I mean it, Mother. Stop writing or contacting Kiki. If you continue, I swear I will file a restraining order. You are not going to drive her into a hospital again." I didn't know if I'd really follow through on a restraining order but she didn't need to know that.

She hung up on me. People who have nice parents never really understand. If you had a bad mother and you survive, you can turn her into a character in funny stories about dreadful parents, to laugh about with friends, though the whole time she will still be there pricking you with the tiny knife of her dislike. Somehow, I was going to keep Kiki free of all that before any more damage was done.

I couldn't go back to work. I needed air and movement to clear my head and calm down my anger so I headed outside. I wandered around until I drew close to the Dutch garden and heard voices.

Marni, Davin, and another man were working on it. Marni and the man stood in the water wearing tall waders. Davin was on the shoreline. I heard Marni say, "And then we built a fire on the beach so we wouldn't freeze to death, and we prayed some boat would come by the next morning to rescue us."

Davin said something in response that I couldn't hear because his back was to me, but whatever he said caused the other two to laugh. Marni bent down and splashed water in his direction. Great. Soon he'd be asking me her age as well.

Marni spotted me and waved. "Come see!" she called.

I felt awkward walking up to them. I didn't want Davin to think I was checking up on the progress. "I just wanted a walk," I said when I got to the edge of the water. It sounded like a made-up excuse.

"Good weather for a walk," Davin said. He motioned toward the man in the water. "This is Joe. You'll be seeing him around quite a bit. He's going to be the manager of all the projects we're doing here."

Joe nodded at me but didn't speak. He was probably mid-twenties and clearly spent a lot of time outside, judging from his tan, which made him appear more Californian than English. He was cute in that Californian way too, with hair a bit shaggy and a casually unshaven face.

"I've been meaning to stop in the house and ask about the dog," Davin said. "Marni tells me he's doing well."

"He is," I said. "He's definitely recovering." Had Davin been checking up on me to make sure the dog was still alive in my dubious care? "We're taking very good care of him. You wouldn't know he's the same dog, He's gaining weight." I probably should have been weighing the dog and making a chart so I could prove I really was watching out for him. "He's fine."

"I'm sure he's in good hands," Davin said.

I felt like I had to come up with a better reason for my presence. "I wanted to make sure the bridge doesn't need work before the wedding. It seemed stable last time I was on it, but I didn't check it over that carefully."

"It's fine," Davin moved around to the other side of me like he was blocking me from the bridge. "You don't need to bother about it. I checked it out. It does need painting though."

"We won't paint it before this first wedding but maybe after that."

"Are you sure? It would look quite a bit better if it was painted."

I didn't know why he cared about the bridge. "I'm sure. It won't fit on the to-do list."

"Davin told us your gang of children believed trolls lived under the bridge," Marni said as she splashed toward the shore.

"We did. But you were the one who made up that story," I said to Davin, remembering details I'd forgotten. "All of the sudden one day you told us we couldn't go there. And Samuel gave you a hard time about it." It was one of the few serious arguments I could remember. Davin had been adamant we wouldn't use it anymore.

"Well, we weren't supposed to play there. It was easier to make up a story than us getting into trouble."

He'd liked the bridge before then. We'd played invading armies, where one side would have to cross the bridge fighting through the defending army, all wielding stick swords. I usually just crept under the sword fighting and made it to the other side first, declaring victory.

"We're ready for another lily," Marni said to Davin.

"We're putting in water lilies to control the algae," he explained, as if he wanted to distract me from the bridge. "The water should clear up very quickly."

"How quickly is quickly?" I asked, knowing that was an unreasonable question. "Will it be clear enough for wedding photos?"

"Possibly, it's hard to predict exactly, but it will at least look better than it does now."

"This spot will make great wedding photos," Marni said. "I'm sure people will post them all over social media."

"Yes, so they can prove to everyone else how happy they are for that one day before it all goes wrong." That came out far more snarky than I intended.

"Whoa!" Marni said. "I'm going to start calling you the Wedding Scrooge, except I won't post that anywhere. That won't get you weddings booked, but maybe you could do divorce parties."

"Sorry. I'm not in the greatest of moods." The crankiness got worse when I realized I'd had the outburst in front of Davin. It would only add to his belief I couldn't handle the job I'd taken on. I needed to get out of there. "Okay, well, I'll leave you to it." I'm sure they were glad when I left so they could go back to the easy mood they'd had before I barged in.

Back inside I looked out the window. Davin was staring up at the house, probably wondering what I was doing wrong at that particular moment.

I returned to my dusting. I had to accomplish at least one thing that day, which might help ease the tension I could feel in my back and neck, tension building to a headache. I managed to finish the library just as my stomach told me it must be close to dinner. Once I had cleaned up, I headed to the kitchen, very ready to eat.

"Something smells good," I said.

Kiki didn't look up from her salad making. "Sweet potato biscuits with apricot jam and ham. Not the British biscuit cookie-kind, the American biscuit kind. And spinach salad." Her voice was a monotone. Not a good sign.

"We're having an after work party," Katie announced as she and Mark set the table. "Which means you can't work tonight." She looked at me and then nodded in Kiki's direction. "I thought we all could use some fun."

I had been planning on doing loads of laundry, though the thought of that was pretty much the last thing I wanted to tackle. "You mean the kind of party where we sit around in a bar and have drinks?" I had a feeling that was not it, because there was a row of flashlights lined up on the kitchen counter.

"Not that kind of party," Katie said. "Too boring! We are hunting for secret passages, of course! What else does one do at an after work party in a giant old mansion?"

I didn't want to tell them I would have known if there were any secret passages in the house.

"I get my own flashlight," Mark said.

"He does. Tell them what you made for dessert after the hunt," Katie urged Kiki.

"Mango passion fruit cheesecake." Kiki did give a hint of a smile at this.

I realized Katie's idea might be just what we needed to get Kiki away from the thoughts I knew were plaguing her. Forget laundry.

"Okay, I'm all in," I said.

"Mark, could you go find your mom and Marni?" Kiki asked. "We're about ready to eat."

Dinner sped by because Mark finished quickly and urged the rest of us on. Kiki didn't talk much during dinner. I wished I could wind the day backwards and intercept the mail before she had seen it.

As soon as we had cleared up dinner, Katie handed out flashlights. "We've got enough for everyone, and they all have new batteries."

Last time I checked, we did have electricity in the house, but since Mark was so excited about the flashlights, I didn't mention that minor fact.

"We need to be able to see really well," Mark said as he turned on his flashlight and zoomed it around the room.

"Not in our eyes," Eleanor reminded him.

"Do you remember the night scavenger hunts you used to make for us?" Kiki asked me while she flicked her flashlight on and off. "Those were a lot of fun."

I did remember. It was mainly to keep my siblings occupied when I was babysitting them, not really for their enjoyment. I'd send them outside with flashlights and a list of things to bring back, like a round rock or a big leaf or a forked stick. It kept them busy for a long time.

"Yes, you really liked those." Her face seemed more relaxed, which spurred me to get in the spirit of Katie's plan. "I'm ready."

"Okay, so is there a plan for this?" Marni asked.

"We tap on all the walls listening for hollow sounds," Katie said.

"What's a hollow sound?" Mark asked.

"We'll know when we hear it," Kiki said. "And then we'll see if anything looks like a knob or a lever that might open a door, so we have to examine all the wood and plaster decorations that are on the fireplaces and anywhere else."

I could have offered to use the stud finder, but I knew that would take away the fun so I kept quiet. I realized even without the stud finder, I was going to have to show them the difference between tapping on a wall with a stud behind it and tapping on a wall in the space between the studs, or Katie would have us punching holes in walls.

Mark carried Pug up the stairs to join us, though at that point the dog was fine going up and down on his own. Mark was still convinced the animal was too weak for too much exertion, but it was mainly because the boy liked carrying the dog around. Betsey followed us, though as soon as she realized Pug had joined our band of intrepid explorers, she went off to sulk.

I had named the upstairs rooms when I was a child, based on either wallpaper or pieces of furniture or paintings that had been in the rooms.

We started with what I used to call the Lost Children bedroom, because the faded 18th century toile wallpaper had a repeat of two little children leading their pet goat about amongst the trees and shrubs. I'd made up stories about their situation, how they were going to have to survive on berries and leaves and make a little hut out of branches for themselves and the goat. Then eventually they'd be rescued by a group of kids playing in the woods, and they'd become part of our gang, because we needed another girl and we certainly could have used a goat. I had kept a sharp lookout for them whenever we played in the woods. For some reason it didn't occur to me back then that the wallpaper children weren't actually going to come alive.

A carved mahogany four poster bed frame was the only piece of furniture that remained in the room. Kiki and I had lugged the unsalvageable mattress downstairs in our initial round of cleanup because the mice had been at it. The first summer I'd come to Pemberley, I'd been a little scared of the bed frame. The legs ended in some large carved animal feet and I used to dream the bed would come to life at night and carry off whoever slept in it. Ideally, we'd get another mattress and more furniture and turn it back into a useable bedroom.

Katie soon decided we couldn't all be knocking at the same time. Kiki got into it, following Katie and Mark around as they knocked. Marni and Eleanor and I were assigned the tasks of checking the molding and the decorations on the fireplace to see if there was any sign of a way to open a secret door.

After much knocking, Katie declared that room didn't hold anything special. "Next room," she announced.

The next room had been decorated in dark Victoriana, with blood red damask wallpaper and dark wood trim throughout. "I used to call this the Egypt Room," I told them. "I had one ancestor who was an amateur Egyptologist, and when I used to come here as a kid, there were still things like Egyptian cat statues and scrolls hanging on the walls."

"Real ancient Egypt artifacts?" Eleanor asked.

"No, just reproductions, because he liked to be reminded of Egypt when he was away from it. I'm not sure he ever actually found anything on a dig but he liked to go there to hang out with the real archeologists."

We took up our same jobs in the Egypt room though there were more decorative plaster elements so it took longer. The fireplace had both a mantel and something called an overmantel, where someone had stuck an extra mantelpiece on top of the one that surrounded the fireplace.

"I feel like I'm in a Nancy Drew mystery," Eleanor said as she pushed on one of the little plaster faces in the scrolling design that ran across the top of the fireplace.

"Ooooh. Let's do Nancy Drew photos," Marni said. "Here, hold up your flashlight and look like you are peering into the dark. I'll take a picture of it." She set down her own flashlight and got out her phone.

Eleanor, to my surprise, did exactly that, and then when Marni had finished taking the picture, they both burst into laughter.

"I actually preferred the Hardy Boys myself," Marni said. "I read all my father's old ones. Let's do a Hardy Girls cover. My favorite was The Tower Treasure. Frank is plastered against a door looking scared and Joe is peeking around the corner of the door, though he has his arm out so he's not really hiding very well. Like this." First she demonstrated Frank and then Joe.

"Okay, I'll be Frank," Eleanor said. She stood against the door and took on an expression where she really did look scared.

"Mommy, you are silly!" Mark said.

She winked at him and then resumed her Frank imitation.

"Libby, take our picture." Marni became Joe Hardy. It was all so ridiculous, I could hardly hold the phone still enough to take the picture because I was shaking with laughter.

"Can I be in one?" Mark asked.

"Sure," Marni said. "Let me think." She snapped her fingers. "I've got it! There's one called the Hidden Harbor Mystery and Frank is pulling Joe out of the water. We can get Kiki's blue blanket off her bed and wrap it around you, like you're in the water. Then your mom can be Frank and pretend she's pulling you out."

Mark pumped his fist in the air. "Yes!"

This one took quite a bit of time to arrange, and didn't actually resemble water and rescue, but no one cared.

We did several more covers like that. I played Nancy in a few of them, including The Ghost of Blackwood Manor. After that one, Kiki said we should write our own book, called The Ghost of Pemberley.

"Speaking of the ghost, has anyone seen her up here?" Katie asked.

"No, she's only appeared on the ground floor," Kiki said.

"Just the perfect place to frighten wedding guests," I added.

"Pug and I want to see her!" Mark said. "Right, Pug?"

Pug wiggled his butt at this, as if he understood and he'd be thrilled to face down a supernatural element.

"Wouldn't you be scared?" Eleanor asked.

"Nah," Mark said. "I'm not scared of silly old ghosts."

"When was the last time the ghost was spotted?" I asked. "Maybe she's moved on to haunt a different house." One could hope.

"I saw her the day after Marni spotted her in the library," Kiki said. "I didn't tell you because I didn't want you to get all worked up, but I haven't seen her since then."

"We haven't seen her at all," Eleanor said.

"Me neither, though I'm keeping a lookout." Katie sounded as irritated as if she hadn't been invited to a party she particularly wanted to attend.

So the ghost hadn't been seen for at least a week. That was a positive. Maybe weather or time of year had something to do with her appearance.

"We should get back to the hunt," Kiki said. "Maybe she'll turn up!" We searched every room on the second floor, though by the last few rooms, we didn't do a thorough job.

Finally, Kiki held up her hand and announced, "I'm getting hungry. Let's call it a day and eat dessert!"

Katie looked downhearted, but only for a moment. "I'm done looking for tonight, but I'm not going to give up."

"Me neither," Mark declared.

Back in the kitchen we turned in our flashlights and then snarfed the cheesecake.

"Delicious," Eleanor said. "A perfect ending to secret passage hunting."

"I never thought I'd actually get to hunt for secret passages. This is such an incredible house," Katie said to me. "You are so lucky to live here."

"We are lucky." I realized I hadn't thought about needing to fix anything up for hours and I'd had fun, both of which were rare occurrences. In fact, I didn't remember the last time I'd had so much fun with a group of friends. Maybe college? When I was with William we'd done a few things with couples who were mostly his acquaintances, none of whom would have posed for a Nancy Drew photo shoot. And the house itself was special. I needed to remember to focus on that sometimes instead of just seeing it as a money pit needing repairs.

"This is a great place," Marni said. "I actually never want to leave. Forget teaching. I'll be the gardener."

Everyone laughed, but I couldn't be sure Marni was actually joking. She hadn't said a word about her job or apartment hunting or anything work-related since we'd talked in the library. It worried me, though I was not really in any position to give advice about life or work to anyone.

"I assume what we ate tonight are all tryouts for the wedding?" I asked Kiki, hoping she'd backtracked on her worries earlier that she couldn't do the catering.

"Yes, Raine doesn't want cake," Kiki said as she put the cheesecake away. "That's why we are doing macarons, cupcakes and cheesecakes. I'm going to cut the cheesecakes into slices and arrange them on a tiered stand so it will look a bit like a cake, and then we're adding flowers all over it too. It's going to be so great!"

Even though Kiki sounded back to normal, I knew I'd have to be vigilant about the mail to keep her that way. And even intercepting the mail might not be enough. She'd sometimes get too down without any specific triggers.

Right before I fell into bed, I checked my email. One from my mother and one from William. I deleted both unread, and that felt like a major accomplishment. A year ago I wouldn't have been able to manage that. There was also an email from Caro Bingley. I didn't delete it but I couldn't bring myself to open it.

I took out my notebook and drew a rabbit with a sword stick defending a bridge. He had extra large ears and extra large feet and was quite dashing for a rabbit. I sighed and turned the page. No turning back time. "Think about the now," I whispered to myself.

Another rabbit appeared from my pencil, this one a Nancy Drew rabbit creeping up some stairs with a lantern held in front of it. Not one of my best drawings. The rabbit looked more irritated than intrigued, but such was the problem with drawing rabbit expressions. The slightest difference in the angle of one line could change the whole look. I was too tired to fix it so I put the notebook away.

I leaned over the bed to look under it, where Betsey had taken to sleeping since the invasion of Pug. "We're good, Betsey," I said. "Really. Pug just wants to be your friend. We all can use friends, right?" That was becoming so much more clear to me. Never again would I neglect my friends and the family I wanted around me.

Betsey crept out and jumped up on the bed beside me. One small victory.

I looked at my phone to check the time. It was after midnight. Eleven days to the wedding.

Chapter 13

Countdown to the Raine Randolph/Stefan Andris
Wedding
11 days

To Do List:
Visit Mrs. Ellis-Casually bring up ghost sightings
Pick up more gilding paint on the way back
Pay more attention to Betsey
Figure out Pug's future

I DIDN'T VISIT Mrs. Ellis until Pug had been given a clean bill of
health at a follow-up vet checkup. I actually wanted to wait until after
the wedding but every day Mark asked me if the dog could stay, and he
was so anxious about it, I felt like I had to do something to settle the
question. By then, the dog had already filled out a little and spent his
days basking in attention from all the humans in the house. Mark and

the dog were inseparable, and Eleanor agreed Pug could sleep in Mark's room.

Betsey had agreed to at least not scratch him to shreds, though she hissed whenever he crossed some invisible perimeter around her. She wasn't eating as much as she usually did, which worried me.

Emmaline had texted me that morning. *Okay if Stefan and the jewelry designer show up around 3:00?*

I'd hoped to have more notice to mentally prepare, but I doubted if a man like Stefan Andris could be put off. *Fine* I texted back. I decided not to tell everyone he was coming that day so Katie wouldn't have time to work herself into a tizzy. She'd been filling us in on every possible fact about Raine and Stefan, as if she was researching them to write their biographies.

The care home where Mrs. Ellis had moved to was in the next village. From the outside it was as nice as the one my grandmother had been in. Flower beds filled the front, paved pathways winding among them. A few people were out in wheelchairs enjoying the sunshine. As I signed in at the front desk, I realized I should have brought flowers or chocolates or something.

"I'm here to visit Mrs. Ellis," I said to the receptionist.

The woman studied me. "I don't think I've seen you here before. Mrs. Ellis doesn't get many visitors. Are you a relative?"

"No, Mrs. Ellis worked for my grandmother. I knew her when I was a child but I haven't seen her for years. I'm American." I realized this last bit was obvious from my accent and I don't even know why I said it, unless it was meant to be an apology for not visiting earlier.

The receptionist motioned down the main hallway. "She's in her room today. Room 211. Most days she likes the sitting room but she's not feeling her best today. I should warn you, she can be a bit sharp at times. It's understandable really, when a person doesn't feel well."

"Oh, I remember. She's always been a bit sharp. I have a question. Do you allow dogs here? We found her dog, which has been lost. I'm sure she'd like to see him."

"Not in the building, though she could see him outside if she'd like. You'd need to call the morning you wanted to bring the animal over."

"All right. I'll ask her when I see her."

The door to her room was open but I knocked on the frame anyways. I recognized her of course, though not surprisingly she seemed much smaller to me than I remembered. She sat in a chair positioned so she could look out the window. When she turned to look at me as I walked in, her expression wasn't exactly welcoming.

"Mrs. Ellis, I'm Libby Darcy, Mrs. Darcy's granddaughter. I used to come visit in the summers."

I noticed her hands were badly crippled with arthritis. She tipped her head and narrowed her eyes.

"Yes, I remember you. Robert's girl, the little quiet girl with that mother." She snorted. "Never understood what Robert saw in her." There wasn't any answer to that. I'd wondered that myself.

I felt like I was six years old again, trying not to irritate her with my requests for glasses of water. "May I come in and talk to you?"

"If you like," she said, showing a distinct lack of enthusiasm.

I went over and stood awkwardly next to her. There were no other chairs in the room. "I'm trying to fix up the house," I said. "Pemberley?"

She rolled her eyes. "I know the name of the house. Where do you think I spent my life?"

It had been a stupid thing to say. I took hold of my bracelet and ran the beads through my fingers. I didn't know why she was making me so nervous. "I have some good news," I said in such a perky voice I sounded like a demented cheerleader. Get ahold of yourself, Libby. This is an old lady who has no control over you. "We found your dog. He's fine, though he's a little thin, but the vet said he'll get back up to a normal weight soon."

"You found Mr. Puggums?" She leaned forward. "That dog! Always getting into trouble, chewing up cushions and being a nuisance. I thought his time was up this time. Are you sure it's him? He's been missing a long time."

"Yes, the vet recognized him." I told her the story.

"Hmm...I suppose it really is him then. I thought the little eejit had been hit by a car or something. I can't believe he's still alive." I couldn't tell if she was pleased by the news. Her expression hadn't changed.

"He's alive and happy. We have a little boy who is staying at Pemberley and who dotes over him."

"Hmmph...children in the house. I hope the child isn't making a mess."

"No, he's not."

"What's going to happen to the dog?" she asked. "You won't turn him over to animal control, will you? He's too old to go to a new home. He was my sister's dog, you know, and when she passed, I took him in. Not that I wanted a dog, but I did get used to having him around, even with all the trouble he caused."

So she did care about him. "We'll keep him," I said, impulsively gifting myself a dog. Not a gift I really wanted. But I didn't have a choice to say anything else. At least Mark would be thrilled.

"Good. Don't let him eat table scraps. He's got a tetchy stomach."

"We'll take care of him," I said. She looked at the clock on the bedside table like she was ready for me to go away.

I forced myself not to take her hint quite yet. "I wanted to apologize for something," I said. "I heard you wrote to my grandmother. I'm sorry no one answered your letters. They...they got misplaced."

"Did they now? Mail usually gets to where it's sent." Yes, she was as sharp as always.

"It usually does, just not in this case." I did not want to explain about my stepmother. "Thank you for staying on as long as you did. I know it was a tremendous amount of work."

"Well, what was I supposed to do! Of course I stayed on. I wasn't going to let that thieving bastard of an estate manager steal everything. Mr. Willoughby would have carted off the fillings in my teeth if he could have got at them. I caught him taking one of your grandmother's favorite vases and that's when I knew he didn't have permission. I put my foot down and told him no more until I got word he was doing what Mrs. Darcy wanted."

"Why didn't you report him to the police?"

She shifted in her chair and turned her head away from me, looking out the window as if there was something she needed to see. "I should have," she said finally. "But it's complicated." She paused for so long I thought she wasn't going to say anything else, but then she spoke again, still looking out the window. "I asked Mr. Willoughby to hire my nephew to help Mr. Mackenzie in the garden. Fred is a good boy but he fell in with a bad lot and he needed to get back on his feet."

I didn't understand what that had to do with Willoughby.

The blanket covering her lap seemed to need attention and she fussed with it, smoothing it out while she talked. "Fred didn't always show up for work but the estate kept paying him. Mr. Willoughby said he'd tell the police it was Fred who stole everything, and they'd believe him over me. That was true. I was letting Fred live in the house so he had access to

everything and he had got himself into trouble in the village in the time
he was there, too much drinking and fighting. I don't know how a good
boy could go so wrong. He is a few sandwiches short of a picnic, but I
didn't think he'd get in to as much trouble as he did."

"Oh." I didn't know what else to say. I could see how it had happened.
One of my stepbrothers was also a few sandwiches short of a picnic, and
managed to find trouble where no one else could.

"I should have realized what Mr. Willoughby was up to long before I
did," she added. "Then when I cut him off and he left, I was worried he'd
come back. I wasn't having any of that. All those trips Fred and I made
up and down the stairs taking things to safety. We must have moved half
the house down there. My knees ached so bad every night for a week.
Fred nearly put out his back moving the shelves in front of the door."

At first I didn't understand what she was saying. "What stairs? What
things did you take to safety?"

"Why, everything Fred and I could carry. Do you mean you haven't
found it yet? I wrote a letter about that too."

I could feel my heart speed up. "No, I haven't found anything. The
house is empty. Where is everything?"

"Everything is in the tunnel in the Dooms. All padlocked nice and
safe. I put the key to the padlock hanging inside the pantry door. It was
all in the letter."

The Dooms was the name for the series of dark interlinked cellars
at Pemberley, but there were no tunnels down there as far as I knew,
and I think I would have known. I'd explored the place thoroughly with
Samuel, as we dared each other to venture into the darkest parts. Davin
had been so jealous he and the other children weren't allowed in the
house to explore with us. Was the woman imagining it all?

"What tunnel?" I asked. "I never saw it on any of my visits."

"Your grandmother didn't want you children playing in it. She didn't even like it when you played in the Dooms. The entrance is behind the racks of old beer casks. It's where supplies used to come in from the village. Big enough for a horse pulling a cart to come right in so they could be unloaded out of the weather. Many big houses have those sort of tunnels."

"They do?" I had no idea.

"Yes, some even had rail tracks going into them, for coal and such. Nice and dry, the Pemberley tunnel is. They built them solid back in the day, all lined with brick. It's next to the boiler room and that helps keep it dry."

"Why wouldn't we have seen the entrance to it when we were playing outside?"

"Oh, the outside entrance was filled in and bricked up years ago, right after the war, when they stopped holding large house parties and they couldn't get staff to run the place like they used to. That's what the old housekeeper told me back when I first started working there."

I tried to picture where a tunnel entrance on the outside of the building might be. The back west corner of Pemberley was covered with huge rhododendrons that had been planted many decades ago. A bricked-up entrance behind them would be easy to miss.

"Not sure how everything will look after all this time," Mrs. Ellis said. "It was dry when we put things in there, but you never know. I just assumed someone would have emptied it by now."

The Damp. I had a horrible feeling we'd open up the tunnel and find everything rotted and covered with mold, with my luck probably some mutant kind of mold that would infect humans and turn us into zombies.

"Thank you." I couldn't wait to get back to Pemberley to see what she'd hidden. But there was one more question I needed to ask. "I feel a bit silly asking this, but did you ever hear any talk of ghosts at Pemberley?"

I thought she'd give another snort and a withering reply. Instead, she looked down at the blanket and picked at a loose thread.

"My sister Kiki thought she saw a ghost," I said, as the silence stretched out. "I don't remember ever hearing anything about one, though I know it's common enough to claim there is a ghost in old houses here."

"Could be," she muttered, still looking at the blanket.

"There could be?" I repeated. "Did you...did you ever see a ghost?"

"I did, but it was a silly old bint of a ghost. Wandering around, scaring the dickens out of a person. More a nuisance than anything else. I just ignored her."

I was staggered. How did I not know the place had a ghost?

"What about my grandmother? She never mentioned it."

Mrs. Ellis looked up at me. "She couldn't see her. Laughed at me when I told her about it. Said she was afraid I was nipping into the cooking sherry too much. If she hadn't needed me to keep the place running, I'd have given my notice right then. But I didn't want anyone else taking over my kitchen."

I felt strangely better my grandmother hadn't been able to see the ghost either.

"What about your nephew? Could he see it?" I felt like I needed to collect some data on this phenomenon, though I had no idea what to do with the information.

"The ghost was gone by then. Disappeared a few years ago and never shown herself since then, at least not while I was there. So she's back, you say?"

"My sister says she is."

"Well, just pay no mind to the old thing. She never does anything but drift around the house. I got to where I ignored her after a while."

Sound advice, since there wasn't much else we could do, strange as it seemed. I still didn't want to have to worry about it appearing at weddings as an unwanted guest but at that moment I was much more interested in the tunnel in the Dooms than a ghost I couldn't see.

"Um...is there anything you need?" I wanted to get out of there and felt a bit of a fraud asking, after I'd made no effort to see her before.

"You don't need to bother with me." She waved at the door. "Go along now, my bridge game is about to start."

I sped home, my heart racing with excitement, and praying that whatever had been saved was still in good enough condition to use.

Chapter 14

- -

Countdown to the Raine Randolph/Stefan Andris
Wedding
11- 10 days

To Do List:
~~Visit Mrs. Ellis-Casually bring up ghost sightings~~
Pick up more paint
Pay more attention to Betsey
~~Figure out Pug's future~~
Cross fingers that the Damp has not devoured everything

THE HOUSE WAS quiet except for the sound of a blender. I found
Katie in the kitchen pulverizing something green so I waved at her and
then hurried over to the pantry door. Inside, on a small hook up high on
the side of the door frame, hung a small key. I could see why we hadn't

noticed it. It hung above a person's sight line, and the single bulb in the pantry cast only a small amount of light in the space.

I grabbed the key and came back into the kitchen. Katie turned off the blender. "This sauce is amazing!" she said. "Kiki took a chimichurri recipe and changed it up. She's left out the garlic and added in a little bit of green tea to add umami. So you want to taste?"

"Not right now, thanks. Where is everyone?"

"Eleanor and Kiki went to a grocery store. Marni and Mark and Mr. Mackenzie took off in his truck to go to a nursery. They took Pug with them."

I took a brief moment to worry about Kiki driving but then decided it was too late to prevent it. "Can you stop what you're doing? I need help in the cellar."

"Sure." She set down a spatula.

I told her what we were doing as we went down the stairs and she nearly exploded with excitement. "That is so awesome! I knew there would be something like that here. I thought it would be upstairs though. I didn't think about the cellar."

The lighting in the Dooms was poor, consisting of a few uncovered lightbulbs hanging from the ceiling. Shelves, both metal and older wooden ones, lined some of the walls. An assortment of no longer useful items collected dust on them, ancient casks that had once held beer and liquor, scores of old tools and random bits of metal I couldn't identify.

Katie shined her phone between the shelves. "I see it!" she squealed. "I see the padlock and the door handle. We just have to move the shelf."

Easier said than done. The wooden shelf was solid and heavy and full of casks that smelled of what might have once been brandy. I put my hands on one side of it and pulled. Nothing happened. "We're going to have to empty it first."

By the time we unloaded it, I was out of breath. The air in the Dooms wasn't great and I didn't want to think too much about what we were breathing in.

"Okay, let's try again." We managed about an inch, because even the empty shelf was heavy and we couldn't slide it on the uneven stone floor.

I heard a voice in the distance. "Hello? Hello? Libby are you down there? We have a visitor."

"What time is it?" I asked as I checked my phone. It was two o'clock. "Stefan Andris is coming with a jewelry designer at 3:00. I hope he's not early."

Katie let out a gasp as I hurried towards the stairs yelling, "We're down here!"

I burst into the kitchen to find Kiki and Stefan Andris, the groom-to-be standing there. Kiki was handing a cookie to Stefan as if he was just an ordinary person, not a drop dead gorgeous and famous actor.

"Oh, I'm so sorry," I said to him. "I lost track of time. I'm Libby Darcy." I held out my hand to shake his and then realized it was filthy, so I wiped it on my jeans. "Sorry, we've been in the cellar and we haven't gotten around to cleaning much down there." We hadn't cleaned at all, but I wasn't going to say that.

"It's all right. I'm early. I hope it's not an inconvenience."

Katie made a choking sound behind me. I hoped she wasn't dying from a bad case of star struckedness.

"No, not at all," I said. I introduced Katie and then asked Kiki, "Everything okay?" I wanted to know if the car and Eleanor had survived Kiki's driving.

"Everything is fine," Kiki replied. "Eleanor went upstairs to make a phone call. What were you doing in the Dooms?"

"The Dooms?" Stefan asked. "What's that? It sounds interesting."

"It's the name for the cellar!" Katie sounded as if she couldn't get enough breath. "There is a secret tunnel down there! Behind some old shelves. We're trying to get into it but the shelves are too heavy to move. Oh, and I'm a big fan of Raine! And...and you too, of course."

He laughed. "I'm a big fan of Raine too. But tell me more about this secret tunnel."

I tried to explain about the tunnel and the estate manager and the housekeeper, all of which I didn't do very well.

He understood at least some of it. "That's terrific! It sounds like something out of a movie. Can I take a look?" I knew he was my age from Katie's recitation of his history, but at that moment from the expression on his face he might have been about twelve.

"Of course, if you want to. Like I said, it's very dusty down there."

"I don't mind. I'd really like to see."

Katie choked back what might have been a squeal. I led the way back downstairs and over to the shelf. "It's heavier than it looks."

He went over to one corner and grabbed hold of it.

"I didn't mean I expected you to move it!" I said.

"I really want to see what's in there too. I love this sort of thing. Maybe if someone else can help with this side, we can move it out enough to get behind it."

Kiki, Katie and I all grabbed hold and between the four of us we managed to shift it far enough away to reveal the door.

Once I could get at the door, I felt a little like Howard Carter breaking into Tutankhamun's tomb. I wished I'd asked Mrs. Ellis more about what she'd been able to save, because the anticipation was almost too much. My hands were actually shaking when I tried to open the padlock.

"Can I do it?" Katie asked.

"Yes, please." I handed the key to her.

She had to jiggle the key a bit, but finally the padlock snapped open. I pulled on the door handle. It creaked but didn't move more than an inch or so.

"It's the damp," I said. "I think it's warped the door."

"I'll try, if you like," Stefan said. He was already moving to take hold of the door.

It took so much pulling that I was afraid he'd pull a muscle and we'd have a groom in a body brace or groggy from painkillers, but in the end he got it open.

"There," he said and let go of the handle. It immediately swung shut again with a bang. "Okay, so I guess I should have propped it open. Let's try that again."

Once he'd reopened it I used the light on my phone to shine it inside. Mrs. Ellis hadn't been exaggerating. They had moved half the house.

"Wow!" Kiki said. "I wish there was more light."

"Um...there's a switch here," Stefan pointed to the wall. He turned it on and the place flooded with light to reveal a long narrow space packed full of objects covered in dust cloths, sheets, old bath towels, even old clothes.

I was overcome. I'd never thought I'd care much about possessions, but then I'd never had possessions that had been an integral part of a house.

"It's almost as good as a secret passage!" Katie lifted a dust sheet to reveal a small square table with an intricate marquetry top.

"I remember that. It was in the drawing room." I unfolded each of the wooden triangle pieces on the top of the table. "It's called an envelope table because it opens up like this, so you could play cards on it." My grandmother and I had played gin rummy on it in the evenings.

We uncovered some paintings and mirrors and while the others were examining a painting of an older woman with two younger ones, I shined my light farther into the tunnel. Something sparkled about halfway down. As I made my way to it, I realized it was the old opera cape I'd loved. When I got close, I saw it was draped over a bust from the sculpture gallery.

I couldn't believe it still existed, though just like Mrs. Ellis, it was smaller than I remembered, and much more faded.

I picked it up, hoping it wouldn't fall to bits in my hand. Some of the boys had made fun of it, though not Robin. His Indiana Jones hat gave him no position to ridicule my cape.

I was a little surprised at how happy it made me to find the cape. I felt the soft velvet between my fingers, memories rushing back. Nostalgia is a tricky lure. It can cloud your judgement so much, you forget the past can't be recreated.

"Look!" I heard Katie's voice. "There's a little dog on the woman's lap. I think it's a pug, though the painting has darkened so much, it's hard to tell."

"Yes, it's definitely a pug," Stefan said. "They have a long history of being lap pets. I know too much about them. Raine used to have one."

"Libby, do you want us to uncover all of this?" Kiki asked.

I couldn't put Stefan Andris to work in my cellar. "No. We'll have to look at all this later. There is so much to sort through and it's all so dusty."

"Do you mind if I take a couple of photos?" Stefan asked. "I want to show my brother this. He'll think it's great too."

"Go right ahead," I said.

Stefan took photos and then we went back upstairs, though I was reluctant to leave our treasure trove. I filled everyone in on what Mrs.

Ellis had told me. Kiki fed us more cookies and some cold fruity concoction while we talked.

"Do you know exactly what the estate manager took?" Katie asked.

"No, and we'll probably never know, but the tunnel is full, enough so the house won't seem so abandoned when we put everything back in place."

"I can see why Raine is absolutely taken with the place," Stefan said. "She wouldn't stop talking about it when Emmaline showed her the pictures. I'd like to take on a renovation project like this."

"It's been a bigger job than I expected," I said.

Stefan chuckled. "They always are. I grew up in a house that was in bad shape. It took a lot of effort just to keep it livable. Of course, it was a closet compared to this but it was still so much work. Can I have the whole tour?" He looked at his phone. "The jewelry designer is running behind schedule."

"Sure," I said. "But the upstairs isn't in great shape. We're concentrating all our efforts down here."

"I don't mind. I'd like to see it all."

We started upstairs first, Katie trailing after us worshipfully. Betsey paced back and forth at the top of the stairs, clearly distressed at the presence of a stranger in the house. I expected her to bolt when she got a good look at Stefan, but she didn't move.

"Hello there." He crouched down next to her and held out his hand.

"She's not very friendly. In fact, she usually hides when strangers are here." I was worried she'd scratch at him. We'd managed to avoid a groom in a back brace but a groom with a cat scratch across his face would be just as bad. I hadn't realized I'd have to be a groom safety manager in addition to all my other jobs. "She hasn't really settled in yet."

"It's all right," he said. "I won't pet her if she doesn't want me to."

She stood up and came over to him, rubbing her head against his knee.

"There you go." He reached out and petted her head. She started to purr.

"Are you some kind of cat whisperer?" I asked. "That's amazing."

"I like animals," he said. "They seem to sense that."

He scratched her under her chin. She purred even louder. "Do you just have the one cat?"

"Yes, she's the queen bee."

"Oh, too bad," he said as he stood back up and surveyed the hallway. "Renovating the house seems like a terrific project. You wouldn't consider selling it, would you?"

At first I thought I had misunderstood what he said. "Are you serious?"

"Sure. The more I see this, the more I really want to renovate a place. I'm kind of tired of acting, to be honest." He went over and took a look inside the Lost Children room. "For a long time, I wanted to live in places that didn't need any work at all. I got sick of everything breaking when I was growing up. But now that I've lived in those sorts of places, it's starting to feel like they are actually hotels meant for just a few people. I'd like to do something real, and fixing up a place like this so it would last seems worth doing."

"Sorry, no, I'm not interested in selling." I said, before I was tempted to explore the idea. "There are lots of other places that need fixing though. I'm sure you can find something."

"Okay, but if you change your mind, the offer is open." He grinned.

I grinned back. I couldn't help it. He was a really nice guy.

I took him through the entire second floor. He was interested in everything and asked intelligent questions about the renovation plans.

We didn't make it to the third floor. As I was explaining about the rotted floorboards, Kiki called out from the hallway that the jewelry designer had arrived.

"She's a bit intense," Stefan warned as we went back downstairs. "Great at her job, but not one for small talk."

"Okay," I said. "That's good to know. If I try to chitchat with someone and they act like I'm being a pain, I want to crawl in a hole." I didn't know why I was telling him my flaws. He just had a way about him that made it easy to talk to him.

The jewelry designer wore all black, and no jewelry except for one tiny gold bead on a thin gold chain. I don't know what I expected but she did have the "I am an artiste" attitude about her and she ignored me after the introduction, even as I showed them the rooms that were going to be used for the wedding. In each one, she walked all around the perimeter, then moved to the center where she slowly turned around in a circle. She didn't speak the entire time until we had seen everything.

"I have some ideas," she said to Stefan. "We could do something with emeralds. The greens in the conservatory are quite vivid. I'd use oval emeralds to mimic the shape of leaves, with smaller diamonds for sparkle, as if the leaves are dusted with drops of water. Or we could do something with a mix of stones. The wallpaper in the drawing room is stunning. We could do rubies, yellow diamonds, sapphires and emeralds. It would be almost a rainbow of colors. Very vivid, just like Raine."

"I'd like to look at both rooms again," Stefan said. We followed him while he went back to those two rooms. It didn't take him long to decide. "I like the emerald and the diamond idea. Raine will too," he declared.

"I'll get started on it right away," the designer said. There was no discussion of price though it was dizzying to imagine how much such a piece of jewelry would cost.

After the woman left, Stefan lingered a while longer, and I got the feeling he wanted to help unpack the tunnel, but then he received a text message. "I have to go," he said. "Thanks for the tour. I'll see you all again soon enough."

We said our goodbyes and watched out the window as he drove away. I assumed I wouldn't hear from him or see him until the wedding.

"Imagine someone like that wanting to marry you," Katie said. "He grew up very poor, you know."

"Yes, you told us that."

She repeated that part of his biography anyway, as if she was practicing to be hired to narrate his life. "His father abandoned the family and Stefan was the oldest child. He supported them all once he started acting in movies. He became super successful, but he has stayed such a nice guy. And now he's marrying Raine. It's like a fairytale."

Fairytales. I'd like to believe in them, at least the grown-up variety of mostly happily ever after. Except I couldn't picture myself in that sort of tale. Maybe you had to be able to imagine the fairytale to have a chance at it. My dreams of how my life would go had always been hazy because I was too consumed with escaping from home to think about the future. Once William had asked me to marry him, I still couldn't picture the future, which is probably why I hadn't pushed for a wedding date or spent any time thinking about wedding dresses and bridesmaid dresses and all that.

We spent the rest of the day carrying items up from the tunnel. At first we put them in the hallway but that quickly filled up. I didn't want any of the cardboard boxes full of knickknacks moved up, because then they'd have to be unpacked and I'd have to find them places to live.

"Wait," I said. "This is a big disorganized mess. We're supposed to be getting more organized, not less." My excitement over finding everything faded as I realized all the extra work they would entail. We needed more items in the house but figuring out what and where to put them would take hours off our wedding prep time. My anxiety rose and I got to the point where I didn't know what to do.

I must have been twisting my bracelet because Kiki came over and said, "Breathe, Libby. This is a good thing, remember?"

I tried to breathe, which did help a little. At this point Eleanor had come back downstairs and we'd filled her in on the situation. "You need a plan and an inventory. I can do the inventory. It will help you decide where to put things. What do you need most for the wedding? Let's focus on that."

The row of gilded mirrors leaning against one wall caught my eye. I remembered my grandmother had said many of them were Venetian, brought from Italy by some ancestor, and that there were so many of them because they reflected light from candles and gas fixtures at night in the days before the house had electricity. "The mirrors first," I said, calming down enough to make a decision. Eleanor's presence helped. "And then maybe some of the paintings, if we can figure out where they went and there are still hooks to hang them."

I'd never paid much attention to the paintings when I'd visited as a child, because most were either of pastoral scenes or ancient relatives in strange clothes. My grandmother had told me none of them were very valuable, but that was years ago, and she never told me a dollar amount that equated to valuable. In her mind, it could have meant something was worth a thousand dollars or she could have meant fifty thousand. I had no idea. But that would all have to wait until later to decide if any of them were worth selling.

"What about the sculptures?" Katie asked. "There are lots of busts of men and stands for them too. Old men, mostly. Not surprising. I suppose you have to be old to be important enough for a bust made of you."

I hadn't paid much attention to them either as a child, because the housekeeper had wanted me to stay out of the sculpture gallery, since she was convinced I might suddenly run amok and knock something over.

"Not those," I said. "Let's leave all of them down here for the moment. We won't be using that room for this wedding so we don't have to haul everything up there. Emmaline said we might want to use it for larger weddings and the sculptures could be placed to take that into account. I need to talk to her before we do any of that." I spotted a piece of furniture I did want to use. A dressing table that would be perfect for the East Room, which meant I could hopefully cancel the one on order.

We took a break for dinner. Katie couldn't stop talking about Stefan and how Raine and Stefan were such a dream couple. After a while, it got on my nerves. The closer we got to the actual wedding, the more the thought of coupledom annoyed me.

"Celebrities don't seem to stay married very long," I said. "Ordinary people have a hard enough time staying married, so imagine how much more difficult it is if you are famous and have to deal with all the gossip magazines."

"They've known each other for so long, they have to know it's right and it will last." Katie said.

I wasn't so sure about that. William and I had known each other since I was ten years old and it had taken me twenty years to know it wasn't right.

"Stefan told me he wanted Raine to have the best day of her life," Kiki said. "It's so cute that he's thinking of her all the time."

"Maybe they are a fairytale couple and they want a fairytale wedding, but that's not how most of the rest of the world works." I couldn't help myself from sounding grumpy.

"Maybe not a fairytale life but a lot of people have good marriages," Eleanor said. "I did."

She and her husband had been happy, from what I could tell. "Oh, Eleanor, I'm sorry. I'm so tactless," I said. "I know you did. I should just be quiet."

"No, it's all right. I've found that when people haven't been around many happy couples, it's hard to imagine that there are such relationships."

That was certainly true. I could count on my fingers the number of truly happy couples I knew, at least those who were still together after a few years.

My phone pinged. A text from Emmaline, which was a relief. I wanted to go back to only thinking of the practical. *What happened at the house today? Stefan was in raptures about the place*

Long story. It all went well. I remembered her previous text. *Why were you texting me about dogs?*

Didn't I tell you?

No

Raine wants her dogs there. They're going to be part of the ceremony. You know, wearing bow ties and sitting up by the altar

I'd been to weddings with dogs in attendance. It was cute, as long as the animals were well behaved.

Okay, that's fine. Do we need to provide dog food?

I hadn't thought about that. I'll ask, though so many dogs are on special diets these days, it might not be easy for you to get the right kind. I'll get the food if necessary

I put the dogs out of my memory since they didn't need to be added to the to-do list.

The next morning when I was working in the study an unfamiliar number came up on my phone. I almost ignored it, fearing it was William again and then I reminded myself I could handle him. I answered.

"Libby?" The voice was familiar, but I couldn't place it. Definitely American and male. A friend of William's calling me to plead on his behalf?

"Yes, this is Libby. Who is this?"

"Hi. This is Stefan. Stefan Andris."

"Oh, of course. Stefan. Sorry I didn't recognize your voice."

"That's all right. I have a big favor to ask and it's kind of a strange one."

I didn't answer right away. Strange? I couldn't even imagine what he might want. All sorts of things flashed through my mind about unusual wedding requests I'd read about. Horses to ride in on? Bagpiper? Releasing doves?

"Raine's mother is a problem," he said. "And Raine's never really gotten along with her. The woman manages to put a damper on everything. She's like a black cloud full of hail, ready to bombard anyone at a moment's notice. We have to take care of her."

Take care of her? I hoped he didn't want a hit organized on the future mother-in-law.

"But I thought of a way so she wouldn't stay long after the ceremony," he added.

"What do you have in mind?" My imagination failed me for once.

"Seeing your cat gave me an idea," he said. "The woman absolutely loathes cats. She's not only allergic to them but she hates them. I thought maybe I could send you a couple of cats to be at Pemberley during the wedding."

Sending me cats? I wasn't sure I was hearing him correctly.

"They'd be taken away right afterwards of course," he said. "Since you said your cat was shy and hid when strangers were there, I thought I could provide reinforcements. Friendly cats who could wander around after the ceremony. Once the ceremony is over, I'd like Raine's mother to go away as soon as possible so she doesn't say anything to ruin the whole day. The cats might be a good incentive for her to leave."

Cats to chase away guests would never have occurred to me. Stefan was right that Betsey would hide, but importing extra cats had not been on my list of possible strange wedding requests, though Emmaline had warned me that I'd have to be willing to accommodate people, especially since they were paying so much money to come to Pemberley.

"Okay," I said, trying to muster some perkiness as if I thought it was a great idea. I could understand not wanting Raine's mother to ruin things. "Sure, why not. We have lots of room. You do know that even friendly cats may not be so friendly in a new strange place, right? They may end up hiding along with Betsey."

"Oh," he said. "I hadn't thought about that. But I'm sure I can find some super friendly cats to borrow. Maybe some that are trained as therapy cats or something. You don't have to worry about that part. If the cats hide, it will be my problem, okay? I know you have quite a lot on your hands already. I just wanted to make sure you'd be willing to let them stay in the house for a few days. They could be fed at the same time as your other cat so they wouldn't be extra work."

"Yes, fine," I said. "The more the merrier." Not really. I was sure Betsey didn't want cat houseguests so they could dine together, but what could I actually say?

"Don't tell Raine, though. If she knows about it, she'll feel guilty for going along with it. Better it's a surprise."

"Of course." We said goodbyes as Kiki appeared in the doorway. She was twisting her hands together and glancing over her shoulder.

"What is it?" My first thought was that our mother had shown up.

"You should stop working and come out into the hall," she said.

"Why? What's happening?"

"It's William. He's here."

Chapter 15

Countdown to the Raine Randolph/Stefan Andris Wedding
10 days

To Do List:

~~Visit Mrs. Ellis-Casually bring up ghost sightings~~

Pick up more paint-(forgot this, add to tomorrow's list)

Pay more attention to Betsey

~~Figure out Pug's future~~

~~Cross fingers that the Damp has not devoured everything~~

Don't be a shriveling little ninny

MY BREATH WENT out of me like I was deflating. Not William. I didn't want him poisoning this space. It was mine and had nothing to do with him and no history of him.

"I don't want to see him," I whispered.

"I can't just leave him standing in the hall!"

She was right. I couldn't make her deal with him because I was a coward.

"Don't worry, Kiki." William's voice came from behind her. "I found my own way." He moved past her into the room. "Surprise!"

I couldn't find the right words to say. He came around the desk and bent down like he was going to kiss me. I leaned away from him, nearly tipping the chair over. I smelled his cologne, which made my stomach clench. I hadn't minded it before, but that had changed. His hair was slicked back, a new look for him, though the rest was the same. He'd always worn double-breasted suits because someone had told him it made his shoulders look wider.

"William, what are you doing here?"

"I had to come to England anyway on business and since I was in the country, I thought I'd drop in." He was using his ingratiating smile, the one that charmed the older women in the church congregation.

"We're a hundred miles from London. You're just dropping in?"

"Very impressive place," he said, ignoring my last question. "Even given the disrepair. Now that I've actually seen Pemberley, I can understand why you want to save it. Historical buildings are so important." I'd never heard William express one bit of interest in history before.

Kiki still stood in the doorway, her expression fierce. She'd never liked William and at that moment looked like she'd drag him away from me if I told her to.

"Kiki, I'm okay," I said. "Why don't you leave us alone now? We have some things to discuss."

"Are you sure?"

"I'm sure." I tried to sound confident though my heart was beating fast. I noticed she didn't shut the door as she left. She was probably standing close by ready to barge in if I needed her. I got up and moved over to the window because I felt trapped behind the desk.

I turned around to face him, but found myself gripping the windowsill for support. "I said I didn't want to meet with you."

He laughed. "I know you, Libby. You say things you don't mean all the time. But there's no hurry to talk things out. Why don't you give me a tour of the place? Like I said, it's impressive."

I had no desire to do that. "What are you really doing here?" I asked. "What kind of business would you have in London?"

Before he could answer, Kiki came back into the room. "Libby, Emmaline is trying to reach you. She texted me because you aren't answering your phone. She says it's important that you call her." I went over and shuffled through the papers on my desk to find my phone. "My phone is dead."

"You can use mine. It's plugged in to a charger in the kitchen."

"I'll be right back," I said to William. I didn't want him to overhear my conversation because if it was urgent, it was undoubtedly something not good.

"No problem," William said. "I'm in no hurry."

"Is Emmaline really on the phone?" I whispered to Kiki as we left the room.

"Yes, but I was about to come in with a different distraction. Do you really want to talk to him? I can say you had to go deal with some emergency."

"I want to talk to him to convince him this is the last time I want to see him. I hope he'll listen."

She took hold of my hand and squeezed it. "You can do it. I know you can. Get rid of Overbearing William once and for all." She smiled and I had to smile back. She'd learned the word 'overbearing' when she was about twelve and immediately labeled William with it, though at the time I'd been furious when she'd called him that. She'd been right all along.

The kitchen smelled of strawberries, which distracted me for a moment before Kiki handed me her phone. The doorbell rang. "I'll get it," Kiki said.

When Emmaline answered, I said, "It's me. I'm using Kiki's phone because mine is dead. Tell me it's not bad news. I don't think I can stand that right now."

"Not bad news! Great news. Astounding news! Are you ready for it?"

"Yes," I said, keeping my enthusiasm in check. Emmaline's 'astounding' was sometimes not my astounding.

"Raine sold the rights to her wedding photographs to Vogue! And Xavier La will be doing the shoot. Raine is going to donate the money she's getting for it to animal rescue and it's going to all be fabulous!"

"And Xavier La is who...?"

"A famous fashion photographer! I can't believe he agreed because he's mostly retired. It's the best advertising we could imagine. It's a dream come true for me."

I knew it was good news, but it meant I had to make sure there were enough spots to take the photographs. That had to move up the To Do list. Was it even on the list? I couldn't remember.

"That's great, wonderful," I said, trying to sound enthusiastic.

"It is!" She paused. "There's one tiny thing."

I should have known. "What?"

"They want to shoot them two days before the wedding so that means some of the rooms will have to be ready by then. The florist will be bringing in some of the flowers for the shoot, and will fix up any arrangements that need refreshing the morning of the wedding. But you don't need to worry about food for them," she said hurriedly. "I'll order some supplies from Fortnum and Mason. I can talk to Kiki about drinks to go along."

Two days less to get ready. And Emmaline was far ahead of me. I was still trying to absorb the idea of more people. She had moved on to feeding them. "How many people?"

"Well, there will be the makeup artist and the dress designer in case there are any last minute alterations and the photographer of course. He has two assistants, and Raine's assistant. So that makes...let's see. That's seven. Not so many, right?"

"Right," I said, though it was not right at all, but I knew I couldn't disappoint Emmaline. She'd thrown herself into believing in me and my plans and it really was a dream come true for her. Even in college she read bridal magazines, not for herself but as a way to analyze everything about weddings. When I went to visit her at her parents' house one weekend, she'd showed me the paper dolls she'd collected over the years, each in their wedding finery from different periods in history. If anyone deserved to make it as a wedding planner, it was Emmaline.

"We'll manage," I said.

"Great!" I could hear the relief in her voice. "I've booked them in for an extra night at the Bingley Dower House. Luckily they still had rooms available."

"They might think this place is a real dump after staying at Bingley."

"No, no, they don't want that smooth luxury look. Remember, Raine could have chosen anywhere to get married and she wants Pemberley. Xavier is going to love it too, I'm sure. It may be one of the reason he agreed to do the shoot. He doesn't do just ordinary photographs."

"Okay, look, I have to go. Lots to do." Like getting rid of William.

"Yes, me too. Love you!"

"Love you too."

Kiki came rushing into the kitchen just as I was leaving. We narrowly avoided a collision.

"Libby, Davin is here and William came out of the study when I let Davin in. They are in the hall talking. I overheard William. He told Davin the house will be a perfect retreat center for the church."

"What? That's ridiculous!" I was ready to physically boot William out of the house.

I dashed into the hall where I found the two deep in conversation.

"Libby, Davin and I introduced ourselves," William said. "Fascinating to hear about the plans for the landscaping renovations."

Davin was looking at me strangely. Not surprising, after hearing what William told him. "I'll talk to you later," Davin said to me. "I can see you are busy. Pleasure to meet you, William." He held out his hand and William shook it.

"You as well. I'm sure we'll see each other again," William said.

Not if I could help it.

"Nice fellow," William said to me as Davin went out the door. "Is he around much?" I knew that note of jealousy in his voice. I ignored it.

"How could you tell him this is going to be a church retreat center? That is absolutely not going to happen!"

"So your nosy little sister is still eavesdropping, is she?" He smirked. "Some people don't change."

"That's not the point. Pemberley is not going to be a getaway for your wealthy parishioners. It's mine and it's going to stay that way. And you'll have nothing to do with it. We're through once and for all. This trip was a waste of your time."

"Was it?" He motioned toward the study. "I just happened to glance at your stack of estimates. And when I saw the place, the idea of a retreat center came to me in a flash. It would be perfect for that."

"You went through the things on my desk?" I tried to tamp down my anger. If I got angry, he'd take the moral high ground and claim he knew women couldn't control their emotions.

"They were right out in the open. Libby dear, you know you don't have the money to restore the place but it could be quite something. That Davin fellow even asked if we'd consider selling it. He said he knew someone who would be interested. That means it must have quite a bit of value even in the state it's in."

"Davin asked that?" Why was he going behind my back? Hadn't I made it clear I was not selling?

"Yes, but I shut him down. Think how great it would be if you didn't have to worry about money, and you could be very involved in the design of a retreat facility. And once it was done and open, if you wanted to spend some time here, you could stay whenever you wanted."

He hadn't taken in anything I'd said when I had broken up with him. "William, tell me, why do you still want to marry me? I'm not the person I used to be. Don't you see I'm a different person now?"

"But we had our whole life planned out. How can you forget all that?"

He'd had our whole life planned out. Not me.

"You need to find someone better suited to you," I said. "Someone who wants the same things you want. I don't. I'd never be the wife you need." He needed someone who would gaze at him adoringly every time he spoke. He claimed he loved my "little quirks" as he called them, but then he constantly criticized them. Too many men want a woman that they can attempt to change, because if they succeed, they'll feel more powerful.

It was time to play on his ego, the best way to approach any discussion with him. "There are so many women who would be thrilled to have a chance to love you," I said. "And who would fit in so much better with the church. I would just cause you constant aggravation, and that wouldn't be good for your work, would it? Not your writing, and not helping your father."

He pursed his lips and I could tell he was actually considering all this. "You're not seeing someone else, are you?" he asked. "You're not dating that Davin guy, right?"

William had always liked me better those times when he became aware other men might be interested in me. That intensified his own interest. I didn't want that now. "No, of course not!" I took a deep breath and clasped my hands together as if I was about to reveal something profound. "I've thought about this a lot, and I've almost decided I'm not interested in getting married. I want to stay here at Pemberley and devote my time to the house and the garden, to live a peaceful life," I said. I was hoping with those words he'd picture me as sort of nun-like, nothing that would make him jealous. "You know I hate crowds," I added. "That's another reason you'd be much better off with a different person. Someone who would enjoy interacting with all the parishioners."

He walked over and looked out the window. "I can see what you are saying. It is very peaceful and quiet here. You could do your little paintings and barely have to see another soul. It would be good for you, maybe even healthier." He turned back to me. "I did notice you are very pale. I hope you are taking care of yourself."

"I am," I said. "But my new doctor says not to expect too much of myself." That was a total lie. I hadn't yet found a doctor in England. "I'd hate to burden you with my health problems."

"Now Libby, it wouldn't be a burden. I am strong enough for both of us."

Bad move on my part. I switched tactics. "I know you are, but you have so many other people depending on you. People with far more serious problems than me. I want you to be there for them, not wasting your time on my trivial health issues. Really, William, I do just want to live quietly here." I wished I'd come up with a plan to make him think it was his idea. That was always the way to get him to agree to something. I was running out of ideas.

He gave a heavy sigh. "Yes, I see that it would be better for you here away from the constant strain of the duties in the church. But I don't want to say goodbye to you forever. We have a history."

"We do." I was getting desperate for him to leave. I was willing to say anything to make that happen. "We won't say goodbye forever. You can go home and think about how the future should work out. What would be best for each of us. We can talk on the phone after some time has passed."

"Yes, all right. We..."

Before he could finish his sentence, I interrupted. "I'll walk you out," I said, heading for the door and hoping he'd follow. He did, and when I opened the front door, he leaned down and kissed me on the cheek. "We can talk on the phone after some time has passed." As usual, he repeated what I'd just said as if I hadn't really said anything at all.

"Good idea. Have a safe drive." After he was out the door, I shut it and leaned against it, relief washing through me.

Marni opened the door to the conservatory. "Is it safe to come out now?"

"Yes, he's gone."

"Good. I was about ready to come out and tell him to leave. I can be your bouncer as well as your gardener."

"Thanks, but this time I managed on my own. It was easier knowing you all were in the house though. I'm ready to pop open some champagne to celebrate."

"How did it go?" Kiki came out of the kitchen.

I told them all about the quiet life bit and how I'd hoped I'd convinced him I was going to lead a nun-like life.

Marni cracked up laughing. "Good one."

"You don't really mean that about not getting married, do you?" Kiki seemed aghast.

"I don't know. I know I don't want to think about it right now. Since when have you become such a fan of marriage?"

"Well, I'm not, I mean, I don't usually care one way or the other, but I always thought I'd be a bridesmaid in your wedding. I'd like to be a bridesmaid at a fun wedding."

"Oh, so that's the only reason you want me to get married?"

"No! Well, yes, maybe. Though it would be great to have a nice brother-in-law."

"How about just really nice sisters and friends of your sister for you to hang out with," Marni teased.

"Well, I've already got that living here. You know, I like that this place is big enough for so many people to stay. We're like a modern...modern, what did they call the places where hippies lived together?"

I laughed. "A commune. I don't think we're exactly that."

"That's what I'm calling us, the Pemberley commune," Kiki said. "Come take a break and try my mini strawberry pretzel buns. I've spread them with strawberry mascarpone cheese mixed with lemon grass. They're pretty good, if I do say so for myself."

"Sounds terrific!" One of the many weights on me had been lifted off. If William stuck to our agreement, I wouldn't get twitchy at every phone call or worry he'd show up at any moment. With two days cut out of part of the renovation timetable to be ready for the photoshoot, we had to move toward the wedding without any distractions. It could be done. Maybe.

Chapter 16

Countdown to the Raine Randolph/Stefan Andris
Wedding
9 days

To Do List:
Gilding repair in the ballroom
Finish rehanging paintings and mirrors
Pick up more paint
Pay more attention to Betsey
Less thinking about Davin, more work, Davin who?

DAYS WERE BLURRING together and the only thing I could focus on was the To Do list. The first item was to finish repairing the gilding on the decorative plaster scrolls on the wall panels in the ballroom. Some people would have considered it fiddley time-consuming work but it was exactly what I liked to do.

As I touched up one next to a window, I looked out to see Mark and Marni carrying flats of flowers to Mr. Mackenzie. There was another little boy with them, the son of the farmer with the cows. Pug trotted after them and when they reached Mr. Mackenzie, the dog flopped down at Mark's feet. Davin drove up as the three of them began to dig holes in one of the planting beds. He got out and came over to them.

I had been watching the action so intently, I didn't hear Eleanor come into the room until she joined me at the window. "I think I may have a gardener for a son now. He can't stop talking about plants and fertilizer. Oh, and soil too, which he informs me is totally different from dirt. According to him, dirt is what is under fingernails, while soil is what is for growing plants."

"I should pay him for being an assistant gardener," I said. "It's great he likes to help."

Mr. Mackenzie listened to whatever Davin was saying, standing with his hands on his hips. I noticed Mark was standing exactly the same way as if subconsciously mimicking the gardener. The other little boy was not as interested. He sat down next to Pug and began to pet him.

"I really should remember the other boy's name, but it won't stick in my head." I'd been introduced to the boy at least twice when I'd gone over to talk to his father. "Has Mark told you?"

"Yes, it's Liam, and Mark has informed me Liam is his newest best friend." Eleanor put her arm around my shoulders and gave me a squeeze. "Thank you so much for inviting us here. I didn't know it was going to help so much."

"I'm glad," I said. "But you don't need to thank me. It's wonderful having you here. I'm sorry I wasn't there for you when you needed it."

"Honestly, I don't know I would have noticed you if you had been there. We had plenty of people who kept us fed and that's all I could take in then."

"How are you doing now, really?" I'd caught her looking sad many, many times, which was perfectly understandable, but she still seemed so tired most of the time as well.

"Better, though the hardest part for a planner-type like me is to realize my life has veered off in a totally different direction. I can't seem to make a plan beyond getting up and making sure Mark has enough to eat."

Mark looked toward the house, and Eleanor waved at him. He waved back.

"I think that's enough of a plan for right now, isn't it? You don't have anywhere you need to be at the moment, right?" I asked.

"I do need to make a decision for the fall, for where Mark is going to go to school. I've decided I don't want to go back to North Carolina. It's not like we had ties there, and I can get a job almost anywhere. I am beginning to feel like we should make a new start somewhere new, so I suppose that's progress. I'm not sure what direction we'll go in, but we'll at least move forward. You're inspiring me, you know?" She smiled at me.

"Me? I've never inspired anyone in my whole life." According to my mother and William, I needed other people to tell me what to do.

"You've moved to a different country and taken on this huge project and are just going all out for it. That's inspiring."

I didn't want to tell her I was teetering on failure. I hoped when I did fail, Eleanor and Mark would be happily settled somewhere else. "Oh, this project may defeat me in the end." I tried to keep my voice light. "You should look elsewhere for inspiration."

"I won't argue with you, but really, I have been inspired." She went back to watching Mark. "Mark has really taken to Mr. de Bourgh, especially after the man told him that he lost his own father when he was fourteen. It was nice of him to share that. I think it made Mark feel less alone."

"I didn't know Davin's father died." After I said it, I realized there was no way I could have known that. I didn't know his family and the last time I'd seen him, we'd been ten. None of the children had ever talked about their families, except to complain their mothers wanted them home at certain times.

We watched for a few more minutes. Marni said something and Davin laughed. "At least Davin seems to like Marni now, " I said. "He wasn't so sure of her in the beginning." I explained about the llama idea. "Maybe they'd make a good couple." I felt a little tinge of regret or jealousy, I wasn't sure which.

Eleanor looked over at me and raised an eyebrow. "I don't really get the feeling that Marni is looking to be part of a couple. She seems a bit of a free spirit. She's told us about some of her travels and how much fun she's had. She talked about a man she went to Thailand with, but when Kiki asked her if he was a new significant other, she just laughed."

"That's her way. She won't say. She didn't date when she was younger, and now I'm not really sure what she wants."

Marni and I hadn't been close when we were younger. She was too wrapped up in her studies. We'd become closer when she started college. Our mother tried to micromanage Marni into joining a sorority in hopes that Marni could find an appropriate husband, as if sorority life was stuck in the 1950s. We'd had something to commiserate about together then. And when Marni had graduated without any signs of an engagement ring, our mother treated her graduation more like a funeral instead of a celebration. I feared Marni avoided relationships just to spite the woman. "Maybe Davin needs a free spirit like Marni."

Eleanor laughed. "You may be misreading the situation. It seems to me Mr. de Bourgh is much more interested in you than Marni."

"What? No. Why do you think that?"

"He spoke very warmly about you. Mark and I heard all about how you and he and his friends played on the grounds when you were children. He said you were always good at getting everyone to agree on what game to play and that you had a terrific imagination."

I didn't remember getting everyone to agree. We spent so much time debating what to play that sometimes half the day would be wasted on whether we'd pretend we were storming the Bastille or were going to make magic potions to become invisible. And it was hard to imagine he'd spoken that warmly about me. He'd not shown any real signs of warmth to me since I'd been back.

"Well, I'm not interested in him," I said, trying to sound as if I meant it. "He reminds me too much of a lawyer, or he did when I first met him and I'm never having anything to do with lawyers again unless it's absolutely necessary."

Eleanor laughed again. "You should hear yourself. First of all, even if you have a dislike of lawyers, he's not actually one, and there are no specific lawyer standards in appearance, at least not that I've ever noticed, except they wear suits a lot."

"He was wearing a suit when I first saw him. I used to like men in suits, until I came across too many who couldn't wait to explain to me about everything I didn't know or understand. Put a man in a suit and the mansplaining button gets turned on."

"Okay, but I think you are protesting a tiny bit too much."

I ignored that.

"I'll stop distracting you," she said. "It looks great in here!"

"Thanks! I hope the wedding guests think so too."

I finished up and went on to finish hanging our long-lost paintings and mirrors back up. Later that day, I passed by the ballroom and spotted Mark, who was lying very still on the floor. "Mark! Are you okay?"

"Yes," he said. "I was just looking at the ceiling. It's kind of weird to have clouds and sky and rabbits and babies painted on it, but I like it."

I came in and sat down next to him. "I like it too." I did, though I mostly spent time thinking about what a pain it was that the ceilings all needed at least some sort of repair, but Mark was right. My neck hurt from craning to see so I lay down too. It felt good to stretch out.

"The rabbits are kind of cute even though I don't know why they are up in the sky," he said.

"Some ancestor of mine went through a rabbit phase, or so I heard," I said. "She had them added in after the original ceiling was painted. I suppose she just really liked rabbits. My grandmother did too," My grandmother had told me the rabbits made her feel more comfortable when she moved into the giant house after growing up poor and struggling. As she explained it, the rabbits were common and a bit silly and not grand at all, but they were an integral part of the house because someone had made them so, and that reminded her she could be part of it too.

I could hear her voice the day she'd talked about the rabbits. *It's a heavy weight to be responsible for such a grand house, and I know your father doesn't want that burden. I hope you'll take it on some day. Remember that while you are keeping the place for the future, you can still make it your own in little ways here and there.*

It was still hard for me to imagine the freedom and the wealth to hire someone to come in and paint animals all over the ceiling just because you liked the idea. I wanted to become more like that, less worried about what anyone thought. Not that I wanted more creatures added, but that I could embrace the possibilities.

"They should have painted over the babies," Mark said. "They are a little creepy, I mean, the idea of babies with wings is creepy anyway, but the faces on these don't look much like babies. They look like grandmother faces in picture books, all round and with red cheeks. They don't have baby eyes or baby mouths."

"It might make it less creepy if you didn't think of them as babies. They are called cherubs, and they are supposed to be a kind of angel. In other cultures, cherubs take all different forms. Some of them are described more like having the face of a lion or an eagle than a baby."

"That would be a lot better," he said, "even if lions in real life don't have wings." He was quiet for a moment and then he added, "Too bad there aren't any dragons. My dad liked dragons. I do too. Do you think some of the angels in heaven look like dragons?" His voice wobbled a bit.

"They might," I said. "I'm not all that knowledgeable about cherubs." As far as I knew, there were no descriptions of cherubim as dragons, but he didn't need to know that.

"My dad was going to teach me how to play Dungeons and Dragons, but he didn't get around to it before...before..." His voice trailed off. I wanted to hug him. I'd hurt so much losing my father when I was already an adult. I couldn't imagine how Mark felt.

"I'm sorry," I said. "It's hard to have something planned that didn't happen. My dad and I were going to go on a trip together to Scotland, to visit where he went to school, but he died before we could go. You know, Marni and I both know how to play Dungeons and Dragons. She's really good at it. Maybe we could teach you. It wouldn't be the same as your dad teaching you, but it still might be fun."

Marni's voice came from the doorway. "It would be fun." I saw Davin next to her. She turned to Davin. "What about you? Are you up for a game?"

"Let me check my schedule," he said, smiling at her. "It's been a while, but I used to be an elven warrior most of the time, if I remember right."

An elven warrior seemed much closer to the Robin of old rather than the Davin of today. I tried to picture him around a game board, playing with the same enthusiasm he'd shown in our games.

"We'll do it then," Marni said to Mark. "But maybe not right away. I'm going to go back to helping Mr. Mackenzie. Do you want to join me?"

Mark jumped up. "Sure. Do you think he'll let me use the pruners?"

"I'm sure he will, if you promise to be careful."

"Okay, let's go."

"Nice room," Davin said to me after they left. "It's in decent shape. I came in to see if you are going to open the terrace doors during the wedding so people can go outside. If you are, we can put some containers around with flowers in them to add some color. Mr. Mackenzie has the original containers stored in one of the outbuildings." Davin was all business. I didn't see any signs of the warmth Eleanor had mentioned.

"Yes," I said as I got up off the floor. I could sound just as business-like. "That's a good idea about flowers. If it's not raining, I thought we'd open up the doors. These at least open without too much trouble." I pushed them open. "Kiki and I fixed them." I didn't tell him what an effort it had been. They were heavier than they looked so while getting them off the frame wasn't too big a problem, getting them rehung again had taken a lot of time and effort. I knew enough basic carpentry from making picture frames for my canvases to do jobs like that, and I would have enjoyed it more if we hadn't had so many other things that needed to be done.

Davin walked out onto the terrace. "I'll have one of my men pull out the containers then," he said. "There's a good nursery nearby. Do you want to pick out the flowers? I can take you over there if you could go tomorrow. I have to go out of town the day after that, but if you can't make it tomorrow, my assistant could drive you a different day."

I got distracted by the news he'd be out of town again. Not that we were likely to have a landscape emergency before the wedding, but I was a little uneasy at the thought he wouldn't be close by. That was silly, though. I didn't need him around to get through the wedding.

"I remember your grandmother let you do the flower arrangements," he added.

My grandmother did let me, though Mr. Mackenzie at first hadn't wanted me to cut the flowers, worried I'd pick too many from the wrong places, but she'd insisted and he'd shown me how to select individual stems across the garden so I wouldn't leave bare spots.

I walked out and breathed in some fresh air. The sun was shining and the warmth felt good. Picking which flowers to use sounded like fun, choosing which colors and combining them. And then I realized how much time that would take. "No, I don't have time. I'll ask Marni if she can do it. Since she worked at a garden store, she'll have good ideas."

He hesitated for a moment and then said, "Yes, I'm sure she will."

We stood there looking out on the gardens in an awkward silence. I should have gone back to my list, but I couldn't force myself to move. He didn't seem to have any inclination to leave either. He went over and examined some shrub that bordered the terrace, flipping over various leaves and studying them carefully like he was trying to determine if they were in need of emergency medical assistance.

I don't know why I found it so hard to talk to him. I felt like a teenager at an awkward school dance.

"So where did you go to school to learn landscape architecture?" I asked, even as I heard how stiff my question seemed. "Mr. Mackenzie couldn't have taught you everything."

Davin turned to me and smiled, looking younger and more Robin-like. "He taught me more than some of my instructors. I went to University College London. They have a good program." He paused, and then said, "I was surprised to hear you went to law school. I was sure you'd study English or some sort of art. I remember you liked to read and draw. Every time we came over, you'd have a book with you and a sketchpad."

I sighed. "I never should have let my mother push me to study economics so I could go to law school. My mother was obsessed with an old television show about wealthy attorneys. I think she wished she would have gone to law school herself." It felt like the right moment to confess my big secret, the one that had been weighing on me, though I couldn't look him in the face. "My grandmother didn't know that I actually didn't pass the bar exam," I said, talking to the shrub instead of to him.

"Oh," he said. "I..."

I rushed on so I could say it all. "She wanted it so badly for me, but she was so close to the end by then, I couldn't disappoint her. So I lied to her." My eyes started to water but I was not going to let myself cry, at least not then. I did not want him to see me cry.

He moved closer to me and when he spoke, his voice was soft. "You did the right thing," he said. "I would have done the same."

A little bit of weight lifted off me. I still felt guilty and always would, but it felt good to have someone agree, someone like Davin who had known my grandmother.

"Libby, where are you?' I heard Kiki's voice in the distance. "The wine and champagne have arrived!"

"Thank you," I said, and stood on my tiptoes to give him a quick kiss on his cheek. His face was warm and he smelled as good as always. I knew I was starting to blush, so I turned away and hurried back inside. "I should deal with this," I said, calling back over my shoulder. I didn't wait for a response, feeling like a teenager who had done something daring.

From the way I greeted the delivery person, my mood so light, I may have been a little overly enthusiastic, because he gave me that British look when Americans are too gushy around them. For once I didn't care. It was exciting to see the amount of wine and champagne and hard alcohol that came out of the delivery van, though it looked like we were going to be throwing a bacchanal for hundreds of people instead of a smallish wedding.

It took quite a bit of effort and trips up and down to the cellar. I made a note to myself to ask Emmaline if we should move it all back up the day before, or just part of it. It was all expensive and I didn't know how fussily I should treat the bottles of red wine.

The delivery person nearly dropped one case, but I spotted him struggling and moved to catch one corner of the box. He sneezed as we stood there on either side of the box, and I caught the full sneeze in my face. "Sorry," he said. "I'm not feeling too well at the moment."

"Luckily no damage done," I said. At least there was no damage done to the wine. I wasn't so sure about myself after being sprayed with germs. Every germ seemed to know I was a good candidate to host an illness, though I'd been so isolated from people, I hadn't been sick since we'd arrived.

"Think positive," I muttered to myself when he finally drove away. Coming down with a cold was absolutely not on the To Do list.

By dinner, I was still in a good mood. "Where's Marni?" Kiki asked as we sat down.

"She's probably kissing Joe," Mark said as he stabbed a piece of roasted potato with his fork.

We all fell speechless.

Eleanor recovered first. "What did you say?"

"She and Joe like to kiss," Mark said. "They go into the garage where there is an old truck there and sit in it and kiss."

"You haven't been spying on them, have you?" Eleanor asked.

"Nah, I just saw them when Mr. Mackenzie told Liam and me we could play with an old croquet set that was kept in there."

Marni came rushing in. "Sorry. I was just putting away some gardening tools.

Her face was flushed and her shirt was buttoned up wrong. Everyone but Mark burst out laughing.

"What?" she asked.

"Nothing," I said, recovering my voice, and feeling even lighter. "Sit down. It looks like you've had quite a day."

The rabbit in my drawing that night had a quiver of arrows slung over his back, though each ended in a flower instead of a point. When I finished the drawing I put the notebook down, happy I'd be able to get a good night's sleep. I completely forgot about the delivery man and his germs.

Chapter 17

Countdown to the Raine Randolph/Stefan Andris
Wedding
8 days

<u>To Do List</u>:
Pick up more paint
Pay more attention to Betsey
Open mail
Wrangle kittens

I DIDN'T WANT to be nosey but the next day I decided Marni needed
to know Mark had seen her and Joe.

"Sorry!" she said. "We should have been more careful, but I didn't
think it would be great if I brought Joe inside, and we can't go to his
place because he lives with his brother in a small cottage, so that's a bit
awkward too."

"Don't be sorry. So if Davin isn't your type, is Joe?" I teased.

She grinned. "He is for the moment. It's just a bit of a fling. It's not like this is going to be long-term!"

"That's a relief. I was afraid you were going to abandon your job to hang out in my garden having rendezvouses with cute gardeners."

She paused for long enough that I was afraid of her response. Finally, she said, "I've thought about it, but as tempting as that is, no. I've decided I am going to give the whole teaching gig a try. It was just nerves, I guess, that made me doubt I could do it. I don't usually have an attack of nerves."

"For someone who can solo travel to the most isolated places, I'm sure you can face down your fears of a bunch of fairly harmless undergrads."

She made a face. "My problem is that I still feel like an undergrad myself sometimes. I'll do it, but I hope I can come back and stay next summer too. I'll work in the garden in exchange for room and board. And spend time at night on my research and writing."

"Absolutely!" I said, but fearing we wouldn't still be at Pemberley the next summer. The latest stack of bills sat unopened on my desk. I hadn't let Eleanor open them because then I'd have to face the bad news.

"You realize what you were doing, don't you?" she asked. "Thinking I was interested in Davin?"

"I'm not doing anything!"

"Really?" she scoffed. "You don't like him yourself, not even a little bit?"

"No! I'm not interested in any relationship either. Not now. Not for a long time."

"That's what I mean. Trying to set the two of us up would be a way for you not to let yourself like him. Putting him off limits, so to speak. You forget, we sociology types have studied a lot of psychology too."

"No, it's not that at all." Though maybe it was. Whatever. "But let's stop talking about it."

She held up her hands. "Okay, but he is a great guy, in case you do get interested." She checked her phone. "I should get going. We're working on the stream today and we should be able to finish Davin's quick fix before the wedding. He's given Joe some really precise instructions on how to do it."

I still felt a little embarrassed I had kissed Davin on the cheek, and it made me wonder how he'd act the next time he saw me.

"Earth to Libby! Where did you go? You didn't answer my question."

"Oh, sorry." I pushed thoughts of Davin away. "What did you ask?"

"Davin said you wanted me to choose plants for the containers on the terrace off the ballroom. Any particular flowers you want?"

"No, you choose. I don't have enough brain space at the moment for that."

"Okay. I'm on it! Now I'm off to get muddy. See you later!"

I watched her practically bounce out of the room, and I remembered back to those childhood days when getting muddy would have been my goal for the day too. I vowed to spend one whole day after the wedding outside, revisiting my old favorite spots. Everything now seemed to be put in one category or the other, either before the wedding or after the wedding. Except for bills. They had to be dealt with before and after.

I was about to sort them when Katie came in. "There's some sort of delivery van out front," she said.

"We don't have anything on the schedule for today. The chaise lounge for the East Room is supposed to be delivered tomorrow, but I think they would have texted me if it was coming early." We both went to the front door. A woman got out of the van and came up the steps. She wasn't carrying anything except a clipboard.

"Hello," she said. "I'm looking for Libby Darcy. I have some kittens to deliver to you, but I'll need to know where to put all the carriers and all the supplies."

I must have gaped at her because she repeated everything she had just said. When the words sunk in, I realized I'd forgotten about Stefan and the cats.

He'd said a couple of cats. She'd said kittens.

I gulped. "All the carriers? How many are we talking about?"

"There are three carriers, six kittens. I told them we could put three per carrier because they are small, but apparently the person who arranged all this insisted they have plenty of space. He made a huge donation to our cat shelter too, so we want to do exactly as he requested."

Six kittens.

"What is all this?" Katie asked. "Kittens?"

"Long story," I said. "Why don't you go get the others so I only have to explain it once." I didn't think I'd mentioned Stefan's call to anyone. I'd pushed it to the back of my brain hoping he'd realize it was too wild of an idea.

The woman hauled out a giant cat tree contraption with multiple levels. I came down to help her with it as she struggled to get hold of it.

"This is like a cat mansion," I said.

"The buyer wanted only the best," she said cheerfully. "And lots of other supplies. Toys, cat litter and litter boxes, and lots of food. They'll be all set."

I wasn't convinced about that. I had already been worried about keeping track of a couple of cats in the vastness of the house, but six would be impossible. We'd have to keep them confined to one room, or kittens might go missing for days.

"And there is one large cage for them to sleep in at night." I felt a bit of relief hearing that. At least we could corral them some of the time.

Katie's mention of arriving kittens brought everyone into the hall within a minute or so, all clamoring for information.

I held up my hands. "Let's get everything unloaded and inside first."

After we had piled everything in the front hall and the woman had driven away, I explained the situation and then added, "But I don't know how two cats became six kittens,"

"Well they are here now and they are adorable!" Katie said as she took a little gray one out of the carrier. Another kitten inside took the opportunity to run out. I scooped it up before it could disappear into the void.

"From the size of them, I think they are about twelve weeks old. Such a perfect age! Do they have names?" Kiki asked.

I looked at the receipt the woman had given me. "It doesn't list any."

"Can I name them? Please!" Mark begged. He was down on the floor looking into another carrier wiggling his fingers at the little faces inside.

"Sure," I said. "But remember, don't get too attached to them. They are just staying until the wedding." I could tell he wasn't listening.

"It's okay," Eleanor said. "I'll keep reminding him."

I realized I hadn't asked who was going to take the kittens away after the wedding. I couldn't imagine Stefan and Raine driving off with a bunch of cat carriers in the car on the way to some luxurious honeymoon getaway. It would have to be Emmaline's problem. Even if kitten removal wasn't specified in her wedding planning contract, it would probably fall under some other category. Nothing like it was covered in mine. The one thing I could do was write a decent contract, but I'd have to make sure the next one had some ironclad clauses in it for unexpected requests like babysitting kittens.

The next hour was taken up with the kittens, the feeding of them and finding them a place to stay. Mark begged for them to stay in his room and Eleanor agreed. She looked happy that he was happy, though once the cat cage and the climbing tree were in his room, pushed up next to Pug's bed of blankets, there was barely space to move around. At least Pug seemed intrigued by them, wagging his almost nonexistent tail every time one came close to him.

"We have to make sure they don't get outside," I said. "They'd get lost for sure. And we need to keep doors closed in any room we aren't in and we should only let them out of the cage when we can keep track of all of them." As much as I liked Stefan, I was irritated he'd just gone ahead and sent all six without asking.

"I know what they should be named," Mark announced. I didn't have the heart to remind him again they weren't staying.

"Let's hear them," Katie said.

He pointed at each one in turn. "Eenie, Beenie, Miny, Moe, Alice and Charlie. The two little gray ones are Eenie and Beenie, the black one is Miny, the orange one is Moe, and the white ones are Alice and Charlie." If only I could make decisions as easily.

"Don't you mean Meenie instead of Beenie?" Kiki asked him, picking up the black one.

"No, I don't want to name a kitten Meenie because that sounds like they are mean."

"That makes sense." Kiki pointed at the white ones. "Why Alice and Charlie?" Alice and Charlie had discovered my shoelaces and were wrestling with them as if they'd caught a couple of small snakes.

"Because they are my two best friends back home," Mark picked up the little orange one and held it close to his face.

Betsey was not going to be the least bit thrilled. First I'd inflicted a dog on her and now a lively horde of kittens. I wasn't sure Betsey even knew she was a cat. She hissed at every animal she saw when we'd go to the vet, lumping all cats and dogs together as 'not to be tolerated.'

As much as I would have liked to play with kittens, I had to go back to work so I picked the kittens up off my shoes and gave them to Katie. I had no idea when we were supposed to bring them out for Operation 'Drive away new mother-in-law.' Would someone need to be designated as kitten wrangler? I typed a note onto the To-Do list.

"I have to get back to the study," I said. Eleanor smiled encouragingly. She had pointed out that avoiding opening mail might lead to late charges on certain bills and I couldn't afford anything like that. I'd known that, of course, but it took a push from her to take some action.

In the study, I shuffled through the stack and spotted a handwritten envelope with the name of the local building conservation officer in the return address, which struck me as odd. All the information I'd read about restoring listed properties in England had been clear that the homeowner needed to develop a good rapport with their conservation officer and to consult them every step of the way. Our person, an elderly retired architect, had been out to Pemberley and I'd spoken with him on the phone several other times. I don't know why he hadn't just called me if he had something to discuss.

It was too soon to hear back about another application I'd made for another stage of the work. After the roof was fixed, we needed to have the rotted flooring replaced on the third floor. Once the floor was repaired, Kiki and I planned to move up there so the damaged ceilings of the bedrooms on the second floor could be redone for guests.

The conservation officer had assured me the application for the flooring was done properly and he could see no reason why it wouldn't be accepted.

The note was short:

Ms. Darcy,

You'll receive the official rejection in a few days. I'm afraid the committee requires that you have the existing boards restored if possible instead of using new boards, and then additional ones added in to match for those that can't be saved. There are several companies which provide reclaimed floorboards.

Also, there is some concern about the order in which work will be done at Pemberley and that priorities still need to be sorted out. I suggest you engage the services of a registered architect or chartered building surveyor to put together a complete package of supporting material for all your restoration plans. Otherwise, I'm afraid any future proposals may be rejected as well. We all want Pemberley restored to its former glory and I wish you success in this project. I am retiring soon so future communications will be from my successor.

I'm truly very sorry.

Sincerely, George Lewis

I had to read it twice for the full impact to hit me. I had planned to have new pine boards replace the old pine boards, finished in the exact same shade. Though they would have been a different width, because wide pine boards were hard to find, it wouldn't have looked much different, except to those who knew the history of flooring.

There was also no way I could pay an expert to come up with a comprehensive plan, not when I was so low on funds. If I had known they'd wanted one, I would have budgeted for that early on, but nowhere had I seen information to suggest a project could be rejected for that reason. Why the change? The people giving the approvals had some leeway in what to accept or reject, but I didn't think new pine boards would be a cause for concern.

Eleanor came in as I was trying not to cry. "You look worried. Another large bill?" she asked.

I explained about the conservation officer.

"That's strange," Eleanor said. "Why would he not have mentioned that before? And if they approved the roof plan without a comprehensive plan, why do they want one now?"

"I don't know," I said. "People keep telling me how difficult it was all going to be, but I thought I was doing it right and had a good working relationship with the contact person, so this is all out of nowhere. I suppose it's good he wrote to me to let me know, but it still doesn't explain what happened." I wanted to sweep all the bills off the desk in some sort of dramatic fit of anger, but I knew I'd be the one who would have to pick them all up again. Better just to put my head down on the desk and think about where I'd gone wrong yet again.

"Bureaucrats! Big time ones and small time ones, they all can be problems. Is there a way to appeal the decision?" she asked.

I took a deep breath. I didn't want to break down in front of Eleanor. "Yes, I think I remember reading I have six months to contest a decision, though I haven't looked into how to do that or what they would want. How do I argue that four-inch floorboards instead of eight-inch floorboards wouldn't be the ruination of the historic nature of the house?"

"I can look into that for you," she said. "And please don't argue that I shouldn't do it. I'm starting to get really invested in seeing this project succeed. If I can help in a small way, it will feel like I'm getting a handle on moving forward."

With an argument like that, I couldn't say no.

As the day wore on, I became aware my stomach was not in a happy state, and by dinner it was downright queasy. My throat had gotten scratchy as well. Kiki set out sandwiches for dinner, plain ham and cheese, and I ate one, hoping it would help. It didn't.

It also didn't help when Katie spilled a glass of white wine on me. She had been talking and waving her arms around as she usually did, hitting the glass hard enough for it to launch itself toward me. I caught it before it fell to the floor but not before all the wine ended up on me. I hadn't been drinking and the smell of the wine on my shirt made my stomach turn over.

"I'm not getting sick," I told Betsey when I finally got to my room, though before I could fall into bed, my stomach rebelled. I barely made it to the bathroom before I threw up. When I crawled back in bed, Whether it was the deliveryman's germs or something else, I knew I was coming down with some sort of bug.

I took out my notebook, hoping to be able to ignore the continuing queasiness. I drew a rabbit digging for buried treasure and uncovering a Roman hoard of gold coins. How nice it would be to go back in time and dig for buried treasure with a young Davin. I sighed. At the rate things were going, finding buried treasure was the only hope to save Pemberley.

Chapter 18

Countdown to the Raine Randolph/Stefan Andris
Wedding
7-3 days

To Do List:
Pick up more paint
Polish the ballroom floor
Pay more attention to Betsey
Visit conservation officer?
Remind everyone we can't lose the kittens
Don't climb on any more statues

I WOKE UP just as the sun rose, my legs stiff from a horrible dream where I was running to take an exam for a class I'd forgotten I had signed up for. It was a reoccurring dream that should have stopped once I'd finished law school, but it seemed to persist as a reminder of my less than illustrious school career. I was surprised I wasn't having dreams where I'd forgotten we were holding a wedding until the guests began to arrive.

Betsey was stretched out next to me, deep in kitty sleep. She was ignoring the kittens and she'd disappeared for several hours in the night. I hoped it was to negotiate with one of the mice clans to vacate the premises, though that was probably not actually what she was doing. Marni had reported she'd successfully transported quite a few of the little sods away in the live traps, but I knew we still had too many.

Betsey hadn't captured any more since Caro Bingley's visit, which was probably a good thing. It wasn't helpful for the cat to just do catch and release, moving the little creatures to potential new homes in rooms that didn't already have mice. I didn't think the kittens were big enough to catch any on their own, or at least I told myself that, because a vision of six little kittens trotting about depositing mice all over the house was just too much for me.

My stomach felt better, though not perfect. I was relieved I hadn't woken up with a fever or a desire to throw up again. I felt a sudden urge to do something, anything, to get away from the pressing list of tasks to do inside. A breeze blew in, bringing with it the scent of green, and an idea came to me. I could tackle the maze, or at least a part of it to see if they could photograph the bride there. The center of the maze with its statue of Aphrodite and the marble rabbits frolicking about her feet would make an amazing place for photographs as long as the statue was undamaged. From the morning room, I could still see parts of it, but it looked as if some weedy vine had taken over the center of the maze and wrapped itself around the statue. It didn't seem like it would be that difficult to get it off. It wasn't on anyone's To Do list because we'd decided there were more important tasks to do first, but somehow that made it all the more an appealing job.

Betsey protested with a sharp meow when I got up. "Sorry, catto," I said as I searched around for something to put on. The shirt I'd worn the night before was on the floor where I'd dropped it. The work on the maze would be sweaty and I'd need to change afterwards, so there was no sense in putting on a clean shirt just to get grubby. Yesterday's would do. I could still smell the wine on it as I pulled it over my head. I hoped the smell would act as a bug repellant.

My stomach rumbled in a good way so I made a stop in the kitchen first. A cardboard box sat by the back door. Kiki had opened it and I went to look, finding the extra floor polish I'd ordered for the ballroom. I almost started on that instead of the maze, but then I pushed away the guilt and thought about how nice the breeze had been. The afternoon would be soon enough to polish.

Pug trotted into the kitchen and went to the back door so I let him out and then grabbed a scone out of a tin on the counter. The scone had some small blue bits in it I hoped were chopped up dried blueberries. I took a bite, only to get a taste of bleu cheese, which was not good. Outside, I tossed the scone into a flower bed, hoping some critter had a refined palate and would nibble it away.

The garden shed was spotless inside and I felt a bit like I was intruding when I took a pair of loppers. As I expected, they were clean and sharp.

Pug joined me as I made my way to the maze. "This isn't going to be very exciting, buddy," I said to him, but he didn't seem to care.

The rabbit topiaries flanking both sides of the entrance to the maze were not as perfect as they looked from a distance. The one on the right had a bit of a wayward ear, which leaned a little too far back and to the side. The one on the left had a nose and a face that were a bit too sharply pointed, as if the rabbit was morphing into a greyhound. Perhaps Mr. Mackenzie's eyesight wasn't as sharp as it used to be. Whatever the reason, eventually I needed to learn how to keep them pruned instead of expecting someone else to do it all the time.

Mr. Mackenzie had kept the first few feet of the maze open, but soon I had the loppers at work trying to clear a narrow path beyond that. I was determined to get to the center. It would take hours and hours to prune it back to the original width, even with some sort of electric pruner, which Mr. Mackenzie refused to use. I'd asked about that when I first came back and he'd scoffed at such an idea. We'd have to have one though, if we were going to use the maze for wedding shots. I added it to my mental to-buy list. If Mr. Mackenzie didn't want to use them, I knew Marni would jump in and try. We wouldn't have to clear all the pathways in the maze. The trickster paths that came to dead ends didn't matter for the photoshoot. Luckily I still remembered which pathways we did need. I'd run through the maze so many times the map of it was imprinted on my brain.

I don't know how long I spent whacking away at branches, but my hands grew sore and sweat trickled down my back by the time I finally made it to the center, Pug still at my heels. As I had thought, a weedy vine had taken over, weaving back and forth around the center like someone had strung party streamers in an enthusiastic burst of decorating. The rabbits at the statue base were completely covered and Aphrodite herself had vines winding around her as if wearing a daring couture dress. Pug stopped and then backed up, whining a little.

"Silly, it's just a statue," I said as I took a step forward. The statue was not what caused the whine. A squelching noise rose up and I felt cold water pour into my sneaker. When I looked down, a couple of inches of water came up over my shoes. The center of the maze had turned into a shallow pond. I wanted to stomp my foot in frustration, but I knew that would just splash more water around. I clacked the loppers together on the nearest overhanging branch and felt a small bit of satisfaction as it dropped down into the water.

Since my feet were already wet, I decided I could clean up the area around the statue. I squelched my way to it and then started cutting and pulling away at the vines that were trying to strangle poor Aphrodite. I cleared the vine away from the plinth that she and the bunnies stood atop, but I couldn't reach all the way up to clear the vines that wound around her head. I could get hold of the bottom part of them but I didn't want to pull too hard in case I toppled her over. The loppers wouldn't reach far enough up with me standing on the ground.

I'd climbed up on the plinth many times when I was a child. How hard could it be to do it again? I found my answer. Not only was it difficult, it didn't help that my shoes were wet. I only managed to get one foot into a nook when it slipped out from under me and I went down hard, a blast of pain shooting through my ankle as I fell on it.

I must have blacked out for a few seconds because when I came back to reality, not only were my shoes wet, but my butt as well, since I was sitting in the puddle. I tried to stand up but another jolt of pain hit me and I sat back down.

"Great. Just great."

I tried again, managing to grab hold of the plinth enough to pull myself up. Somehow I was going to have to hobble back through the maze. I looked around for the loppers, hoping I could use them as a cane of sorts. They lay in the puddle where I had dropped them. When I picked them up, I realized they were only long enough for a very short cane, and the blade end stuck in the soggy ground every time I put it down.

"I don't suppose you'd go for help or fetch me a big stick," I muttered to Pug. He cocked his head at me and gave another little whine. "No, I don't suppose you are like one of those hero dogs in movies." At least he took one step forward toward me, but when his little paw hit the water, he jerked it out and moved backwards again.

I knew I needed to force myself to move so I could get back to the house and put ice on my ankle before it swelled up. No one was going to come rescue me. No one even knew where I was. No one would see me unless they happened to go to the morning room and look down at the maze, which was unlikely to happen. I pictured myself sitting there waiting for help until the vine grew over me and I faded away, my bones discovered years later. Who all would mourn my loss? Kiki and Marni and Eleanor and Emmaline at least. Would Davin? My cold feet kept that ridiculous vision brief, and I stood up, taking one hobbling step forward, which nearly brought me down again. If I could just get out of the blasted puddle, it would be easier and I'd be less likely to fall again.

My progress was slow. Not only were the loppers too short to be a cane, I was afraid if I used them, I'd accidentally stab Pug, who had decided he must stick very close to me. I finally just dropped them, deciding they could be retrieved later.

I had made it about a third of the way out when I nearly ran into Davin. He came around a corner so fast, we bumped into each other. I almost toppled over again but he caught me, managing to avoid squashing Pug in a rather nimble maneuver.

"What are you doing out here?" he asked. And then when he took a closer look at me, he added, "What happened to you?"

"I fell and twisted my ankle. If you could just lend me an arm back to the house, that would be great." My vision blurred and there were two of him as I felt myself sway to one side. I was so distracted by the two Davins that I didn't realize he was already moving to pick me up until I found myself in his arms. "I'm too heavy," I said. "You'll hurt your back." I was short but I was solidly built. William had never been able to lift me.

"No problem. I move small trees around all the time."

I didn't care at that moment he'd just compared me to a tree. "Okay, Paul Bunyon, go for it," I said, not wanting to admit the relief I felt with the weight off my ankle.

Of course Pug suddenly became the perfect dog, trotting along far enough away from Davin that the animal was in no danger of being stepped on and Davin was in no danger of tripping. I struggled to keep from resting my head on his shoulder like some damsel in distress. Yes, I was in distress but I didn't want to be a damsel, and I was too grubby anyway. I closed my eyes trying to make the double vision go away and became aware that Davin smelled like an herb garden. It was a good smell.

"I didn't know you were going to do some gardening projects yourself." Davin shifted me around a bit.

"I really wanted to get the maze cleared," I said. "It was a great maze."

"It was. I'm sorry it got so overgrown. If I had known Mr. Mackenzie wasn't able to keep it up, I would have volunteered to do it myself."

We reached the back door. Davin yelled for someone to open it. When Kiki saw me, she gave a little shriek. "What happened? Are you hurt?"

"Just my ankle. I'll be fine." I didn't actually feel fine.

Davin put me down in a chair. "You need someone to take a look at that," he said.

"I don't have time. Kiki, can you put some ice in a bag for me?"

"No," she said. "Davin is right. You need to go to a doctor."

All at once the kitchen filled with what seemed like more people than we had in the house, as if they had multiplied overnight.

"Pug!" Mark cried. "I thought you were lost again!" He scooped the dog up and then there were lots of voices all talking over me until I explained what happened and again asked for ice.

I got a cup of tea instead. Katie pushed it in front of my nose and the fragrance made me feel a little better. I took it and took a big gulp, then nearly choked it back up, tipping some of it on my shirt. "What's in this tea?"

"Brandy," Katie said. "That's what they gave people in the olden days when someone got hurt. Or was it whiskey? Anyway, it's supposed to make you feel better."

I did feel a tiny bit warmer. Why not? Anything to make the rest of the day better than it had begun. I took another sip and then another until it was all gone, only spilling a little on my shirt because my hands were still a bit shaky. I felt a giggle rising out of nowhere, though I knew I couldn't be drunk on a few sips of brandy.

After asking for ice one more time and none appearing, I gave up and agreed to go to a doctor. I thought about changing clothes but the image of all the stairs daunted me.

"I can drive you," Davin said.

"No, I'm sure you have too much to do." I looked around. There were plenty of drivers in the room, except neither Eleanor nor Marni had any experience driving on the opposite side of the road, and Kiki needed constant reminders every time she turned. I had no idea how well Katie could drive.

"It's no problem," Davin said.

"I don't know any doctors here," I said.

"Not a problem. You'll need an x-ray anyway, so I'll take you to the closest A&E."

"What is that?" Kiki asked.

"Accidents and Emergencies. What you Yanks call an ER."

I refused to let Davin carry me to his car, insisting I could hop along with help, but by the time I got to it, my ankle was hurting so much, I could hardly concentrate on anything else. I did let him lift me in.

"You've gotten very pale," Davin said once I was in the car. "Best to put your head back and close your eyes."

"But we need to talk about how everything is going to get done," I said, though I could barely manage to get the words out.

"Later," he said.

We drove in silence for a few minutes and then I heard myself ask, "Why didn't you recognize me when you first saw me?"

He glanced over at me. "What?"

I repeated the question, though I don't know why it had popped into my head.

"I didn't recognize you because you look completely different," he said.

"I do?" I seriously thought I looked very much like I'd always looked.

"You do. Your hair was lighter back then and you kept it so short." All my siblings and I had short hair, because my mother didn't want to deal with tangles. "And I remembered your hair as more reddish."

"It used to be, especially when I was out in the sun, but it darkened as I got older."

"Plus your legs and arms were always bruised or scratched up and you had a lot of freckles. I suppose I came to Pemberley expecting just a larger version of that girl."

"That would have been really attractive," I said. "Woman who looks like she's been mauled by a bear with a home haircut and freckles."

"It made for a cute girl," he said as we pulled into the parking lot of the A&E.

I couldn't think of a way to respond to that, so I was glad we'd arrived. The place was bustling but they were moving people through rapidly. We didn't have to wait long before a nurse approached us. "You're next," she said to me. "Your partner can go back with you."

"Oh, he's not...we're not...," I started to say. She had already turned away.

"If you want me with you, just go along with that," Davin murmured in my ear. "Or I'll stay here, whatever you want."

I realized I did want someone with me. My head felt like a fog had invaded it and all I really wanted to do was curl up next to Davin and put my head on his shoulder.

When I saw the doctor, he was brisk. After I told him I twisted my ankle, he asked, "Have you been drinking? I smell alcohol."

I started to explain about the shirt and Katie and brandy and olden days but I must have been rambling because Davin jumped in with a more coherent explanation, for which I was thankful. It seemed odd the brandy had hit me so hard, because it had only been a few sips, but I assumed it was because I hadn't eaten enough.

"Do you have any existing medical problems?" he asked. "There's nothing on the form you've filled out, but I like to check."

"I have chronic pernicious anemia," I said, wondering why I hadn't written that down. I'd lived with it so long, I automatically told every doctor I encountered.

"I see," he said. "And are you taking your medication or do you get regular injections?"

"Medication," I said. Had I been taking it? I thought I had, because I usually didn't forget, but now I couldn't remember.

It was all a blur after that. After getting x-rays and being taken back to the examination room, I was listening to the doctor explain it was a bad sprain, when everything grew very small and I heard the doctor say, "Don't faint on us," and then someone put his arm around me. I leaned into him and realized the someone was Davin. "Why do you smell all herby?" I asked him.

"What?"

"You smell good, like something Kiki would make." This struck me as funny, and I heard myself giggling.

"Something seems off," the doctor said. "Did she hit her head?"

"I don't know. She didn't say she had." I heard Davin's voice but once again it seemed far away.

"Ms. Darcy, did you hit your head?" the doctor asked.

"Maybe. I don't remember." I realized my head was hurting. Why hadn't I noticed before? "I was climbing up on the statue and then the next thing I remember I was sitting on the ground."

The doctor felt around on the back of my head and when he touched one spot, I winced.

Bright lights shone into my eyes. "She might have a slight concussion," the doctor said. "Someone will need to watch over her the next 24 hours. Bring her back if she gets very drowsy suddenly or if the pain increases. And have someone wake her up every few hours tonight. Make sure she can respond. Ms. Darcy, I do recommend you get a more thorough checkup from a general practitioner."

They let me go with my foot in a boot contraption and so many instructions, I couldn't take everything in. Davin helped me back to his car.

"Thanks for all this," I said as I settled into the seat. "I'm sure this wasn't on your to-do list for the day."

"No problem. It brought back some memories seeing you in the maze." He maneuvered out of the parking lot. "I remember you used to love it. We always knew where to find you when we showed up. You and Samuel. You two were inseparable."

"Samuel didn't actually hang out with me that much when the rest of you weren't there," I said. "His grandfather always had him working on projects."

"He used to make it sound like the two of you spent hours together there. He even said he kissed you there."

"Kissed me! Samuel? No! I was ten. I didn't want a boy kissing me." I did vaguely remember one time when Samuel found me there and stood around awkwardly for a while without anything to say, which was very unlike him.

"Really? We certainly believed him. I always thought you liked Samuel better than the rest of us."

"Well, that was true. I did, but mainly because he could identify lots of birds and he was good at drawing dragons."

Davin laughed. "Hmm...yes, that was hard to compete with. I can see why you liked him best."

I glanced over at him. He was smiling. That made me smile too. "How did you find me in the maze? I didn't tell anyone what I was going to do."

"Mr. Mackenzie told me his loppers were missing. I don't know why but I just had a hunch you'd taken them to the maze."

"That's odd, but I'm glad you did." I put my head back and closed my eyes.

"Are you all right?" Davin asked.

"Just sleepy," I said. "You didn't answer when I asked you why you smelt like herbs."

"It's just soap. A friend of mine makes herbal soap as a small business and I buy it to help her out."

A friend? What kind of friend? A girlfriend? I pictured a woman in floaty skirts and long beautiful hair flitting about in a cute little cottage as she made her soap, all while singing to a bunch of cute little animal companions. That image morphed into Snow White and I began to think I really had scrambled my brain.

The next thing I knew we were pulling up to the main door at Pemberley. "Did I fall asleep?" I asked.

"Yes. I'm going to tell your sisters what the doctor said about a possible concussion. If you stay sleepy, you'll need to go back to the doctor."

I was already feeling more awake because my to do list had come rushing back into my head.

"Do you want me to carry you up the steps?" he asked.

I did, but instead I said, "No, you've done enough." I had to pull myself together.

"At least hold onto my arm while you go up the steps."

I did let him do that as I tottered inside. Everyone appeared in the hall as if they'd been waiting for us and they all went back to asking questions all at once. As I tried to explain what happened, I saw Davin talking to Kiki. She kept nodding her head and looking over at me. At one point she gave him a quick hug and soon after that he left. Even though Kiki was a very huggy person, it surprised me she felt comfortable enough hugging Davin. I'd have thought he'd come across as too formal to hug, unless he was much more relaxed with her than he was with me, just like he was more relaxed around Marni.

"Okay," Kiki announced. "We're putting Libby in a chair with her foot propped up and she can direct us all on what needs to be done."

I spent the next day trying to do that, but it was too frustrating, so the days after that I hobbled around working as much as I could, falling into bed each night too exhausted to even draw my rabbits as the wedding edged ever closer.

Davin did not appear inside, though Marni told me he asked how I was doing each day. I had to admit I spent too much time replaying our conversations in my head. I almost wished he and Marni had hit it off, so I wouldn't have an excuse to think about him. He was definitely too distracting.

"I only need you, Betsey," I said as she settled next to me. "Cats rule, right?"

Chapter 19

Countdown to the Raine Randolph/Stefan Andris
Wedding
2 days

<u>To Do List</u>:
Prep the dining room for painting
Pay more attention to Betsey
Investigate the bridge

THE DAY OF the photoshoot dawned cloudy. I texted Emmaline to let her know, as if she could do something about the weather.

She replied back, *Don't fret. Xavier is used to dealing with all sorts of light and he'll bring what he needs. Maybe cloudy will even be better for the kind of shots he wants.*

I could still fret about a ghost sighting and kitten chaos, which I preceded to do.

We'd arranged to keep the kittens in their big cage for the day, since Raine wasn't supposed to know we had them. I didn't want them crawling in camera cases for naps or scampering into a room unexpectedly to climb up Raine's wedding dress, all of which I could imagine in vivid detail. I checked the East Room one more time. It was ready but still wasn't quite right. "Flowers, it needs flowers," I said to Betsey. We'd recovered some vases from the stash of hidden furniture so I went to the kitchen to get one and then hurried outside, hoping I had time to cut some flowers.

Cutting flowers was more fun than I had thought it would be. Once I saw all the colors spread out before me, It was like picking colors for a painting.

"That one is a weed," Mr. Mackenzie said as he came up to see what I was doing. He pointed to one I particularly liked. It had small creamy yellow flowers with a scent of honey and the color of good butter. "It's called lady's bedstraw."

I pulled the bundle closer to me. "It looks good with the rest of the flowers and it has a nice scent," I said. "Who decides what is a weed anyway?"

I didn't really want an answer at the moment, and Mr. Mackenzie just made a huffing sound, not bothering to answer what he obviously considered a silly question. I wanted to ask him about Samuel, but he had already moved off with his shovel, obviously on a mission to do something important garden-wise.

I just managed to get the flowers arranged, sort of, in the vase when two vans pulled up. Emmaline had told me I'd like the dress designer. *She's quiet and unflappable. You have to be, to design wedding gowns.*

When everyone got out of the vans, one woman took charge, first coming up to me and saying, "I'm Charlotte Heywood. You're Libby

Darcy, I presume." Charlotte was older than me, but not by much. Her hair was pulled back in a bun, and she wore no makeup and a plain blue top and trousers. The most noticeable thing about her was her voice. It was lovely, very melodious. I could see where it would be a calming sound to hear for nervous brides.

"Careful now!" she called out to two people unloading a giant suit bag. Another person carried a stand.

I showed them to the East Room. Charlotte walked around the room, examining every little bit of it, even running her finger along the windowsill. I was glad I'd been so obsessive about dusting.

"All right, lay the floor cloths and unpack the dress," she told the assistant.

A froth of a dress emerged from the suit bag, a froth of the palest blush pink tulle, such a subtle shade that it seemed white at first glance. The ruffles cascaded down the front of the skirt at an angle like breaking waves. The corset-style bodice was in the same pink, in what was surely silk, unadorned except for three pearl strands draped off each side. The underskirt of creamy white fabric added structure, and I could tell from the way it gleamed it was also silk. I must have gasped because the designer smiled at my reaction.

"It's stunning," I said. I'd never paid too much attention to wedding dresses, but this one looked like nothing I'd ever seen before.

"Thank you. Raine particularly wanted the waterfall-style skirt with no train, and she picked the pink color herself. It looks lovely against her skin tone."

The assistant brought in a square case and opened it up to reveal a mannequin head, which held a delicate circlet of gold leaves and pearls. "Raine didn't want a veil, so she chose this look," the assistant explained. "It goes well with the dress."

"That's gorgeous too," I said. "It's all so gorgeous." I could suddenly see why people dreamed of the perfect wedding and the chance to wear a once-in-a-lifetime dress.

The designer made some tsking noises. "It's far more wrinkled than I expected. Get out the steamer please."

I heard cars coming down the driveway and then Eleanor's voice from the hallway. "They're here."

We hurried out to the front entrance. The line of cars and vans that pulled up made me feel like we were about to greet a head of state.

A young man all in black got out of one of the cars and opened the passenger door. A much older man dressed all in gray emerged, the color of his outfit matching the long gray hair he wore swept back from his face.

"That's Xavier," the dress designer murmured to me. "He does like a dramatic entrance."

More and more people piled out of the cars, all dressed in monochrome, mostly black, but with a few taupe outfits mixed in. I wondered if that was de rigueur for wedding personnel. I pulled at my pink shirt, which obviously didn't match my blue slacks. I realized I'd have to come up with my own wedding venue owner wear so I didn't appear as if I'd just wandered in like a stray tourist.

Emmaline and Raine got out of the same car. Emmaline waved at me as Eleanor went down the steps and greeted Raine, who hugged her. "I'm so glad you are here!" Raine said. "Everyone, this is my new sister! She's the one to thank for finding such a fabulous place." Raine took hold of Eleanor's hand and raised it in the air as if they were celebrating a victory. "Isn't it just like I said. It's like a dream, like right behind every door is a fairytale. I can't wait for you all to see it." She led the way inside as if she were a tour guide, urging us to hurry.

When we were all assembled, Emmaline introduced us and Raine took hold of my hands. "You're so lucky to have this place. It's marvelous. Thank you so much for letting us come here." She really was stunningly pretty, and her voice was lovely too.

"You're welcome," I managed to say. I'd felt a little weird in Stefan's presence because I'd known he was a famous actor, but with Raine, it was more than that. I'd never really understood stage presence before and she wasn't even on stage, though clearly she was the center of attention. It was as if people couldn't look away from her.

She let go of my hands and twirled around, her face taking on what could only be described as a blissful expression. We all just stood there and watched her, until the makeup artist said, "At some point, I'd like to see Raine in the room where the ceremony will take place so I can take a look at the lighting." The woman turned to me. "It needs to be right."

"Of course." I hoped the lighting was up to her standard. That hadn't been on my list of worries, though as soon as she said it, it jumped right on to the list. I suppose if the lighting was wrong, we could put in different light bulbs if we had them, which we didn't.

Raine was still drifting about in the entrance hall. "I want to look like a princess in a fairytale, but all blurry around the edges, sort of. I don't want to look totally real, because sometimes fantasy is better. Does that make sense?" she asked the makeup artist.

"Perfectly," the woman said.

Mark came running in from the kitchen. Pug followed him with tongue hanging out, struggling to keep up. Mark slid to a stop when he saw all the people, and then darted behind his mother. "It's Raine, Mark," Eleanor said. "You remember her, don't you?"

He peeked out from around her, ducking his head and giving a quick glance up. Raine came over to them. "He may not remember me, but I remember him." She rummaged in the large bag she was carrying and brought out a book. "I remembered you liked dolphins. I hope you still do, because this is a story about a dolphin."

Mark nodded. "Well, good," Raine said, handing it to him. "Once you read it, you can tell me all about it."

With that, I could see Mark falling under her spell. He practically glowed as he clutched the book.

"And who is this little sweetheart?" Raine knelt down and held out her hand to Pug, who came forward and licked it.

"That's Pug," Mark said. "We found him on the island."

"Long story," Eleanor said to Raine.

"Well, isn't he just adorable! I used to have a pug." As Raine petted the dog, I swear he gazed at her with an adoring look. "My pug was a sweet little thing too and looked so adorable in his little sweaters. Now I have two big dogs. I wish I could have brought them today, but I was afraid they'd slobber all over the wedding dress."

The makeup artist cleared her throat and looked over at Emmaline.

"Maybe we should get started," Emmaline said, "so no one has to rush."

"I'll show you to the East Room," I felt a little silly saying it because it made the room sound far more grand than it was. I'd have to consider whether we'd need to change the name.

"I wish to see the possible sites for the photographs," the photographer announced.

Marni had volunteered to show off the sites and I'd agreed, thinking she'd be better at selling them on any particular site, since her enthusiasm for the garden had only increased with working in it. Several of the group followed them out the front door, which was good because there was no way the whole herd of them would fit in the East Room. Emmaline's assistant took over the florists as they went to unload their vans.

Raine exclaimed over everything, including my poor attempt at the flowers. "Isn't it all just perfect?" she said. "Everything looks like it's all been here for years and years."

"I want a picture of the dress hanging by itself before we get started," Raine said. "Can someone please go get Xavier."

Emmaline came in just in time to hear her, but there was dead silence for a few moments.

"What?" Raine asked.

"I'm not sure he likes to be told what to photograph," Emmaline said. "Perhaps we can get a shot of it the day of the wedding with the wedding photographer?"

"That's fine," Raine said. "I wasn't thinking." Emmaline nodded at her other assistant who typed something on her tablet.

"Are you sure about the dogs being here for the ceremony?" the dress designer asked. "I don't know how we're going to keep them away from the dress."

Emmaline stood up a little straighter and her eyes widened. "What's this?" she asked. "Why would they bother the dress?"

"Oh, in all the fittings, my babies had a hard time staying away from it," Raine said, picking up the skirt and fluffing it. "I don't know if it's the scent of the fabric or because it's so soft, but they just wanted to snuggle up to it the whole time. They can't miss the ceremony, though. They're family. I'm sure they'll behave."

From the look on Emmaline's face, I could tell she wasn't going to leave that to chance. "Maybe you could spray the room with some sort of scent that would change the smell of the dress," she said. "A perfume misting spray that wouldn't hurt the fabric?" She looked over at the dress designer.

Charlotte nodded. "Yes, that might work."

"I'll get some," Emmaline said and nodded to her assistant who typed it into her tablet. I decided it would be nice to have an assistant of my own, someone who would follow me around with my lists and remind me what to do when.

"And shall we designate someone to be in charge of the dogs when you are busy?" Emmaline asked Raine.

"Oh, that's a good idea," Raine said. "Except they only like certain people. I'll have to think about that." Worry flashed across Emmaline's face and once again I knew I could never do her job.

I took myself off to work on prepping the dining room for painting, taping along the window frames and the ceiling while keeping one ear open for anyone who might need me.

They photographed for hours, and I began to understand why they didn't wait for the day of the wedding to do it all.

I had moved on to doing the brush painting when Emmaline found me.

"Xavier wants to see the tower room to determine if it's suitable for pictures," she said. "He thinks the sun coming in the windows will light Raine beautifully, and the curved walls will add a great feature to the photos."

"It's full of my painting supplies!" I said. "I didn't get it ready because I didn't think anyone would want to use it. It's just bare stone walls."

"Why don't you take him up there and explain? He'll have to see it to be convinced it isn't right."

When I explained all my objections to them photographing in the tower room, including the fact that it could collapse on them, Xavier waved all that away. "We won't be in there for long, and the wind isn't blowing. Why would it fall down?"

I didn't have a good answer for that so I tried a new tactic, speaking at the dress designer about how the room wasn't all that clean and the painting materials would have to be moved around. At this information, she snapped her fingers and then fired off instructions to her assistants.

"You will show them the room first, all right?" she said to me. "If Mr. La likes it, we'll clean up an area and move things as needed. Mr. La, if it needs to be cleaned, could you photograph somewhere else until the room is ready?"

"The bridge," Emmaline suggested. "I could show you where it is."

"Oh, yes!" Raine said. "I loved the photograph of it."

He agreed and followed me up to the tower. "Yes," he said as soon as he saw it. As he left the room, people began to scurry about in it.

I had two canvases on easels, which is how I usually painted, a pair of not quite identical works that I alternated between. I'd been playing with shades of pale green and touches of gold, the gold inspired by the gilding. *These are so weird*, William said every time he saw one of my paintings. *Why don't you just paint rabbits, since you draw them so much, instead of these...abstract things.* He'd always make air quotes around the word 'abstract' as if they weren't quite good enough to even merit that description.

"Can we move everything on either side of the door?" the assistant asked. "If the photographer wants to put Raine in front of the window, he won't need that space."

"Yes, fine," I said, though it wasn't really. "I'll move the easels first and then we can put things in front of them so they won't get bumped. The oil paint on them isn't dry." After I moved them, I got the assistant a broom and dust cloths, once she declared there wasn't time to mop the floor.

"I suppose it will do," she said when we finished cleaning. "I'm so glad there isn't a train. We'd be in trouble if there were."

We waited around until Raine came up the stairs, people on either side of her holding the dress up off the floor.

"The bridge is so cute," Raine gushed to me as she came into the tower room. "But Libby, tell us, are you the "L" carved in the heart on the bridge post? Who is "R"?"

"What?" I didn't remember anything carved on the bridge.

"The heart. I had Emmaline snap a photo of it. Show her." Emmaline held up her phone. There was indeed a carved heart and in the middle of it were the letters L+R. Libby and Robin. No. That was silly. It was probably some ancient carving from a hundred years ago. Except I would have seen it on one of my visits.

"I don't know," I said. Would the Robin of my childhood have carved that about the two of us? I'd never had the sense he particularly liked me. It was understood that Samuel and I were the better friends. Most likely someone had carved it to tease him. It would fit with that particular group of boys.

"I never noticed that," I said. "No idea who it's referring to."

Xavier came in. "We must hurry," he said, "to get the light right."

I stayed in the hallway while they were photographing, as if I could rush to save them in case the tower fell. Every time I shifted around and the floor creaked, I gave a start, worried I was actually hearing masonry heaving itself from the mortar.

When they finished, the dress designer tried to hurry Raine downstairs as if the paint was going to leap off the canvases onto the dress. I could see where it would be nerve-wracking to keep a wedding dress pristine until the ceremony. If it had been me, I would have needed tranquilizers to watch Raine moving around to so many different locations, any one of which provided dress hazards.

Raine resisted the designer's efforts, coming over to look more closely at my canvases. "These are beautiful," she said. "Like an image is there but I can't quite make it out, because it's hidden in the mist. Is that what you meant to do?"

I was so embarrassed to have her examining my work, that my throat went dry and I could feel my face getting hot. "Yes," I croaked.

"Raine, we should go," one of her assistants said.

"Yes, I am ready to get out of this dress, as much as I love it," Raine said. "Thank you, Libby. We'll see you soon!" She blew a kiss at me and swept out of the room.

I debated about putting everything back in place but decided it didn't need to be done right then. It wasn't like I'd be painting there in the near future or maybe not at all, depending on how concerned I'd decide to be about the tower falling down.

When I went back downstairs, they were busy loading the vehicles. Raine swept out of the East Room, back in regular clothes, waving at everyone still bustling around. "Thank you! Thank you, my lovelies! You're all spectacular!"

Emmaline sent one of her assistants with Raine, and then came over to me. "We've decided to leave the dress here," she said. "The designer says there's no sense in putting it back in a bag to get all wrinkled again. No problem with that, right?"

"Um...I guess not." I didn't really want to be responsible for that beautiful dress, but I didn't see how I could say no.

"Great! I have to go. Text me if there are any problems. Today went great! After the wedding though, let's get together for some real fun. I feel like we haven't had a chance to talk about anything but the wedding for months."

"We will," I said. "We both need it."

Someone called out for Emmaline, and she dashed off.

I needed to get back to my list though I was tempted to go investigate the carved heart on the bridge. Before I could make up my mind, Mark ran up to me.

"Libby! Libby! Pug is sick!" He was practically in tears.

"Sweetie, calm down. How do you know he's sick?"

Eleanor came down the hallway. "Mark, I told you not to bother Libby right now."

"But Pug is really sick! He won't get out of his bed and his eyes look funny."

"Are you sure?" I asked. "He seemed fine earlier."

"I'm sure."

"Okay." The list would have to wait. "Let's go see him."

Mark was right. Pug lifted his head and gave a small wiggle when we went into Mark's room, but then the animal put his head back down.

"He's not going to die, is he?" Mark said in a small voice.

My heart wrenched. "No, of course not. But let's take him to the vet so he can be checked out. Maybe he just played too hard yesterday and he's tired. Or maybe the kittens are keeping him awake at night."

"Can you drive with your foot in a boot?" Eleanor asked. "I'd offer but I think I'm too much a nervous driver to drive here, using the other side of the road and all."

The doctor had said I could take the boot off the next day. I could take it off a day early, though I'd been warned my foot would be stiff at first and I'd be uncomfortable driving. "Kiki can drive," I said. "I'll go with her. Mark, why don't you stay here?" Kiki wasn't a good enough driver to be trusted with a child in the car.

"But I want to go with him!" the boy cried.

"I know you do, but the kittens need you too," Eleanor said. "They won't be gone long."

"That's right," I added. "They need some exercise since they've been shut up all day, but they need someone to keep track of them so they don't get lost." I almost suggested he take them into the library, and then realized how bad it would be if the ghost appeared. "Why don't you take them to the conservatory? They'll love that. It will be like a big rainforest to them, but make sure the doors are all closed."

He agreed so I went to find Kiki. I was afraid she would be too frantic with wedding food prep, that she'd be extra nervous driving me, but she was perfectly calm. "Everything is fine," she said as we started down the drive. "My spreadsheet timetable is working out just great, so don't worry."

I didn't talk for the rest of the drive because I didn't want to distract her, except to remind her which lane to turn into. The three of us made it to the vet with only one close call.

"He was doing fine for a while," I said to the vet as the man examined Pug. "I don't know what's happened."

The vet looked in the dog's mouth. Pug just sat there. "He does seem a bit off, and he's dehydrated. It doesn't appear to be a respiratory virus, which would be my first thought considering he'd been out as a stray for so long. I'd like to keep him overnight and run some tests."

"Okay, but what do you think it might be? That little boy who was with us before has already gotten very attached to him, and he'll want to know why we're leaving the dog here."

"For the moment, just tell him the dog got rundown living on his own for so long and we're testing him to see if he needs some medicine to get him back up to normal. No sense in having the boy worry too early."

I was worried myself. The vet didn't say Pug would be all right.

"I'll call with the test results," he said.

When I told Kiki the news, she looked like she was going to cry. "I was afraid of that. I've been googling Pug's symptoms and it's not looking good."

"Kiki! The vet said he didn't know what was wrong yet. You know you shouldn't google medical things for dogs or people. The worst things always pop up first."

"But it might actually be bad. It could be cancer, or pancreatitis, or the dog could have eaten something poisonous and gone into kidney failure. What are we going to tell Mark?"

She was as good at catastrophizing as I was. "We'll tell him what the vet said."

Those were exactly the words I used when we got back. I must have been convincing, because Mark didn't seem too worried. The kittens were so absorbing he didn't have time to dwell on Pug.

I was so tired that night I only managed to draw one rabbit ear before I put down my pencil. As I drifted off, I remembered what Raine had said about the heart carved into the bridge. I dreamed that night I was a child again, and Robin and I were running through the woods, laughing and laughing, not a care in the world.

Chapter 20

Countdown to the Raine Randolph/Stefan Andris
Wedding
1 day!

<u>To Do List</u>:
Paint the Dining Room
Try not to explode
Set pride aside and do the right thing

THE DAY BEFORE the wedding Betsey took on the overseer job as I rushed to finish painting the dining room. The windows were all open and I very much hoped that not only would the paint dry quickly, the paint smell would go away just as quickly. I had taken the boot off my foot that morning and thankfully, my leg wasn't as stiff as predicted. The rose pink paint color, Fredericka's Blush, made the room look just as I had envisioned it and for once, the job went fast and I wasn't interrupted. I had just about finished when Marni came in.

"How did it go?" I asked. "Did you get some fabulous flowers?" The visit to the garden store for the container plantings had been put off until that morning and I hoped she'd managed to get enough plants. We were cutting it very, very close.

She came farther into the room. She wasn't smiling. In fact, she looked downright serious.

"What is it?" I asked. I couldn't imagine a sudden flower shortage accounted for her expression.

"We need to talk," she said. Her voice was odd and strained.

"Okay. Come with me into the scullery so I can deal with the brush." I left the paint can because I needed to do a tiny amount of touch up with a smaller brush. She followed me without another word. I set down the brush in the sink. "Go ahead." She was making me so nervous, I grabbed hold of my bracelet and let the beads run through my fingers.

"Davin's office assistant took me because the crew were all assigned to other jobs today. His name is George. He was very interested in hearing about Pemberley. Said he'd always wanted to see the inside and the whole village is talking about the place."

"Okay," I said. That wasn't surprising. I knew how small towns worked. I didn't know why she was telling me all that.

"Libby, it was weird. George knew so much about you. About our whole family. When I asked how he knew so much, he got very uncomfortable, but I pressed him on it until he told me. Davin has a report on you done by some investigator in the States. An actual private investigator."

I couldn't take in the words right away and I made her repeat herself.

A private investigator? I knew they existed outside of television and movies but I'd never met one in real life and didn't know anyone who had ever used one. "Why would Davin have someone do a report on me?"

"I don't know. George didn't know either. It came when Davin was out of the country for several days on a business trip and George opened the envelope himself. After I wouldn't stop asking him, he admitted he read it. It made you sound, well, not like you at all. It focused mostly on things that have gone wrong, about our family and the finances and the bar exam and you leaving North Caroline all of the sudden. It made William's church sound bad too, like they are doing something shady."

I didn't tell her that part was probably accurate.

I felt my face go hot and my jaw clench. "That's why he thought I might sell the place," I said, more to myself than to Marni. Any report about my past life wouldn't show any real signs of accomplishment or give any indication I could actually restore Pemberley. I thought my head might explode in fury. How dare he investigate me?

"And Davin's office wasn't at all what I expected," she said. "It's very fancy. I mean, really upscale. Lots of framed landscape plans on the walls of major projects at huge estates and high-end hotels. George said they even do plans for some members of the royal family, though he's sworn to secrecy as to which ones and those aren't displayed. Davin must have some good connections somehow for a village kid."

I didn't care about Davin's connections at that moment. I wanted to storm into his office and ask about the report.

"Thanks for telling me," I said, trying to keep my voice calm. I felt like I was going to throw up at any moment. "I'll ask him about it."

"I can ask him if you want."

"No, I need to do it myself," I said.

"One more thing," Marni said.

I didn't know if I could handle one more thing.

"Have you talked to Mr. Mackenzie yet?" she asked. "I guess the latest news about Samuel isn't encouraging, according to George, who seems to know everything about everybody in the village. You may have to drag Mr. Mackenzie onto an airplane because he won't be easily convinced you can survive without him. He's so attached to the estate, he doesn't want it to fall into complete disrepair. According to George, some wealthy family near here offered him a position as head gardener years ago for twice the money. Mr. Mackenzie wouldn't take it. George says everyone in the village knows Mr. Mackenzie was always in love with your grandmother. I wouldn't have believed it except I saw a picture of her in the garden shed. It's behind the little bin he uses to store seed packets. It's in a frame and it isn't a bit dusty, so he must take it out and look at it sometimes."

"What? Mr. Mackenzie? He barely spoke in my grandmother's presence." Though it would explain a lot. I wondered if my grandmother had known.

"Love is weird." Marni looked at her phone. "And with that profound statement, I've got to go be productive. I need to answer some emails and then I'll plant those containers. Are you okay?"

"Yes. Thanks," I said.

After she left, I finished washing the brush. I knew I needed a bit of time to pull myself together before I went back to painting or I'd make a mess of it. I both wanted and didn't want to read the report about myself. How could he have had something like that done? It was such an invasion of privacy.

I headed for the study, planning to close the door and sit for just a moment. Eleanor was at the desk. "Do you want your desk?" she asked. "I've just finished adding these latest estimates to your spreadsheet."

"No, I'm just taking a break." I knew if I told her about the private investigator report, she'd be sympathetic and indignant for me, but I couldn't bring myself to talk about it.

"Well, I can leave you to some peace and quiet before tomorrow. I need to iron Mark's shirt for the rehearsal dinner. I told Raine that Mark was too young to attend but she has really embraced the idea of having a step-nephew."

"And a stepsister from what I saw yesterday. That's good, right?"

She straightened the papers on the desk. "Yes, except I think I'm supposed to be a buffer between her and her mother. I can't believe my father married the woman now that I've seen her true colors. It's like he can't see how awful she is. I don't understand it."

I could have said the same for my own father. Even though if he hadn't married my mother, I wouldn't be around, I still never understood how he'd picked his two wives. Or rather, I supposed I could understand it a little, given that I couldn't see William clearly for what he was until years after I'd first known him.

"But at least you'll get to see your father for the wedding," I said. "I should have told you to invite him here for dinner or just to hang out with you if you wanted." Once again I was angry at myself for not thinking enough about my friends.

"He didn't come. He's been having trouble with his lungs and a doctor told him not to fly."

That made me feel even worse because I had no idea what was happening in Eleanor's life beyond our immediate day to day. "Oh, I'm sorry. I hope he'll be okay."

"He will. It was just going to be a short trip for them anyway." I was relieved she didn't sound worried. "Well, I'll leave you to it," she added. "The ironing isn't going to get done by itself."

I knew I didn't need to see the estimates right at that moment, but it was as if I wanted to try and make the day worse than it already was. I went over to the desk. The estimate for the heating repair was on the top of the pile of bills. The old boiler was in such bad shape, it spit out little bits of heat at only a few random points during the day, which is why we froze the first few months we were here. The behemoth contraption crouched in a corner of the Dooms and whenever I'd venture down to look at the thing, it wheezed away like it was on its death bed. Not that I'd ever do anything to it beyond banging on it with a wrench. I was too scared to touch any of the knobs or levers.

We'd survived the cold those first few months with a series of portable heaters that got moved around as we worked, though some days they barely managed to raise the temperature of a room even a few degrees. I'd promised Kiki we'd get a new boiler before next winter, though that promise had come before I'd seen the estimate for the roof.

I'd told the estimator I wanted a range of options, from just replacing the boiler to what it would take to make the place more energy and cost efficient. He'd gone into raptures describing the possibilities of a solar thermal heating system on the roof to help with the hot water supply and a solar photovoltaic array on a section of the roof to produce some of our own electricity.

I had known right away those options wouldn't be possible initially, but I had been trying to get in the frame of mind that I had to plan long term to make the place successful.

"Just do it," I muttered to myself as I picked up the bill. When I read the numbers, I set it back down on the desk trying to remember to breathe.

I spent the next hour poring over my spreadsheets, my jaw clenching more and more until it became clear the situation was hopeless. We'd either have to go another winter without heat but with an intact roof and the possibility of a tower collapse, or we could stay warm with a leaking roof that would cause more damage and still have the possibility of a tower collapse. There just wasn't enough money.

I sat back in the chair and closed my eyes until a ping came from my phone.

It was Emmaline: *Going through my notes. Did you do something about that vicious swan?*

I'd completely forgotten about Palmer. I hadn't seen him for a couple of days and I'd spent so much time inside, I hadn't even thought about him. Had he crossed the rainbow bridge to some great swannery in the beyond? I felt only a tiny bit guilty for thinking I wouldn't be broken up about that.

I closed my laptop, and opened and closed my mouth a few times, which made my jaw crack. It didn't help the headache that had come upon me with a vengeance.

"One thing at a time," I said to myself. "Focus, Libby. Deal with the swan and the wedding."

I found Mr. Mackenzie putting mulch around some of the newly planted annuals. He straightened up when he saw me, and I noticed a grimace pass across his face at the motion.

"Mr. Mackenzie, do you have any ideas how we can keep Palmer from attacking the guests?" I asked. "Can we sprinkle some swan food away from the house right before the guests are due to arrive?"

"You didn't know?" He put his hand on the small of his back and gave another grimace.

"Know what?"

"Mr. Davin brought him a mate," Mr. Mackenzie said. "The two have taken to each other like they be made for each other."

"Davin brought a swan here?"

"Aye. Palmer's mate got killed a number of years ago by a marauding great beast of a dog. The bird's been cranky ever since."

"That was very thoughtful of Davin," I said, though I wasn't sure how I felt about him doing that. Of course, Davin had just gone ahead and assumed I had forgotten about the swan problem because he thought I was a ditz. So what if I had actually forgotten? He had no business dropping off random swans unasked. Solving the swan problem didn't make up for the private investigator report.

"Aye, Mr. Davin's always been one to look out for others." Mr. Mackenzie's admiration came through in every word.

Since we were actually having a conversation and Mr. Mackenzie stopped digging, I realized it was a good time to get him to talk about the future. "Marni told me that Samuel was ill. I'm very sorry to hear that."

"He'll be fine." The gardener averted his eyes from me. "There are good doctors down under from what he says."

"I'm sure there are. I just wanted you to know if you wanted to go see him, don't feel like any obligation to Pemberley is keeping you from doing that. I'm sure he'd like to see you."

"You need the help with all the flap about this wedding," he said, stabbing the shovel into the ground. "I can't leave now."

"You've been a major help. We couldn't have gotten ready without you. But it will all be over soon and we don't have another wedding scheduled. We can get by without you." He jerked his head back as if I had slapped him, so I hastened to add, "though of course things won't look as good. I'm sure the estate owes you some backpay as well. I just realized you haven't had a raise in a long time. I'm intending to pay you for a retroactive raise."

Again he looked at me like I'd slapped him. "I don't take charity!" he said as he pulled the shovel back out of the ground. "And I'll be minding my own business, as people should." With that, he spit on the ground and then stomped away.

"Okay, Libby, you really mucked that up," I said to myself. I heard my mother's voice in my head. *I'm not surprised. You can never do anything right.* It was true. I had only one employee and I couldn't figure out how to have a conversation with him. My head was throbbing so much I could hardly concentrate. I didn't know how I was going to get through the wedding. I wanted to go away and forget all about everything.

From that spot on the grounds, I could see the village. I looked back up at the house. A bird landed on the top of the tower and some small bits of render fell off from the edge. Rain clouds were gathering in the distance. In the darkening light, Pemberley looked more like a looming ruin than it did in daylight. What a silly dream I'd had. I'd been so foolish to think I could bring it back to life myself. It needed to be in the hands of someone with money who could renovate it the right way. Someone like Stefan Andris.

Davin's report had been accurate about the me I'd been in the past. Maybe I was mostly still like that, but I could still try to set one thing right. I headed to the village.

Chapter 21

Countdown to the Raine Randolph/Stefan Andris

Wedding

1 day!

To Do List:

Finish painting the dining room

Face facts

Keep it together

~~Set pride aside and do the right thing~~

THERE WAS ONLY one real estate agent in town. I'd seen her about the village, a woman with graying hair who always had on a bright purple or red blazer. Her office sat on the main street, one small building between the pub and an Indian restaurant.

"Why, hello!" she called out from her desk when I walked in. She gave a little start when she looked more closely at me. "You're Mrs. Darcy's granddaughter, aren't you? You do look a bit like her."

I'd never heard that before. "Yes, that's me. Libby Darcy."

"Welcome. I'm sorry we haven't been formally introduced." She got up from her desk and came around to shake my hand. "I'm a bit surprised to see you in my office. You're not thinking of selling Pemberley, are you?" I couldn't tell if she was making a joke or just getting right to the point.

When I didn't respond right away, she added, "While I'd hate to see it go out of the family of course, everyone in the village knows what a massive task you took on trying to restore it. No shame in getting it off your hands." So getting right to the point. No flies on her, as my stepfather would say. Her eyes practically gleamed at the thought of the commission.

"No," I said. "I'm not here to talk about selling Pemberley." She didn't need to know of my plans for the place. "I am here for a reason though. I want to buy Mr. Mackenzie's cottage."

She deflated a bit. "Oh...oh...oh...I see. I see. I see." Her hands fluttered about in confusion. It took a few more moments until she actually seemed to understand what I wanted, and then she was back to being all business. "That can be arranged if he's made the final decision to go ahead. I know he's worried about his grandson in Australia."

Of course she would know everything about Samuel. I was sure everyone in the village had known long before me. "There's one condition though," I said. "I want to buy it through the company I've set up to run Pemberley and I don't want Mr. Mackenzie to know I'm buying it until the contract is signed." I'd set up a private limited company when I'd made the decision to turn the estate into a wedding venue and most of the bills were paid through that account, except for Mr. Mackenzie's salary. That was still being paid through the household account. So Mr. Mackenzie would not know the name of the company, unless he'd been on our placeholder website, which I very much doubted. He'd know once he saw my name on the contract, but by then it would be too late for him to object.

She nodded. "All right. If that's what you wish. News gets around fast in the village though, so if you don't want him to know, you shouldn't tell anyone."

My grandmother had always said any news spread through the village as if carried by air currents the moment anyone opened their mouth. "You and me and my solicitor will be the only ones to know for the time being. What is the asking price?"

She named a sum that was just slightly under the amount I had in the estate's bank account, money that had been there for the new roof. When Stefan Andris bought Pemberley, he'd have plenty of money to put on a new roof himself.

I hesitated only for a moment. "Fine, I'll take it."

She stared at me. "You...you don't want to make a counteroffer? Are you approved for a mortgage?" Now her eyes narrowed and I could imagine her radar going off that something was wrong. I'd have been the same way.

"No mortgage," I said. "I'll pay cash."

The word 'cash' dispelled all her concerns. We spent a little longer discussing the process. "Send the contract to my solicitor," I said and gave her the information. We shook hands and then I headed back toward Pemberley. I'd thought I'd feel like a huge burden was lifted from me, but instead I just felt resigned. It was still a failure, even if a self-declared one in place of an actual bankrupt failure. But with the sale of Pemberley, there would be enough money to send Kiki to culinary school and for me to go somewhere to live for a few years while I figured out my next steps. I'd rent out the cottage because I didn't want to live in a place where my failure would be looming over me each time I looked out the window. I'd call Stefan as soon as possible after the wedding and take him up on his offer to buy Pemberley. It would be in good hands with him.

As I walked back up the drive, a car came down it, one I didn't recognize. It passed and I saw an older couple inside. They smiled and waved so cheerily, I knew they were Americans because only Americans would be that friendly to a complete stranger.

When I came into the house, Betsey was waiting for me in the hall. I picked her up and put my face against her fur. "Maybe you'll be happier in a smaller place," I said. She purred in response. I could hear voices from the kitchen. Not surprising. It had turned into meeting place central in the house. Kiki was in there all the time as it was her natural habitat, and so everyone else migrated there too. There were lots of excited voices, more than usual.

"What's going on?" I asked as I walked in. "Who were those people in the car?"

"There you are!" Kiki said.

I looked around at all the happy faces. Something was definitely up.

"Sit down," Kiki said. "We've been scheming behind your back, scheming in a good way. Here, have a macaron while we talk." She waved a plate of them at me.

Betsey squirmed her way out of my arms so I did sit down. "Okay. But I really want to know about the people in the car."

"They're just a small part of it," Katie said. "They knocked on the door and asked if they could see the house. I didn't see why not so I showed them around and told them all about the history. Good thing

I'd stayed up so late reading about the Darcys and the Bertrams." She tapped the book I hadn't noticed that was lying on the kitchen table. "They ooohed and awed all over the place, and when they left, they gave me thirty pounds! Said it was the best house tour they'd had so far." With a flourish, Katie took some bills out of her pocket and put them on the table. "Here, put it toward my room and board."

"That's...good," I said. "Amazing, in fact. But I'm still confused. What is the scheming?"

"I'll do this part," Eleanor said. "We know you are under tremendous pressure to get the place fixed up before it falls down. And I've been doing some research about what it means exactly to have the building listed with English Heritage."

I was confused. "I thought we already talked about this. It means we have to get permission to do repair work and everything has to be done just so and it makes everything extra expensive and takes an extra long time."

She smiled. "Yes, but it also means you can apply for grants to do emergency work . You'd have to open it up to the public, though only for a few times a year. It would be a terrific way to get some funds. I've looked at the application online and it's not too daunting."

"You can charge admission too," Katie added. "I'm happy to stay around and give tours. I had so much fun telling stories to those tourists. You don't have to pay me. I can work up some possible handouts and maps of the garden. I like to do that sort of thing. And it would be a great opportunity to write my book."

"Having tourists in won't bring a big income, but it will help with day-to-day expenses," Eleanor said. "I've done some estimates with how many days you'd have to be open and how many tourists you'd need, to see how it would all work."

Too much coming at me at once. "I thought people visited houses that were part of the National Trust and we aren't that."

"There are other organizations to join that would work with this house better, and they help put out the word," Eleanor said. "I've been researching that too."

I don't know why I was asking questions. I'd already committed the roof money to the cottage instead. Even if some grant money became available, there was no way it would cover the tower repairs, the electrical repairs and a new heating system.

They all looked so pleased with themselves, I didn't want to disappoint them. Not right then. I forced a smile. "That sounds fantastic. Thank you. I'm just so overwhelmed with the wedding, let's talk about all this afterwards." That's when I'd tell them what I'd done and explain about the new estimates and how I just couldn't carry out the plan. I didn't want to imagine their reactions to all that. I had to focus on getting through the next day. "Thank you. I love you all!"

"Even me?" Katie asked.

"Even you," I said.

Everyone but me turned toward the hallway.

Kiki gasped. "Who's that?"

"I hear a woman's voice." Marni got up and went to the door. "It's the same voice I heard the other night in the library."

We all moved over to where Marni stood. She put out her arm like she wasn't going to let us pass.

"I don't see anything," I said. The hall was dim but I could see all the way down it.

"There is a woman in a long white nightgown," Eleanor said. "I can't believe it. I didn't really believe any of you had seen a ghost, but there she is."

"I can see her!" Katie tried to push past Marni but Marni grabbed hold of her shirt. "A real ghost! I've got to try to get a picture of her."

"I don't see anything," I said. I would have thought it was an elaborate practical joke if Eleanor hadn't been there. Eleanor was not the type of person to participate in practical jokes.

"I thought ghosts only came out at night," Marni said. She got a better hold on Katie who was fumbling with her phone.

"Not this one. The first time I saw her was in the middle of the day," Kiki said.

"Awesome!" Katie held up her phone and clicked away, though her hands were shaking badly. "This will make the house tours even better."

For the third time, I said, "I don't see anything." Everyone continued to ignore me. Why could they see the ghost but not me? "Hello! Okay, I don't see her but why is everyone not terrified out of your minds about this?" Besides Katie's shaking hands, no one looked particularly worried or upset.

"If you saw her, you wouldn't be terrified either," Kiki draped her arm over my shoulder. "I was scared the first time because I was startled, but there is absolutely nothing scary about her."

"She's right," Marni added. "Same with me. It's weird but I just know she's harmless."

"And I've always wanted to see a ghost. I knew they existed somewhere." Katie's response didn't surprise me. I looked over at Eleanor, sensible Eleanor.

"I don't feel frightened either, for some reason," she said. "I'd like to find a logical explanation because I don't believe in ghosts, but at the moment, I can't think of one."

"I can't think of one either," I said. "Is she still there?"

"No, she went into the dining room," Kiki said.

Katie pulled away from Marni and darted down the hall. She slid to a stop at the dining room door and leaned in. I found myself holding my breath.

"She's gone," Katie called. "I hope I got some pictures of her."

"That was...weird, but exciting in a way," Kiki said. "We can all agree that I didn't imagine her, right?" She nudged me in the side.

"Right," I said. With four eyewitnesses, they clearly weren't all having a mass hallucination. I couldn't really take it all in at the moment. My brain went right back to the wedding. "Let's just hope she doesn't appear during the wedding to snack on the canapes. I don't suppose anyone knows how to keep ghosts out. I know garlic works for vampires, but ghosts?"

Katie came back toward us as she scrolled through her phone .I looked to her as the one most likely to have the right knowledge. "They're all blurry! My hand was shaking too much. I can't believe I messed that up."

I repeated my question to her.

She sighed. "We could smudge the house with sage," she said. "That's supposed to work."

"That means walking around the house with a piece of sage we've set on fire, right?" Marni asked. "There's sage in the garden."

"Right. It shouldn't be too hard." Katie gave a grimace and then frowned.

"What's wrong?" Kiki asked.

Katie put her phone back in her pocket. "I have a bit of a sore throat. It's hurting when I swallow, but anyway, I know people who've done sage smudging."

I held up my hand. "Um...no. I don't want to take a chance of catching the house on fire."

Katie stared back down the hallway. "You know, that ghost looked familiar somehow, but I can't think why. Weird."

The doorbell rang, making us all jump.

"Hopefully not an extra ghost coming to stay," Marni joked.

"It's the pizzas," Kiki said. "I've ordered from the village for dinner because we don't have room to store any ingredients that aren't for the wedding."

"And it's almost time for the car I arranged to pick Mark and me up," Eleanor said. "I'm going to have to pull him away from the kittens."

I'd forgotten they were going to the rehearsal dinner. I'd been too preoccupied to notice that Eleanor was all dressed up.

Kiki brought in three large pizzas. "Veggie, plain cheese, and pepperoni. I thought we'd want leftovers, or cold pizza for breakfast. We'll have breakfast pastries, but everyone is on their own for figuring out their own breakfasts."

"I'm not hungry," Katie said. "And my throat hurts. I think I'll skip the pizza and lie down for a bit."

"I'll make some tea or heat up some soup for you," Kiki said.

Katie waved her off. "Maybe later. Go ahead and eat the pizza while it's hot."

After she left the room, I said to Kiki, "Do you think she's coming down with something? This isn't good if you were counting on her for tomorrow."

"I don't know. She said this morning her throat was scratchy. Maybe it's just a twenty-four hour thing. I'm sure she'll be fine tomorrow."

I hoped so. I didn't know anyone to call in to help. I was angry at myself for not having a back-up plan. I thought about texting Emmaline to see if she could add in another person to the servers she had already arranged.

"I'm planning on helping," Marni said. "I'm not a great cook, but I'm a good sous chef."

"We'll be fine," Kiki said, though I wasn't sure she meant that. I knew she had worked out an exact timetable with Katie about how to get everything done.

"Really?"

"Really," Kiki said. "I'll deal with it. Don't worry."

"Okay." I told myself she knew better than I what it would take to deal with the food. I went through my own list in my head while I munched away, a little distracted by the pizza. The village pizzeria did make excellent pizza and I was hungry.

Kiki's phone buzzed when we were just finishing. "It's Eleanor," she said. "Mark asked her to text so one of us would check on the kittens."

"I'll do it. The kittens. I still had no idea how we were supposed to carry out Operation Kitten to chase away Raine's annoying mother.

When I brought up the problem, Kiki had an easy solution. "Call Stefan and ask."

"Would it be weird to call him?" I asked. "He'll probably ignore the call because he won't know it's from me."

"Then text him, silly!" Kiki got up and began to clear the plates. Marni jumped in to help.

"Okay." They were right. I shouldn't be so timid. He'd called me, after all, so he had to know I had his number.

I typed in *Hi Stefan. This is Libby from Pemberley. The kittens are all fine and adorable of course. Do you have a plan for them for tomorrow? Just wanted to get everything right here.*

No response. Of course he wouldn't be glued to his phone. He hadn't looked at his phone the whole time he'd been at the house, except to take photographs and to read the jewelry designer's message. And he was at a rehearsal dinner. Probably for a guy like him, a phone was more an aggravating demand on his life than anything else.

The kittens were fine, of course, all in a pile and all sleeping, though the orange one opened an eye when I came into the room. I left them to their slumbers.

I had started one last walk through of all the rooms we were going to use when Eleanor and Mark came back from the dinner.

"How was it? I asked.

"Interesting." Eleanor looked over at Mark and said, "I'll tell you all about it when we have time."

I hoped that didn't mean there was going to be some sort of problem. I hadn't heard from Emmaline except for a text asking if we were on schedule.

"How are things going here?" Eleanor asked.

I was about to say everything was on schedule when I remembered something. "I forgot the floor in the ballroom! I was going to polish it the day I hurt my ankle. It looks terrible." I didn't know how I could have forgotten except that I hadn't been in there since I'd finished the gilding.

"It shouldn't take too long, right?" Eleanor said. "I can help after I change and get Mark to bed." He was yawning huge yawns.

"Thanks, but it's just a one-person job. We have a floor polisher." We'd inherited an ancient floor polisher with the house. It looked a bit like a cartoon robot and it ran, though very slowly and with much creaking, as if it had developed machine arthritis over the years.

I hauled it up from the cellar to the kitchen and explained what I was doing to Kiki, who was busy chopping something.

"Do you think it's still working? Remember last time how it gasped a lot."

"Fingers crossed," I said. I plugged it in and turned it on. It gave one exasperated wheeze and then quit.

"Fabulous, just fabulous," I muttered.

Eleanor came in and surveyed the dead appliance. She picked up the can of polish. "You know, I have an idea," she said. "I saw it in a movie or a tv show. I don't know if they really did this, but in the movie which was set in the days before electricity, maids used to attach polishing cloths to their feet and skate around the rooms to do the floors. We could do that."

"Oh, that sounds like fun," Kiki said. "I know I should go to sleep since I'm getting up so early, but I'm too wired. Libby, put on your renovation playlist and we'll have a dance polish party."

"Yes, let's do it!" Marni said. "I'm wired too. We've spent so much time building up to this wedding, it's hard to wait for it now."

It didn't sound fun to me, not in the least, not as the clock ticked down, but I knew we had to do something. "Okay," I said. "But Kiki, you do need to go to bed soon. One of us has to be alert tomorrow and it's most important you are that person."

It took a while to figure out how to best attach the cloths to our shoes and then figure out the right amount of polish. I wasn't very good at it because my ankle ached from all the day's activity. I'm not sure the method was terribly efficient, but we kept at it and it sort of worked. It was better than leaving it unpolished because if it had been only me, I would have given up.

As one of the songs on the playlist finished, I heard a voice in the door. "Hello, I knocked but no one answered."

Raine Randolph stood in the doorway with two large dogs, or what might actually have been wolves. They were huge and grayish and their yellow eyes scanned the room and then locked on me. Betsey took one look at them, arched her back and hissed, then bolted away in a blur.

Raine held their leashes in one hand and an open bottle of champagne in the other. A large bag was slung over her shoulder and when she leaned against the door frame, it clinked.

"I hope you don't mind." Her words were slurred. "I had to get away from everything, and I couldn't think of any place else to go. There are so many people wanting my attention." She waved the champagne bottle to one side as if pointing to somewhere. "Aren't weddings ridiculous? I'm not sure I want one of my own."

Chapter 22

Countdown to the Raine Randolph/Stefan Andris Wedding

1 day!

<u>To Do List</u>:

Finish painting the dining room

Do a check of all the rooms

Face facts

Keep it together

Keep track of the bride

WE WERE ALL frozen in place until Eleanor broke the silence. "Come in!" she said. "What's all this?"

I didn't speak, too overcome with the thought I'd have to deal with a bride who was having doubts. That was Emmaline's job, maybe, but certainly not mine because I was the last person to convince someone to go ahead with a wedding if they weren't one hundred percent sure.

Raine didn't answer Eleanor. She was too busy looking around the room. The dogs sat down on either side of her, both watching her intently as if awaiting a command to clear the room of us.

"Um...what beautiful dogs!" Marni managed to say. Beautiful was not the word I would have chosen.

"They look fierce." Kiki echoed my thoughts as she backed away a little.

"They do but they are really lambs, aren't you, my darlings?" Raine made kissing noises at them and the dogs relaxed a little. "People think they are fierce so it makes them keep their distance, especially the paparazzi, but the pups really wouldn't hurt a flea."

"What kind are they?" I asked, trying to sound very friendly and unthreatening, because a wolf dog might actually still be a wolf dog only pretending to be a lamb.

"They are Tamaskans. The poor darlings don't like to be left alone. When I came here for the photoshoot, they got upset and ate part of a sofa at the hotel. We didn't really like that sofa anyway, did we?" She made more kissing noises and then set down her bag, nearly tripping over it, which she thought was very funny. "Oops, stop moving," she ordered it. I looked over at Eleanor. Clearly her stepsister was a little inebriated.

"I hope I'm not bothering you," Raine said to me. "I brought champagne."

"You're not bothering us." I smiled as brightly as I could. Did Emmaline know the bride was here? What would happen if someone discovered her missing?

As if she could read my mind, Raine said, "Please don't tell anyone I'm here. They will make a lot of fuss. I told them I was going to take the dogs for a quick walk and then go to bed. No one will notice I'm gone. I paid a maid to let me use her car until tomorrow. She's sworn to secrecy."

I very much doubted no one would notice Raine's absence.

"What are you all doing?" she asked. I explained about polishing the floor.

"Oh, that looks like fun! Can I help?"

I was confused. Had she already forgotten what she'd said about not wanting a wedding? Did she want to polish the floor anyway?

"I'm trying to learn more about cleaning," Raine said with the same enthusiasm as if she'd wanted to learn something actually fascinating like wine making or piloting an airplane. "Someday Stefan and I are going to have a little cottage in the middle of nowhere and we can be all alone, not even with a cook or a housekeeper, so I have to know some practical things. Stefan knows all that sort of thing and I'd like to surprise him." I wondered if she knew Stefan was actually in the market for a fixer up mansion, not a self-serve cottage. I suppose they had enough money for both. She picked up the bag and held it out to me. "Let's put on more music and open more champagne and have at it."

No more mention of not wanting a wedding, which was an enormous relief. We did have at it, though by the end, I'm not sure the floor looked much better. The dogs sat in the doorway watching us, but sometimes they'd look around behind them as if to make sure no one was planning a sneak attack on Raine. Occasionally they'd growl at the empty hallway as if putting out warnings. Each time Raine would shush them, and they'd fall silent again. I was relieved they did seem to be well-trained.

Somehow all the champagne bottles were opened and everyone had their own. I restrained myself, putting mine out in the hallway. I noticed Kiki drank some but then set hers aside as well. She gave me a thumbs up, and I knew she was thinking about how early she'd have to get up as well.

When we finished with the floor, Raine looked around at all of us. "I suppose I should get back," she said. She didn't seem very eager to go and I knew she'd had way too much to drink to drive. The others were probably over the limit too. I'd have to do it.

"Why don't you stay here?" Kiki suggested before I could offer to drive. "It's really late."

Too late to shout "NO!" We had nowhere to put Raine, at least not in any sort of room she'd be accustomed to.

"Really? I could do that?" Raine asked.

She seemed so eager, I cast about for a solution. She could have my room and I could sleep on the sofa in the library. I'd done that early on. Maybe she wouldn't notice the piles of laundry all over the floor.

"She can stay in my room," Eleanor said. "I'll take a different room."

I didn't want to point out we didn't have any other rooms with actual beds that had mattresses in them.

"Oh, you are such a lovely sister!" Raine said, going over to hug her. "Thank you! We won't cause any problems, I promise."

The dogs. They'd have to stay too.

"You can sleep in my room," Marni said to Eleanor. She mouthed 'sleeping bag' at me and then mimed putting her head down.

Eleanor nodded. "That will work. But I'll take the sleeping bag. Mark is asleep in the little room off mine, so you'll have to be quiet," she said to Raine. "He hasn't been waking up in the night at all since we've been here, but if he does and can't go back to sleep, call me and I'll come down."

"I'll be quiet as a mouse," Raine made tiptoeing motions with her fingers. She didn't know our mice, with their little feet sounding as if they were in tiny mouse tap shoes. "I'd like to visit my dress, then I'll take the dogs outside for a wee. And then I suppose I should go to bed."

I didn't ask why she wanted to visit her dress, but if that was what she wanted, it was better than hearing about wedding doubts.

Raine looked around, as if she was confused. "Which way? There are so many rooms."

Eleanor and Kiki were deep in consultation and I heard something about clean towels so I said, "I'll show you."

The dogs padded after us. I glanced over my shoulder to see them looking from side to side like two silent bodyguards watching for any threats. Good thing Pug was at the vet's. They might consider him a threat just because he was another dog. At one point, one of them stopped and growled at the entrance to the dining room, and then the other stopped too. I hoped Betsey wasn't in there. I assumed she'd placed herself under my bed.

"Oh hush, you sillies," Raine said and snapped her fingers. "Come on." The dogs obeyed though they seemed on high alert as we went into the East Room.

I wished we'd put a heater in the room. It was chilly and had an abandoned feeling even with the few bits of furniture we'd moved in. I realized it needed more flowers and decorative pillows and knickknacks, but it was too late for any of that.

Raine didn't seem disturbed by it. Her attention was totally focused on the dress.

"It is really beautiful," I said.

The dogs padded over to it and sniffed at it. One tried to get his nose under the skirt like he wanted to burrow under it.

"No, silly, don't touch," Raine ordered. "Back!" The dog gave a tiny whine but did step back. "It did turn out well, didn't it? The designer took all my ideas and made what I wanted. Other people have been dressing me my whole life, so I wanted to do this all on my own. That's why I love it so much."

She reached out to touch it and then drew back her hand and turned to me. "But I don't think I should get married." Her voice trembled. "Stefan will get tired of me. Everyone does. I should call it off."

I tried not to panic at the thought of her canceling the wedding. Emmaline needed the wedding to happen, and I wanted to prove I could manage at least one before it all folded. When I noticed a tear running down Raine's face, I remembered it wasn't just about me. And then I realized what she was actually saying, that she thought she wasn't the kind of person her fiancé would stay in love with.

"He's known you a long time," I said. "If he was going to get tired of you, it would have already happened. He's obviously madly in love with you." I felt sure about that from the way he'd acted during his visit.

As soon as I said it, I wished I hadn't. She didn't know I'd met him. I couldn't tell her because that would give away the secret of the bracelet.

"That's true, he has known me for a long time," she said. "Do you know, we made a pact a long time ago to try not to annoy one another. That's the secret, I think. Don't annoy each other. But it has to work both ways. It can't be just one person trying not to upset the other. Stefan would get annoyed that I was so messy and I'd get annoyed that he'd wear his clothes until they were falling apart. Now I try to be less messy and he dresses much better." She laughed. "Such little things when you think about it, but they still make a difference."

I had tried not to annoy William but he'd certainly never bothered to figure out what annoyed me. I tried to tell him one time it really bothered me the way he wanted to know every single thing I'd done all day, as if he was always checking to make sure I was accomplishing enough. That discussion had gone nowhere. He'd said, *I'm afraid if I don't check on you you'll just drift away in that dreamy space you inhabit sometimes.*

"My mother doesn't want me to marry him. She thinks I should marry an Italian count or a British lord." Raine made a face. I had a feeling that if her mother had been present, Raine would have stuck out her tongue at the woman. "I have a dreadful mother, did you know that? It's apparently not a big secret."

I couldn't mention that Stefan had told me. "I'm sorry," I said. "To be honest mine is a bit dreadful too."

"Oh that's too bad. Stefan says dreadful parents make us stronger. His father abandoned them so he knows about really, really dreadful parents. I'm not so sure it does make you stronger, but I'll drink to it anyway." She looked around as if she expected a champagne bottle to appear and then giggled. "Or maybe not. I think I'll call him and ask if he still wants to get married. It will be easier for him to back out over the phone than in person."

I backed out of the room, thinking she probably wouldn't want me there. She didn't notice, though the dogs watched me go. I went into the kitchen and called Emmaline, who answered the phone right away.

"Good, I didn't wake you," I said.

"I can't sleep. What's wrong? Why are you calling so late? Please don't tell me your roof collapsed or anything."

I explained about Raine.

"Thank goodness you called! We would have been in full panic mode tomorrow morning if we found her missing. Is she coming back here?"

"No, we've convinced her to stay. She's had way too much champagne to drive. I don't know what she'll do in the morning. I suppose she can take a shower here, but she doesn't seem to have brought much with her, like makeup and everything."

"Don't worry about that. The makeup artist will have all that. I'll text Raine in the morning and let her know we can bring over whatever she needs."

The dogs began to bark. Angry, upset barks. I ran back to the East Room to find Raine with tears running down her face. I felt sick and then angry. I couldn't believe Stefan would drop her, not the man who had seemed so in love a few days before.

Raine looked as young as Kiki with her teary face. "What...what did he say?" I asked, though I was very afraid I already knew.

"He...he...still wants to marry me. He says he's never wanted to marry anyone else and he'll stay with me always." She burst into full-fledged sobs as I took a moment to understand she was crying from happiness, not sadness.

The dogs whined at her distress. I thought about going over and giving her a hug but I was afraid the beasts would think I was trying to squeeze her to death and therefore sentence me to death. Instead I made encouraging noises from a safe distance. Eventually her sobbing moved into more of the sniffle range.

Finally, she took a step back and wiped her eyes. "It's silly of me to cry. I should stop so my face isn't all puffy in the morning."

The relief nearly overwhelmed me. "I'm glad everything is fine." I fought back a yawn as a wave of tiredness came over me. It made me even more tired to realize I'd have to be up in a few hours.

"Oh, I almost forgot. Your grandmother is looking for Pug," Raine said as she went toward the hall. "I told her I'd help her find it when I got off the phone. That's why the dogs were barking. They were startled when she came into the room. Did she find him?"

"My grandmother? Pug?" I knew I sounded drunk but I was completely confused, and anyway she didn't notice.

"Yes, she wandered in here calling for him. I hope the dog is not hiding because of these love-a-doves." She petted one of the beasts and they both thumped their tails.

The ghost. Raine had to be more drunk than I'd realized if she thought the ghost was an actual woman. Was the ghost calling for a pug or did Raine just hear that because she had met our pug? Looking for a pug made a lot more sense than looking for a pig while wearing a lacy nightgown. Not that it explained a ghost in the first place, but if one was going to have a haunted house, the ghost's story needed to make sense. Our ghost could have had a pug at some point in her life. Something about that tugged at my memory, but I couldn't catch hold of it. Not that it was important at the moment. I was definitely not going to explain to Raine she'd seen a ghost instead of my grandmother, so I just said, "Thanks, she gets confused late at night."

"I should take the dogs out," Raine said. "And then I'll go to bed. I'm sure you want to go to sleep too."

"I'll wait until you're back in and then lock up, okay?" I didn't want Raine roaming about the grounds in the dark and either falling in the Dutch pond or getting lost in the maze. Emmaline would not appreciate that sort of text from me. While I waited I roamed around looking for the ghost. Was it common for ghosts to search out lost pets? Was my brain addled that I was even considering such a thing because I was so tired? In any event, I didn't see any ghostly specters and I had to admit to myself I did not have the gift of sight or whatever ghost viewing is called.

I closed the door to the East Room. It was too warped to shut firmly so when Raine and the dogs came back in at last I asked if the dogs might try to get in the room in the night.

"Oh no. They won't wander around. They'll sleep by the bed all night."

I hoped she was right. Once the front door was locked and they were safely in Eleanor's room, I trudged upstairs. Betsey squeaked at me from under the bed and then turned her face away, as if it was my fault there were giant dog creatures inhabiting the house. "I'm sorry, baby. They won't be here all that much longer," I said, but she continued to ignore me. I knew she'd come up onto the bed at some point in the night so I let her be.

I sketched a quick rabbit in a wedding veil and then as I was drifting off to sleep, I was overtaken by the thought that I needed to remember to tell everyone the ghost was looking for her pug, not her pig. There was something about the information, which was important, but I couldn't think what. I was just too tired.

Chapter 23

Day of Wedding

<u>To Do List</u>:
Put on a happy face until after the wedding
Then deal with Davin

I DID REMEMBER to set my alarm, which was good because by the time I woke up, it had been dinging for at least five minutes. After fumbling around in a daze to shut it off, I lay there for a moment forcing myself to come alert. The house was completely silent. I thought I remembered hearing barking in the middle of the night but I couldn't be sure it wasn't just a dream. Had the dogs been barking because they'd seen the ghost again during the night? Dogs were supposedly able to sense ghostly presences.

As I pondered our ghost, I realized it seemed extra dark in my room. I looked over at the window to see a sky covered in dark gray clouds. No rain yet, but it had to be on its way. We'd bought some decorative bowls to place around the floor of the conservatory if it rained, but it was a poor solution. I just knew someone would trip over them but I hadn't been able to come up with a better idea.

It also took me a moment to realize what else was wrong. No Betsey. She was not at the foot of the bed or on the chair. I leaned over and looked under the bed. No Betsey. I went out into the hallway. All the other doors were closed except for an old cleaning closet where we kept one of the litter boxes.

No Betsey there either. A little tremor of worry snaked its way through me. What if Betsey had gone downstairs in the night and Raine's big dogs had found her?

I saw the footprints as I was halfway down the stairs. Even in the dim light, they stood out on the hall floor. Dark pink dog prints, large wolf-sized pink dog prints leading from the dining room. They got fainter as I traced their path but they led right to the East Room.

And the wedding dress. I ran, ignoring the pain in my ankle.

Inside the East Room the dress lay on the floor on top of the drop cloth. One of the dogs was on the chaise lounge and the other sprawled out on the floor. The orange kitten lay curled up fast asleep on top of the floor dog. I took a step in and the beast on the chaise lounge lifted its head and growled, which woke the other two animals up.

I took a step back. "No problem," I said. "See, I'm leaving."

I couldn't get a good look at the dress. I could only pray it wasn't damaged.

Eleanor came down the stairs as I backed into the hall. My stomach turned over at the thought something might have happened to that beautiful dress. I remembered I'd left the can of paint in the dining room intending to finish the touchups, but then Marni had told me about the private investigator report. I'd completely forgotten about the paint, and I'd left the can so that the open door would have hidden it from view when I looked in the day before. So, so careless. I cursed at myself.

"Good morning!" Eleanor said. As she drew closer, she must have seen something on my face. "What is it? What's wrong?"

I choked out the words. "The wedding dress is on the floor and the dogs got into some pink paint. They are both in there with it. I can't tell if they got paint on it or not." I pointed down to the footprints. "I did something so stupid. I left a can of paint in the dining room. They must have knocked it over when they were chasing one of the kittens. The kitten is in there with them too."

With each word out of my mouth, her face grew as sick-looking as mine must have been.

"And the dogs won't let me come into the room."

"I'll wake up Raine," Eleanor said. "Mark must have had one of the kittens out of the cage. I told him they had to stay in it during the night but I guess he didn't listen."

I twisted my bracelet, trying to think what to do. "It's not his fault. It's mine for forgetting about the paint."

Raine stumbled of the bedroom rubbing her face. "What did they do again?" she asked Eleanor.

"They don't want us to come into the room," Eleanor said, "but we need to pick up the wedding dress. It's on the floor. I think they knocked it down. We need to make sure they didn't get paint on it."

"They must have been chasing one of the kittens...a kitten we have," I said, stumbling over the presence of the kittens. "I shouldn't have left out the paint. I completely forgot about it. So stupid of me!"

"They love cats," Raine said. "If they were chasing one, it was because they wanted to play with it." She went into the room and snapped her fingers at them. "Be good!"

Eleanor and I followed her and picked up the dress. I was relieved not to see any obvious tears or snags.

"See, nothing's wrong, though you are bad, bad boys." Raine shook her finger at the dogs, who thumped their tails, not convinced they were anything but good dogs.

Eleanor made an odd sound in her throat and when I looked over at her, I saw she was pointing at the bottom of the dress.

There were two fuzzy pink blotches, smudgy pawprints, on the back bottom edge of the underskirt. She pulled the tulle down over it but they were still very visible, much darker than the pink of the tulle.

I waited for Raine to become the bridezilla I'd expected all along.

"We can wash them out, I think," Raine said in the mildest of voices. I shot a closer look at her to make sure she hadn't already been tipping into more champagne.

"It's already dried, so it's not going to come out with water," I said.

"Let's call the designer," Eleanor suggested. "There must be some sort of cleaner that will get the paint out."

I thought I should call Emmaline as well.

Raine acted as if she wasn't listening. She knelt down next to Eleanor and studied the damage.

"You know even though they aren't really clear as dog prints, they are actually kind of sweet, a reminder of my babies. Let's just add some more paint so they really do look like dog prints."

She must have been into the champagne. The idea was completely bonkers. I couldn't believe what I was hearing. I looked over at Eleanor.

"I don't know," Eleanor said in a calm voice. "If we add more paint and you don't like it, it will be that much harder to get out."

"I want to do it!" Raine cried. "Besides, it will make a fun story Stefan and I can tell our children someday. Who wants a boring wedding where everything went just right? And Libby can do it. I saw her paintings. She knows what to do."

If I hadn't been sick over the dress, I might have been touched by her faith in me even if it was just for painting dog footprints. It was still a bonkers idea.

Then I remembered the dress designer. I dreaded to think what she would think of me. I tried to talk Raine out of it but she was adamant.

"Really, it's what I want. Please!" She put her hand on my arm. "It will turn out fine. I just know it."

Eleanor nodded at me and I gave in. After all, we didn't have much of an alternative. I knew there was no chemical that would remove the paint from the fabric without damaging it.

I got a brush and brought in the remains of the paint, shutting the door of the dining room behind me. Most of the paint was in a puddle where the can had tipped over and it wasn't all dry. We didn't need any more creatures running through it and decorating any more of the floors with paw prints until I could get it cleaned up.

I got a cup to put a little paint in from the remains in the paint can and thinned it with water. When I dipped the brush into the cup, my hands were shaking. "Are you sure? I could make it worse."

"I'm sure," Raine said. "Do it."

I took a deep breath hoping I'd thinned the paint enough. I made a few strokes and then stopped, not wanting to overdo.

Raine studied my efforts. "I like it. They are sort of impressionist dog prints. It's different."

That was one word for it. I decided I'd make myself scarce when the dress designer saw it.

Raine yawned. "I should take a shower, right?" she asked. "After I take the dogs out."

"Right," Eleanor said. "And I'll make us some coffee."

And that was that. Something to record if I ever wrote down my memories of my brief career as a wedding venue manager.

I still had to deal with the paint spill. I couldn't get it all up, certainly not in the time left before the wedding, but I managed to make it all less noticeable. The worst of it, the origin of the spill, was mostly hidden by the door. To hide the rest of it, I moved one of the plant stands the florist had brought so that it looked like it had been placed there to keep the door open. I caught myself thinking that at some point we'd have to have the entire dining room floor refinished, which had been on a wish list anyway, and then I remembered. I didn't need a wish list anymore. Raine and Stefan, the future owners of Pemberley, would be the ones having the floors refinished.

I did the best I could with the dog prints in the hallway. I hoped I'd be the only one to notice the traces of pink paint that remained. No one would be looking down, I reasoned. And the lights weren't all that bright.

The doorbell rang. I realized I was still wearing my pajamas, but I didn't actually care if any of the wedding suppliers saw me like that. Except when I opened the door, it wasn't a wedding supplier. It was Davin. He was carrying a large cardboard box.

"I thought you were going out of town," I said, realizing how bad my hair must look. And then I remembered I shouldn't care what he thought, not after he'd had a report done on me. I was still furious at him for that, but somehow with him in front of me, the fury eased a bit.

"My plans changed."

Kiki came into the hall before he could explain why he was at my door. I noticed an older woman standing behind him.

"That was fast!" Kiki said.

"Good morning," Davin said to her. "I brought you some help since Katie is not up to it. This is Anne Taylor. You remember, I told you I had a friend who makes herbal soaps?" he said to me. "She's also an amazing cook."

This person was not the woman I'd imagined in floaty skirts and long beautiful hair flitting about. She had short gray hair and a round face. How had Davin known Katie was not feeling well still? I didn't know that. I was completely confused.

"Delighted to meet you," the woman said, holding up a bag. "I brought my apron. Lead the way to the kitchen and tell me what you want me to do."

"Oh, I'm so glad you are here!" Kiki said. "The kitchen is right this way. We've got breakfast pastries and tea and coffee to get us started too. And leftover pizza as well."

"Lovely," the woman said. "I could do with a cup of tea and a pastry."

The two went off chattering like best friends.

"How did you know Katie was ill?" I asked Davin.

"I texted Kiki and asked...asked how you were and how everything was going. She told me. And I got a text from Marni as well, asking if I thought it was really going to rain because you still have the problem with the leaking conservatory. It is going to rain, so I need to get the ladder I brought once I put these down." He held the box a little higher.

"Wait. A ladder? What can you do?" I had visions of him trying to repair the conservatory roof in the next few hours.

"It's easier if I show you. Where's Marni?"

"I'm here!" Marni called as she came down the stairs. She was all dressed, which made my pajamas look even worse.

"I've got a solution," he said to her. "I've been thinking about it but it finally came to me a few days ago and I wanted to see if I could get hold of the supplies before I mentioned it. I'm sorry it took so long. Come on, I'll show you."

I followed after them as they went into the conservatory. Everyone seemed to know what was happening except me.

Davin set the box down and pulled out a long chain made of copper spirals.

"What are those?" I asked.

"I know," Marni said. "They're Japanese rain spirals. The rain runs down them."

"Exactly," Davin said. "And then it's going to run into the large containers I have in my truck. We'll float flowers in them, but we also need to place small pots of flowers around them to make them more noticeable and to keep people from accidentally running into them. I've got everything we need."

"That's brilliant!" Marni said.

"It is," I said. I loved the idea.

"Let's just hope I can get the spirals attached without breaking any panes of glass." Davin looked at me. "That glass is so old, I'm a little afraid to touch it. Libby, you'll have to give me the go ahead. I might make things worse."

The sky was still a very ominous gray. "Go ahead," I said.

"All right. I'll get what I need from the truck."

"I can help you unload," Marni said.

I held the door for them, acting as if I didn't care I was only wearing pajamas. As soon as I could, I'd get dressed.

Once they had everything inside, I watched for a few minutes as Davin and Marni worked together, but it was too nerve-wracking each time Davin touched one of the supports. I made an excuse about needing to get dressed and left them to it. If it was a disaster, I'd learn soon enough.

I had a dress ready, a dark blue one in a simple cut that I'd kept from my law office internship days. If I left off the suit jacket, it worked as a fade-into-the-background dress, which was the look I needed as a wedding venue manager. Kiki had made sure she and Katie and Marni all had black trousers and white shirts just like the servers Emmaline had hired, but I didn't want to look like them because I'd mostly be lurking trying to deal with any problems. When I was hanging about, I didn't want to be mistaken for a slacking server.

I'd told Marni she didn't need to help or dress up in server wear but she'd insisted. "How else am I going to see who all is here? It will be fun," she'd said. "Besides, it's an interesting real life example of social mobility, dear to my sociologist's heart. I've learned everything about Stefan and Raine's background from Katie, and Stefan is certainly an example of upward mobility. I'm very curious to find out who the other guests are."

If it interested her from a scientific standpoint, I wasn't going to argue with that.

When I came back downstairs, I went to the conservatory. Only Marni was still there, positioning pots of flowers around the larger containers.

"Isn't it great?" she asked. "I think it looks fabulous."

"It does," I said. "I want to thank Davin."

"He had to go change. He said he'll see you in a few hours."

"What? Why?"

She shrugged. "I don't know. I wasn't paying that much attention."
She pointed at one of the pots. "Do you think each rain spiral should
have one color of flower around it or should we mix them all up?"

"Um...one color around each." I realized Davin would be coming
back to pick up Anne the kitchen helper at some point. That must have
been what he meant. In any case, I needed some coffee or I'd never get
through the day.

Kiki and Anne and Mark were all in the kitchen. "I can help," I said
as I poured myself a cup.

"We're all under control with Anne's help," Kiki said. "Katie and I
did so much prep work in advance that it's all good. We don't need you
now."

"I'm helping too," Mark said. He was wearing a large apron and
wiping off trays with a dish towel.

" I can see that," I said. "Thank you. And thank you too, Anne." I'd
have to figure out how to pay her without it seeming weird.

"I'm happy to help." She was chopping dill very fast, just like Kiki
could. Impressive.

"Did you know Anne was Davin's nanny when he was a little boy?"
Kiki asked. "She's been telling us all sorts of things about him."

"He was a handful, he was," the woman said.

Davin had a nanny? What was a village boy doing with a nanny?

"And I heard quite a bit about you, Miss Libby. Once Davin was too
old to need me, I took care of his younger cousins. He'd come home and
talk all about you."

"He did?

"He did," she said.

The doorbell rang. "That's surely Emmaline. Find me if you need
anything," I said to Kiki. She nodded and gave me a thumbs up.

I came into the hallway to find Emmaline, her assistant, Eleanor and an older woman. The older woman was wearing a white sequined dress, which I thought a little odd. I had assumed wearing white was still not done for weddings, so as not to distract from the bride. As I got close to them, I got a whiff of a very strong perfume.

Emmaline gave me a quick hug. "Today's the day!" she said.

"Libby, let me introduce you to my father's wife, Mrs. Ferrars," Eleanor said.

"How do you do," I said. I couldn't see any resemblance to Raine, deciding Raine must take after her father. I realized I didn't know anything about a father. Katie had not brought him up in her detailed recounting of Raine's life.

The woman nodded at me and then said to Eleanor, "Where is Raine? I'm sure she needs my help."

"The room she will get dressed in will get very crowded soon with the makeup artist and all." Eleanor motioned away from the East Room. "If you like, I can get you some coffee."

"No, a mother should be with her daughter before her wedding! I'm sure she wants me."

I was sure Raine didn't, though I didn't see any way of stopping the woman without bringing out the kittens, and it was too early for that. Eleanor gave the tiniest of sighs and led the woman away.

I stood there for a moment trying to figure out if I needed to do anything right then. Emmaline and I hadn't talked about what exactly I'd be doing, except being there to troubleshoot any problems. She was already back at the door greeting scores of helper people, which she directed here and there.

When they had all been dispersed to their proper places, I asked, "Where should I be?"

"Stay with me at the front door initially," she said. "I'm going to direct people toward the conservatory. Some guests are going to be curious about the house, and it will be good to have you there to answer questions. Once everyone is in the conservatory, I'm going to put you by the bartending station, again, so if anyone has questions, you can answer them. I'll be back with Raine by then, but one of my assistants will be at the entrance to the conservatory in case I'm needed." I was beginning to understand why she had so many assistants.

When the guests began to arrive, it all moved perfectly. No one asked any questions about the house, so I was lulled into almost dozing on my feet.

I came awake when I thought I heard Davin's voice. But he wouldn't be here. Not during the wedding.

A group of people moved through the entrance and I saw him in the middle of them. He was wearing a suit again, a very nice one, and he blended right in with all the wedding guests. It took me a minute to realize Davin de Bourgh was an actual wedding guest. In my house, where he'd somehow neglected to mention that fact in the weeks since he'd first appeared at my door.

Chapter 24

- -

To Do List:

Remind Emmaline to assign a groom minder at her next wedding

Tell Kiki and everyone they did a great job

HOW DID DAVIN go from landscape architect to guest at a posh wedding? How had he neglected to mention he was a guest?

He saw me and I froze, like I was the one who had appeared out of nowhere.

"I'll be with you in a moment," he said to the rest of the group as he walked over to us.

Emmaline was obviously confused. "Hello," she said. "You're Davin de Bourgh, right? I'm Emmaline Knightley, the wedding planner."

"How do you do?" he said. "Hello, Libby. Everything seems to be running smoothly. You should be relieved."

"Oh, you know Libby?" Emmaline asked, looking over at me.

"This is...well...you know his name." I stumbled over my words. "This is the landscape architect I was telling you about."

Emmaline raised an eyebrow at me and then turned back to Davin. "So nice to meet you, Libby told me about your work here, but she never mentioned your name so I didn't make the connection. I've met your brother Giles."

I didn't remember Davin having a brother. The brother certainly never came to play with us. "You didn't tell me you were invited," I said. All this time he'd listened to me talking about getting ready for the wedding, he could have mentioned it. And how did he know Raine and Stefan?

"I didn't think I'd be attending. I was supposed to be speaking at a conference in France today but they cancelled the in-person part because the venue had a fire. I'll do a Zoom talk later. I thought I told you I was going to be away."

"You didn't tell me you were invited," I repeated. I know I was making it sound like an accusation, because it was.

"It wasn't intentional. I don't think we've ever had a conversation where I thought to bring it up. I didn't know the wedding here was for Raine and Stefan. You never mentioned their names and they didn't tell anyone this location on the original invitation because they didn't want it to leak to the paparazzi. I only realized it was here at Pemberley a few days ago when they called everyone to give us an address."

Was that all true? I couldn't remember our exact conversations, but surely it would have fit in somewhere. Davin's phone rang and he excused himself. "Libby, I hope we can talk more later. Very pleased to meet you, Emmaline." He moved off until he was standing to one side of the conservatory doors to speak into his phone.

"I don't understand," I said to Emmaline. "How does he know Raine and Stefan?"

"Darling, don't you know anything about your dreamy landscape architect?" Emmaline asked. "Haven't you seen the pictures of Giles and Davin on the gossip sites of them skiing with Raine and Stefan at Gstaad? They met when Raine and Stefan were in Switzerland filming a movie. Now they have an annual ski trip with a whole group of friends. Davin dated one of Raine's friends for a while. Very exclusive group. I know many people would do anything to get invited along."

Gstaad? I knew it was a fancy place to ski, but that was all. "I don't really follow the celebrity news," I said. I knew the British paparazzi focused on wealthy Brits but I hadn't followed any of that in the states, and I hadn't had time since I'd been at Pemberley. "I don't know anything about Davin beyond knowing him as a child when he played here. He was just one of the scruffy boys from the village."

She laughed. "Seriously? A scruffy village boy? You don't know anything about his family?"

"No. What's to know?"

She laughed. "He's not just a village boy. His family is extremely wealthy and very well-connected. I can't believe you didn't realize that. His accent is so posh, even a clueless American should have recognized that."

"I can't tell the differences in most accents!" I tried to take in all she'd said. "But he ran around here as a child. He was just like all the other kids." Except he wasn't, exactly, now that I thought about it. And all those items he brought to play Robin Hood? They were nicer than what most ordinary people owned. Then there was Mr. Mackenzie calling him Master Robin, unlike the other boys. And his former nanny was in the kitchen at the moment. A posh family would explain why he had a nanny.

"His grandfather's estate is right next to Pemberley. Bingley House? And the Bingley Dower House Hotel? And the Bingley Hotel Group?"

"Wait, he's related to the Bingleys?" The people who wanted to buy Pemberley. No. How could that be? I was getting even more confused.

"Yes! His mother was a Bingley. Surely you've heard of Caro Bingley. She's his cousin and always on the gossip pages. And known as a real bitch, not to be crossed. Giles, his brother, is one of the vice presidents of the hotel corporation, and Davin's firm does all the landscaping. In fact, Caro will be here soon. Somehow she got Giles to bring her as the plus one. He's between girlfriends and I suspect she wants to say she'd been at the wedding."

I had to put my hand on the door frame to steady myself. "Are you sure?" The words were hard to get out, like they were stuck in the back of my throat.

"Sweetie, you're looking a little strange here, like you might throw up." Emmaline glanced around as if looking for help. "Do you need some water? Do you need to sit down?"

"I'm fine." Though I did feel a bit woozy. "Are you sure he's a Bingley?"

"I'm positive. Google him. You'll find a whole history of the family. Giles is on the gossip pages all the time, Davin, not so much, especially these last few years. Oh, more people! We're about halfway there. Are you sure you're okay? I should get back to the door."

"Yes, go." I waved her away.

Davin was still on the phone. As I watched him, I realized his Bingley identity explained so much that had confused me. Why he kept trying to get me to sell Pemberley. Why he'd had a private investigator look into my life. Why he was being so nice and helpful, so he could soften me up and convince me to sell. I felt completely betrayed.

I marched over to him just as he had finished his call. "I need to talk to you," I said. The new Libby was not going to put up with sneaky maneuvering, not from William, not from my mother, and not from Davin.

"Are you all right?" he asked me. "You look like something is wrong."

Emmaline appeared next to me. "Libby, I'm sorry to interrupt, but who is wandering around the halls in an nightgown? Have you got some older woman staying here? I don't want any of the guests to see her."

The ghost. The last thing I needed at the moment.

"I've got to go, but I do need to speak with you," I said to Davin as I took hold of Emmaline's arm and dragged her away.

"You're going to tear my sleeve," she said. "Slow down. Who is the old woman?"

I came to a stop and took a deep breath. Better just to come right out and say it. "You're not going to believe this. I don't believe it and I can't even see her, but everyone else can. It's a ghost."

"Oh, not funny, Libby." She took a step back and shook her head. "Not funny at all. This is the biggest job I've ever had and you're actually playing a practical joke on me?"

"I'm serious. It's a real ghost. Look at my face, my serious face." I waved my hand around it so she would see I wasn't joking. "Have you ever known me to play a practical joke? I'm telling you, it's a ghost."

She stared at me, as if waiting for me to laugh and admit after all it was a joke. When I didn't, she said, "You're serious. I thought I'd considered every possible thing that could go wrong, but I never, ever considered 'ghost appearing' as something we might have to deal with. I don't know what to do. What do we do?"

"I'm sorry. I didn't believe it either. Like I said, I can't see her. Kiki saw her first, then Marni, then Eleanor and Katie. Maybe they are the only ones, well, besides you."

"What do we do?" Emmaline's head jerked in one direction and then another like she feared the ghost was right there. "What makes it go away?"

"Nothing, as far as I know. It just wanders around like it's looking for something. It's okay. It doesn't seem to be dangerous."

"Dangerous!" She put her hand to her forehead. "Headache incoming. No! I hadn't even thought of danger. I just don't want the wedding guests to descend into hysteria if they see it. If someone forgets Raine wants to keep this private and a guest posts about a ghost to social media, we'll be swarmed by paparazzi within the hour. It will be horrible for all of us! I can't just say, 'Oh, it's the resident ghost. Don't mind her!'"

"She hasn't appeared much." I was grasping at anything that would calm Emmaline down. "Maybe the one sighting is all that will happen today. There really is nothing we can do."

"Okay, okay, we're staying calm and we're breathing, right?" She did take a couple of deep breaths. "I'm not hyperventilating, I'm not."

"Right, you're not. Just keep breathing. If she does appear, I will pretend it's my grandmother, okay?"

"Okay. Okay," she said the word like it was a sort of mantra. She walked away without another word as I heard a crack of thunder and then the sound of rain. I hurried to the conservatory in case Davin's efforts hadn't worked and we'd need to move the guests somewhere else.

The rain spirals were doing their job so well people gathered around to watch them, murmuring in what seemed to be appreciation. Maybe I wouldn't get the conservatory roof repaired after all.

With the rain problem solved, I was still left with the ghost. Could she be shooed away by someone who could see her? Maybe I should have taken Katie up on the idea to sage the place. And then there was Davin. He was back in the midst of a crowd of people, all of them drinking and laughing. Caro Bingley was there too in all her polished perfection. I hadn't seen her arrive but she was next to a man who looked enough like Davin to be the older brother Giles. I shrank back trying to be invisible so the woman wouldn't notice me. I didn't think she'd want to talk about selling Pemberley at a wedding, but I wanted to make sure that wasn't even an option. I did notice she wasn't talking with the rest of the group. Instead, her gaze went from the conservatory roof to the floor to the walls as if she was calculating either how to fix it or remove it.

Davin saw me watching him and smiled. I didn't smile back. I couldn't believe I had come close to forgiving him for having a private detective look into me. I was such a fool and so easily taken in, just like I had been by William.

As Davin took a step toward me, my view of him was blocked by Emmaline, who had come back into the conservatory and was scanning the crowd. She didn't seem to be finding what she wanted. I didn't think it had anything to do with the ghost because she appeared more puzzled than anything else. I went over to her. "What's up now?"

"Have you seen Stefan?" she asked. "We're about ready to go and Raine wants him to be the one to make an announcement for everyone to go to the music room."

"I haven't seen him. I saw him earlier with a younger man who looked a lot like him, but I haven't been paying attention."

"That's his brother. He's the best man. I don't see him either."

"They must be looking around at some of the other rooms. I can check."

"Thanks," she said. We went to the door and Emmaline spoke to the assistant. "Look outside and check with the valets," she told the woman. "See if anyone left or any of the cars are missing." I wanted to ask why she thought Stefan would leave but she'd already hurried off.

I popped my head in the kitchen first. "Anyone seen the groom?" I asked.

Kiki was busy placing appetizers on a tray. "I caught a peek at him earlier. He's so gorgeous in his tuxedo!"

"No, I mean recently, like in the last few minutes. Nobody knows where he's gone."

"We haven't seen him," Marni said. "But we've just been moving between the kitchen and the dining room."

"If you do, tell him to find Emmaline."

I did a quick look through all the rooms on the first floor and then went to the door of the East Room to see if he'd been found. He hadn't.

"Someone like Stefan doesn't just disappear into the woodwork," Emmaline said.

There were still people gathered around Raine, fussing with her hair. Eleanor hadn't been successful in keeping Raine's mother away because the woman was there lounging in a chair and drinking some sort of green cocktail.

"What's going on?" Raine asked. "I'm ready."

"Um...Stefan seems to be taking a walk about the property," Emmaline said brightly. "We need to get him first."

"Taking a walk?" Raine's mother said. "That sounds suspicious. Darling, has he scarpered? What did you do to chase him away?"

"Mother! Of course I didn't chase him away!" Raine's lower lip trembled.

"I'm sure he's just wandering about," I said. "It's a big place. We'll find him."

Emmaline and another assistant went out the door with me. "Let's not cause a stir," Emmaline said. "Everyone is enjoying themselves in the conservatory, so they're fine for the moment."

"He may just be wandering around on one of the other floors," I said. "He was really interested in the place when he was here with the jewelry designer."

I remembered Stefan wanted to take pictures of the tunnel to show his brother. Maybe he wanted to show the brother the actual tunnel. "You check the upstairs rooms just to be sure, but I think I know where he is."

As soon as I reached the bottom of the cellar steps, I heard pounding coming from the tunnel door. I yanked on the handle and nearly put my shoulder out when it didn't budge. "I'm getting someone to help!" I yelled. Some muffled response came but I couldn't make it out. I went back up the stairs and ran right into Davin.

"Stefan...the groom...he's stuck in the tunnel and I can't get the door open!" I said.

"Tunnel? What?"

"I don't have time to explain but I need help."

I zipped back down the stairs, nearly falling in my rush. Davin came after me. "Libby, slow down! You're going to hurt yourself."

I ignored that, sliding to a halt in front of the door. "Here! Can you pull it open? Stefan," I called, "Someone is here to help. Push on the count of three. Ready?" I asked Davin,

"Ready," he said, grabbing hold of the handle.

"One, two, three!" I yelled.

Davin got the door open more easily than I expected. Stefan and his brother stood there, both with sheepish expressions on their faces. They looked like children caught doing something forbidden.

"Hey, there, Libby, Davin," Stefan said. "Boy, am I glad to see you. I just wanted to show my brother the tunnel and I thought I had the door propped open but it swung shut. Weird, huh? Almost like someone pushed it shut."

His younger brother was sweatier and more agitated. "The place isn't haunted, is it? When we came down the stairs, I thought I saw an old lady in the corner mumbling to herself and acting like she was looking for something, but Davin laughed at me. And then I thought I saw something white and filmy pass by the door as it shut like the old lady had pushed on the door."

I laughed, or tried to, though it actually came out as a choking sound. A ghost haunting the wedding was bad enough, but one trying to trap the groom in a tunnel was worse. Davin put his hand on my back as if he was ready to do the Heimlich maneuver if necessary.

"I'm okay," I told Davin. "That's very weird," I said to the brother. "But I've never seen any ghosts here." This was not a lie. I did not want the story to spread, not at that moment. "Look, everyone is waiting for you. We need to get upstairs."

"We uncovered some of the paintings to look at them. I should cover them back up." Stefan motioned to a large one we hadn't gotten to in our excavation of the tunnel. It showed the same older woman we'd seen in the other portrait with the two younger women and a dog, except this one was of just the older woman with three little dogs, one on her lap and two on either side of her. Pugs.

"Don't worry about it," I said, my brain spinning. "You have a wedding to get to."

"Right." Stefan's brother punched him on the shoulder. "Let's do this before Raine realizes she's made a bad choice."

"Funny," Stefan said. "Watch it or I'll tell everyone you thought you saw a ghost."

I hoped he was only joking.

We all trooped back up. "What's with the tunnel?" Davin asked. "You never said anything about it."

I realized I hadn't. I'd just assumed he'd heard it from Marni or Mark or someone.

"Later," I said. "I have something important to do."

Kiki had seen the ghost before we found Pug, and then Marni had seen it in the library, again before we found Pug. But once we found Pug, no one had seen the ghost. The next sighting occurred after I got back from leaving Pug at the vet.

We'd been here for months without a ghost sighting. There had to be a reason Kiki hadn't seen it before, if there was any logic to ghosts at all. We had no way of knowing how long the dog had been in the folly but he could have been there a few days before, and just not miserable enough to howl. Mrs. Ellis had said she stopped seeing the ghost a few years before. Had the sightings stopped when she'd brought Pug to the house? The ghost was an old woman looking for her pug. Katie had said the ghost looked familiar. She had seen the painting of the old woman with a pug. We currently had no pug in residence, but there was a solution to that problem.

I made a phone call on my way out the kitchen door and finished it right as I got to Mr. Mackenzie hiding out in his shed. I realized I should have just told him to stay home. He raised his eyebrows at my appearance. "Could I ask you a favor?"

He nodded.

"Pug, you know, the dog." Why did I say that? He knew the dog's name was Pug. "Pug is at the vet and ready to come home. Could you go get him and bring him into the house when you get back? Just bring him into the kitchen."

"I can do that," he said. "The little boy will be happy to have him back." He didn't ask why I needed him to get the dog right then and I was thankful I didn't have to come up with a story.

By the time I got back inside, then explained to Kiki and the rest what was happening, the ceremony had started. I stood out in the hall to one side so that I could see in but not be seen.

Raine and Stefan looked so stunning, it was hard to imagine they were real. I knew we'd been incredibly lucky they had been so agreeable and easy-going for our first attempt at a wedding. I felt a surge of pride that the music room was as stunning as they were, the floral arrangements matching the rest of the room as if it was meant to be decorated like that.

The giant dogs were out of place, their bow ties doing little to make them appear domesticated, but at least they sat calmly to one side, as if they'd never dream of going on a rampage. I hadn't had a chance to find out the dress designer's reaction to the painted paw prints, but I hadn't heard any screaming when she'd arrived, so that was a good sign.

Pemberley was holding up well. We'd managed one great wedding. That would have to be enough. I could be proud of that. I wiped away a tear and then scolded myself. No crying, not then, though probably later. I made myself concentrate on keeping an eye out for the ghost, hoping she wouldn't float through the middle of the ceremony.

I heard Stefan say, "I promise to never assume I know what you are thinking." And then in a less serious voice, he added, "because I usually don't get it right." The guests laughed. "And I promise always to be honest with you," he added.

I hoped Stefan meant what he said. Honesty was in short supply in so many relationships. I saw Davin listening intently to the service. He turned around and looked in my direction as if he knew I was there. I moved farther into the hall.

When the ceremony finished and the bride and groom had kissed, everyone clapped. Stefan turned to the guests and said, "Please everyone, help yourself to food and drink in the dining room. We'll get the music started in the ballroom soon."

I hadn't had a chance to look into the dining room once it was all set up, so when I saw the table laid out, I wanted to clap for it too. Kiki and team had outdone themselves. I was so proud of my sister. I needed to make sure I remembered to tell her that.

First, though, there was a ghost to dispatch. I found Mark and Eleanor, and asked if I could borrow Mark. She nodded. "He's had enough of strangers anyway," she said. "And I think he sampled all the food earlier."

Mark patted his stomach. "I'm really full."

The two of us went into the kitchen as I explained Pug was coming home. "Don't let him run around though," I instructed.. "He still needs rest. Could you take him into my study or your room?" I didn't think the ghost actually needed to see the dog. Hopefully she'd just be aware of his presence.

Mark nodded. "I'll take care of him. I'm kind of tired of weddings anyway." He rolled his eyes. "Too much kissy, kissy."

Since a wave of tiredness had overcome me once the ceremony had ended, I could see his point. What a joy it would be to fall into bed when it was all done.

As soon as I left the kitchen, I ran into Stefan and a gaggle of children of assorted ages. "Libby, my relatives would love to see your kittens." He winked at me. "I told them they could bring them out for everyone else to see. Would you mind showing us where they are?"

The kittens. I'd forgotten about the kittens.

"Of course," I said. Now that we were actually carrying out his scheme, it seemed even more mad, but at least it was Stefan's mad scheme, not mine. And anything to please the bride and groom, as Emmaline often said.

We collected the kittens from their cage, and the children did much cooing about how cute they were. Each child got a kitten and I realized Stefan must have planned for that in the number of kittens he sent us.

A procession formed back to the wedding guests as Stefan and I went first, followed by children two by two, holding their little bundles of Mother-in-Law repellant.

Except before we reached them, a shriek came from outside one of the guest bathrooms and then I saw a woman in white rush toward the dining room.

Not the ghost, Raine's mother, looking absolutely panicked.

I hurried up my pace. She shrieked again, her hand on her chest.. "A ghost! A ghost! I saw a ghost. Over there!"

Chapter 25

Day of Wedding

<u>To Do List</u>:
Consider hiring self out as ghostbuster

THE WOMAN'S HAND wobbled and I watched in horror as she swayed and then crumpled down in a faint. Some guest nearby acted quickly and caught her, so she didn't crash to the floor. They both slid to the ground until he was sitting with her practically on his lap, still in a dead faint.

Another woman hurried over. "Clear the way please. I'm a doctor." Everyone began to talk. People crowded out into the hall. Raine's dogs ran out and set up a furious barking.

"I think I saw it!" A guest shouted. "Something white went right through that door over there."

Raine's mother came to. Her eyes fluttered and then she opened them wide. "I'm not feeling well at all," she said.

I was about to offer to let her lie down when she noticed Stefan's group of small kitten minders. "Look at how cute they are!" one little girl said, holding a kitten up to show Raine's mother. "Kittens will make you feel better. Would you like to hold one?"

Raine's mother shrieked again and tried to scoot away from them, nearly knocking over the man who was still supporting her. "Keep them away from me!"

In a somewhat cowardly way, I left the woman to Emmaline and Stefan, who was trying to hide a smile as he knelt down and took her arm and said something to her that I couldn't hear. I'd rather deal with a ghost than a fainting guest. Raine was busy trying to control the dogs who were still barking in the direction of the East Room.

"Did it go in there?" someone said. "The dogs sense something."

Emmaline's assistant came up to me. "Libby, there is an old man at the front gate with a dog. He says he works here and you asked him to bring the dog."

I'd forgotten about the security guard at the gate. "Yes, let him through! The guard must have seen him drive out. Of course he can get back in!"

She spoke into her phone. The guests continued to stream out into the hall. I heard someone mention something about forming small groups to search for the ghost as if we were in the middle of a Scooby Doo episode. There was lots of excited chatter. The dogs were making such a racket I didn't know what to do. They certainly weren't listening to Raine. The whole thing was descending into a fiasco.

I went to the back door to wait for Mr. Mackensie and Pug. He pulled up and I ran out to get Pug, opening the door of the vehicle and scooping the animal up.

Pug licked my face as I carried him back inside.

"Can I hold him?" Mark asked.

"In a minute," I said. I carried the dog out into the hall. After a few more barks, Raine's dogs fell silent, tipping their heads back and forth, and then whining a little. One thumped its tail and sat down, looking up at Raine.

I gave the dog back to Mark and moved over to climb partway up the staircase.

"Hi, everyone!" I said in as loud a voice as I could manage. It wasn't loud enough because while a few people stopped talking, most didn't notice me.

Davin came over to the foot of the stairs and gave a loud whistle.

That did get everyone's attention.

All the faces turned in our direction. I took a deep breath and plastered a smile on my face.

"Hi, everyone," I repeated. "I'm so sorry for the disruption." I saw Caro Bingley in the middle of the group. She looked amused. I looked away from her before I continued. "This is an old house and often people think they see strange things in the shadows. Air currents, you know, sunlight coming and going out of the windows. light hitting the mirrors at just the right angles, things like that." I couldn't think of any other explanations to add, so I hoped one of those would do the trick. Time to finish. "No ghosts here, I can assure you. Please get back to enjoying yourselves."

There were murmurings and no one moved until Raine called out, "Let's get back to the eating and drinking and the music!"

That did the trick. The guests began to move to the dining room and the ballroom. After some drama which most of the guests didn't have to watch, Raine's mother was helped out the door and taken away by someone. We decided Mark, Pug, the kittens and their young minders could play in the conservatory, with one of Emmaline's assistants to oversee.

I went back to the now empty hallway, wishing the party would finish soon, though I knew it would still go on for hours. I couldn't leave in case something else happened, and I didn't want to go to the kitchen to join everyone else. I couldn't keep up the pretense that we were staying at Pemberley much longer but I didn't want to spoil the success of the day for Kiki.

The East Room and its chaise lounge beckoned. I went in and was nearly overwhelmed by the scent of lilies from the many small floral arrangements that had been placed around the room. It was too much for a small space so I opened a window and leaned out to breathe some fresh air.

The grounds that I could see looked good. Mr. Mackenzie and Davin and crew had done a good job. The Dutch pond was clear of algae and even had blooms on the water lilies. The bridge looked picturesque in its slightly rundown state. I hadn't had time to go look for the heart, not that it mattered anyway. The Robin of long ago was gone, as was the girl Libby.

I wiped a tear away as I heard someone come into the room.

"Libby?" It was Davin's voice.

I turned around. "Why didn't you tell me who you were?" I asked.

He frowned. "Who I am? What do you mean? Are you all right? You are still looking very pale."

"Yes! No! I mean, I'm fine. Why didn't you tell me you were a Bingley?"

"Why would I need to tell you that? I've always been related to the Bingleys."

"I didn't know. I thought you grew up in the village. And I certainly didn't know you were related to Caroline Bingley. You lied to me."

"I did not lie to you. How could you not know I lived at Bingley Manor?" He did look confused, and though I was bad at detecting lies, I wanted to believe he was telling the truth.

"No one ever said." The room was still very hot. I brushed my hair back from my face. "And your last name isn't Bingley."

"No, my mother was a Bingley and I have my father's last name. You really didn't know who I was?"

"Of course not. I thought your name was Robin, remember? Now I understand why you kept trying to convince me to sell the place. So your family could buy it. All this time, you've been willing to go out of your way to help with things just so your family could get their hands on it."

"That's not why. I don't want my family to buy it and turn it into a Bingley hotel."

That staggered me. It took me a moment to respond. "Why do you care so much about the place? And why wouldn't you want your family to own it?"

He waved an arm around. "If it's a Bingley hotel, they will move every existing piece of furniture out of here, including all the books, paintings, everything and replace it all with a generic furnishings that look old and expensive but are actually bought in quantities from a factory which gives the company a significant discount. They'll even strip all the wallpaper, no matter what condition it's in and replace it all with something very pricy and very dull. I didn't want that for this place. I've always loved it. I got worried when your fiancé said it was going to be a retreat center. I wanted to buy the place myself. That's why I said I knew someone who would be interested in buying it. It was me."

"My fiancé? I'm not engaged and this will never be a retreat center."

"He said you were, that you were just taking a break from each other."

"William lied!" I snapped. That weasel. "It's a permanent break."

"I swear to you I thought you knew who I was," Davin said. "I didn't realize my cousin had been to see you. I knew she'd sent a letter, but she told me you had turned her down."

I wanted to believe him. I really did. "If that's all true, why did you have a private investigator do a report about me?"

His head reared back. "I didn't! I don't know how you found out about that but Caro is the one who hired the investigator and she sent it to me. Why would you think I'd do that to you? I thought we were friends. What exactly do you think of me?" He looked genuinely shocked. "I guess we don't know each other at all any longer."

I was so confused and it was still so hot, I felt light-headed and nauseated. "I...I need to be alone." I didn't want to throw up on him.

Emmaline's assistant stuck her head around the edge of the door. "Sorry to interrupt. Libby, Stefan has been looking for you." Stefan was right behind her.

"I didn't realize you were busy. We can talk later," Stefan said when he saw the both of us.

"No problem," Davin said, brushing past him. "We're finished here."

I didn't feel like we were finished but I couldn't talk to him right then. And there was no time better to talk to Stefan about selling Pemberley to him. I hoped he'd come in to talk about just that.

Stefan pointed at a chair. "Do you mind? I need a bit of peace and quiet away from the crowd. Families!"

"No, of course not. Go ahead." I waited for him to make the offer again.

"I just wanted to thank you for making the wedding great for Raine. Our kitten scheme worked out well, didn't it?" He grinned at me like I was a co-conspirator.

Okay, we could do small talk first. "Yes," I said. "You were certainly right about how much your new mother-in-law hates cats. And I'm so grateful you held the wedding here. I'm sure you and Raine will be very happy together."

"We will," he said. "Sometimes you just know, well, I knew, even if it took her awhile. I didn't know you were with Davin. I'm glad to see it. He's a good guy."

"Oh, we're not a couple! Not at all." I could feel myself blushing.

"I thought...you seemed...sorry. I shouldn't have assumed. The way you were arguing was pretty intense and I just assumed...whatever is going on, don't stay mad at him for long. Like I said, Davin is a good guy."

"I didn't know you knew him that well." I said it like it was a question. I couldn't help asking.

"Pretty well. We go skiing with him every year. In our business it's hard to meet someone who doesn't want something from you, so when we meet people like Davin, we like to hang around with them."

"I can understand that. Emmaline told me he dated one of your friends." Now I was flat out obviously fishing for information, but Stefan didn't act as if he noticed.

"Yes, well, it was one of Raine's friends, not really mine. Raine set them up but it didn't work out. A woman named Alexandria. They got engaged and then Alex broke it off unexpectedly. She'd met someone who was much more into the party scene and city life. That was the lifestyle she really wanted, not Davin being based here, even though he travels a lot. Raine still feels badly for introducing them. She says she should have known they weren't all that compatible. He's been unwilling to go out with anyone else she's suggested since then. Turns out his own mother had a nickname, The Bolter, from some old book, because she was always bolting off from various husbands."

That explained why Davin seemed to be unattached. But enough about Davin. I wanted to get to the house.

I was about to just tell him I wanted to take him up on the offer when he said, "I hope I can call on you for advice. I bought a property somewhat like this about 50 miles away as a wedding present for Raine and it's going to need a lot of work. Raine wanted a smaller place but then I told her with a bigger place she can have as many pets as she wants. As long as the animals are happy, she's leaving it to me to deal with the actual renovation details so..." He threw up his hands and laughed. "I guess I'll just jump right in."

My breath caught. "You...you bought a house?" I choked out the words. No, no, no. He had to buy this house, not some other house.

"Yes, it came on the market and I wanted to snap it up before someone else did."

I couldn't think what to say, or even if there was anything to say. My plan had just been torpedoed into shambles. I could back out of buying the cottage. I hadn't signed any papers yet. But there was still not enough money for the repairs, not even if we got a few more bookings for expensive weddings. I knew that unlike Raine and Stefan, most couples would book a wedding for months in the future and we wouldn't be able to ask for more than deposits up front. I didn't want to sell it to Caro Bingley. That left Davin. Had he really been serious about buying it himself?

"Yes, it's going to be great. I can't wait to get started on it."

I heard someone calling Stefan's name. "Oh, that's me," he said. "Back to the crowds. So it's okay if I get in touch with you if I need recommendations and such?"

"Of course." I managed to smile through the sour taste in my mouth, I was getting closer to throwing up.

"Great! Thanks again," he said as he left the room.

I took hold of the back of a chair to steady myself. An ice bucket with an open bottle of champagne sat on the dressing table, so I went over and took some of the melting ice out of it and ran it over my face. When that was all gone, I took another and another until I was almost dripping. It took away some of the nausea, but it left my makeup a mess.

I had to make a plan, any sort of plan, though my brain was having a tough time focusing.

A voice came from the doorway. "Miss Darcy! There you are. I was a bit worried about you when you were speaking to the guests. You were looking extremely pale. Such stress, I know!" It was Caro Bingley.

I wished everyone would stop telling me how pale I looked. "I'm fine," I said.

"I'm glad to hear that." She came into the room, looking all around her. "I thought it might be a good time to let you know our offer still stands to buy the place, and now that you've experienced some of the difficulties that come with owning a wedding venue, you might be interested in talking more."

I didn't know what to say.

"It was a charming, if somewhat eccentric wedding," she said. "And the food, well, interesting, if a bit twee. But of course, your sister is the...I won't say chef since she's just barely out of her teens, right? She's the cook, and as I understand, she's self-taught. Not culinary school trained, is that right?"

"That's right, but she did a lovely job, just what Raine wanted." A bit twee! Not a very subtle putdown.

Caro did a slight eye roll. "You do understand that the most upscale wedding venues get that way partly by the caliber of their chefs, don't you? We feature all our chefs on our properties' websites because they are such an important part of the package. They've all been to the best culinary schools and have worked in Michelin-starred restaurants. Our clients expect nothing less. Will your sister, being so young and inexperienced, be able to handle less than positive reviews? Because they will come, even for the slightest imperfection."

I wished the woman would stop talking, though what she was saying rang true. Would Kiki be able to handle any of that? It would take so little to shatter her confidence. I had been such a fool to throw her right into such stress.

Caro tapped her foot. "So, Miss Darcy, are you interested in discussing a sale?

"Possibly. I'd need to see the conditions of the sale in writing first, though." Who knows what they'd try to sneak into a sale contract. If I was going to do this, I'd need enough money to make a fresh start for both Kiki and me.

"Caro, don't push her right now." It was Davin again. He held out a bottle of water to me. "You look like you could use this."

"I don't need your help," I said to him, though I took the water.

"Libby, please don't jump into anything," Davin said.

"Davin! Why are you interfering?" Caro's voice rose. "You know we've wanted this property for a long time. Grandfather has his heart set on it."

"He's just jealous it's a better property than his own." Davin said. "He always has been. And the fact that the owners were somehow related to us in the distant past makes him think he should have a claim, but he doesn't. He doesn't actually care a whit about the place itself. Libby does."

"Davin!" Caro said again. "Have you lost your mind? What does it matter to you? Grandfather will be furious if he finds out you interfered in this, and you can be sure I'll tell him why if this sale doesn't happen."

"Let him be furious." Davin said. "Someone should tell him no once in a while. I've seen him bully owners to sell for years and I'm tired of the underhanded maneuvering the company does to get people to sell. Libby, have you had any of your applications for improvements denied?"

It took me a moment to understand. "Yes...yes." Things suddenly become clear. "I just had a renovation plan for the third floor work rejected."

"That's what I mean," Davin said. "I suspect someone put pressure on the approval board for that, someone associated with the Bingley Corporation."

I shouldn't have been as shocked as I felt at that moment. I'd hoped to move away from devious behavior by extricating myself from any connection with William's church. Little Libby fooled again by assuming most people were good and honest.

"I can't believe you are making such accusations against your own family's business!" A vein throbbed in Caro's smooth forehead "You say you don't care what Grandfather does, but if he pulls all the Bingley contracts from your business and cuts you out of his will, you'd care about that. He'd be angry enough to do that."

"No, I wouldn't care," Davin said. "Libby, my offer still stands to buy the place."

The fury on Caro's face changed her look completely. She was actually a little scary.

"You! You don't have the money to offer her what we can. That really would drive Grandfather over the edge. He'd never speak to you again."

"I'll take that chance. And you're right. I couldn't offer her the money the Bingley corporation could but I could offer her a fair price. Libby, you and I need to talk in private. Can we go somewhere?" he asked me.

"Miss Darcy, think carefully about this. My offer stands. You'll get much more money from us." She turned and flounced out of the room.

"I need to get outside and breathe some fresh air," I said.

He followed after me, but once I was outside, I didn't know where I wanted to go.

"You keep saying you are fine, but you look like you're going to faint," Davin said. "We put in a bench by the Dutch pond. At least, let's go somewhere you can sit down."

I nodded and followed him to the bench. We both sat down and I took a long drink of the water.

"Now, tell me, why were you considering Caro's offer?" he asked. "The wedding has been a success, even with that ghost business. I want to hear more about that later. I'm sure you'll get many more bookings."

"I can't afford to keep the place." I was tired of keeping it all to myself so I told him about the roof and the tower and the heating system estimates. "It would be better for Kiki if she could go to culinary school anyway. And since I can't afford it, I've taken the money I set aside for the roof so I can buy Mr. Mackenzie's cottage. He wants to go to Australia to live near Samuel."

"I wish you had told me." He ran a hand through his hair and he looked so distressed, I was surprised. "You haven't spoken to Eleanor?" he asked.

"No. What does Eleanor have to do with this?"

"Eleanor just told me she wants to buy Mr. Mackenzie's cottage. She's decided it would be good for Mark and for her to spend some time here, to make a new start in a totally different place. She asked me if I knew someone she could speak to about the local school system. I suppose she was waiting to tell you after the wedding when you had less on your mind."

I didn't know what to do. I couldn't buy the cottage out from under Eleanor if that's what she really wanted.

"I'll loan you the money for the repairs," Davin said.

"I'm not going to take charity!"

"It won't be charity. It will be a proper loan for a good investment. And if you let me do a complete renovation of the grounds, I can add it to my portfolio. It will be an excellent way to attract new clients."

"I can't let you do something that would estrange you from your family. Caro said your grandfather would cut you off."

"The old man is more bark than bite. He has fits of temper and then he gets over it. I'll take the chance. He actually likes it when people stand up to him, though he'd never admit it. And I'd actually prefer to completely dissociate my business from the Bingleys. I've only been involved because of family loyalty, but it's not the sort of work I really want to do. I'm far more interested in historic restoration. It would free up my time to take on more of those projects."

"You seemed to think Kiki and I could not manage to pull off this venture. Are you sure you have faith in us now?" I didn't want him to be constantly judging us for what we did and how we did it.

"I'm sorry." He had the grace to sound as if he meant it. "I did jump to a few conclusions the first few times I saw you. It's a bad habit of mine. I need to be better about that. You and your sisters were a bit outside of my experiences. I have faith in you now, absolutely."

Would taking a loan from Davin make me dependent on someone again? I wanted to be free of all that. And if I took the loan, I'd have to get over being too proud to admit I couldn't do the project exactly the way I'd planned.

"So it would just be a strict loan with interest, and you would have no say in the management of the place?"

He held up his hands and laughed. "I know nothing about putting on weddings. It would simply be a loan. And during the time the renovations were taking place, maybe Kiki could do some sort of culinary program. I don't think you'd be able to book weddings with larger renovation projects happening."

It was sounding very, very appealing. But Davin and I would be entering into a business relationship. Did I want that? "Why were you so cold to me when you came to the house with your proposal that first day?" I asked.

"Was I that bad?"

"Yes!"

He got up and looked at the bridge for a moment before turning back to me. "I made some assumptions about you before I saw you again. I have an acquaintance who knew you when you were here doing a study abroad. I shouldn't have believed what he said about you."

I also knew which of his acquaintances had told him about me.

"Henry Crawford?" My ill-fated study abroad romance.

"Yes, Henry Crawford. He originally told me you broke his heart when you bolted back to the states. I did not want to get anywhere near a situation where the same thing would happen to me. I was afraid because I found myself looking forward to seeing you again. I didn't want to be attracted to you."

I thought of what Stefan had said about Davin's last romance, and his mother, the bolter. "Did Henry tell you why I broke it off?"

"No, but Marni did a few days ago. I should have realized there was a good reason. Henry is on his third marriage already, so he hasn't changed much. I'm sorry. I should have been a better judge of who to believe. But let's not talk about Henry. Do you feel well enough to walk up on the bridge?"

I nodded and he reached out a hand to pull me up.

Once we got to the middle of it, he pulled something else out of his pocket. "After you left that last time when your father and your grandmother had the big blowup, I thought you'd still come back the next year. When I found the Roman coins, I used my allowance and bought a chain so you could have one too. I was going to give it to you the next time you were at Pemberley."

He held out a silver chain with a small Roman coin dangling from it. It sparkled in the sunlight. I took it from him, feeling a flush on my face, this time not from the heat.

"But that necklace was the child's allowance version," he added. "I got you a better chain after I saw you again. I hope it will match your bracelet. That is, if you want to wear it. You don't have to, of course."

I took the necklace. It was made of tiny silver beads, smaller than the ones on my bracelet but made to look as if they went together. "Of course I'll wear it."

He smiled. "Back then, I was hoping it would convince you to like me better than Samuel, because I knew I'd never match his drawing ability. Do you remember the first time we met?"

"I remember coming outside and finding a whole group of little boys staring at me. I remember wishing there had been at least one other girl."

"Do you remember what you were wearing?"

"I wasn't wearing that silly opera cape, was I?"

"Yes. You marched out the door and stood there as if daring us to tell you that you couldn't play. You wore that cape like you were some tiny superhero. I was impressed."

"I suppose I'd decided to take a stand right away. I'd dealt with enough younger siblings to know how to take charge when faced with a group of children. But if you grew up at Bingley Manor, why did you spent all your time here and why didn't you invite us over there?"

"My grandfather didn't want village children running around the grounds. He only opens up the grounds one day a year for the locals, for the church fete. I wasn't just going to hang out there by myself. At first when I tried to join in with the group that played here, they weren't so sure they wanted me. That's why I started bringing all the Robin Hood items, so I could be part of a game. They eventually accepted me, though it wasn't until you showed up that I started bringing the really impressive items."

I remembered the fabulous chalice that had looked so real. "That magic chalice was actually an antique, wasn't it?"

He chuckled. "Yes, and extremely valuable. At least three hundred years old. When my grandfather finally found out what I was doing, I got in big trouble. I got in even more trouble when Mr. Mackenzie found out I'd carved a heart in the bridge." He pointed down at one of the posts and I saw it, just like Raine had said, a small heart with our initials in it. "If I hadn't been a Bingley, Mr. Mackenzie would have banned me from the place. As it was, I volunteered to weed the kitchen garden to get back in his good graces."

I decided right then that even if we repainted the bridge, we were not going to paint over the heart.

"So, Libby Darcy, could we possibly go on an actual date to get to know each other a little better, even if I still can't draw dragons?"

"Yes," I said. "I'd like that very much. Will you help me get the necklace on?" I handed it to him and turned around lifting my hair up.

I wanted him to touch me, and when his fingers brushed the back of my neck, I shivered.

"There," he said, his voice soft as he leaned in and spoke in my ear.

I turned back around and put my arms around his neck. No more waiting around and hoping for a scrap of attention from someone. I was not going to play it cool again or hide my feelings. If we had a chance at anything, it would have to be without any games.

I kissed him and he kissed me back, putting his arms around me and pulling me in close. I forgot about everything and everyone else but the two of us, giving only a brief thought that I'd been close to missing out on this.

Someone made gagging noises behind me. I looked over my shoulder to see Mark scowling at us. "Not more kissy, kissy!" he said. "Yuck! Libby, my mom and Raine and everybody are looking for you. Raine wants to make a movie here or something. You should stop kissing and go talk to them."

"That sounds promising," Davin murmured, and then kissed me again. "You should go, but let's take this up again later."

"Definitely," I said. "Okay, Mark. Lead the way."

The end...of this story, but only the beginning for Libby and Davin.

Continue on for a Book Club/Readers Guide and more about Dee's other books.

Book Club/Readers Guide

Contact Dee at deegarretson@gmail.com to discuss a phone call or Facetime meeting with your book club.

1. Libby has taken on an enormous job without fully realizing how difficult it will be. This is often the case in real life, which may be a good thing because otherwise people wouldn't take chances. Have you experienced this yourself?

2. Libby's self-doubt and guilt are in large part due to her lie to her grandmother that she passed the bar exam. Should she have lied? What would you do in a similar situation?

3. Davin comes from a very orderly world, which is why at first he has trouble understanding the Darcy sisters and is a bit suspicious of them. If he had never met Libby as a child, do you think he would have fallen in love with her as an adult?

4. Difficult family relationships mean difficult choices. Did Libby make the right choice in cutting contact with her mother for both Kiki's sake and her own?

5. Do you believe in ghosts? Have you ever had a paranormal experience?

6. Libby eventually overcomes her pride to let her sisters and her friends help her. As Emily Bronte wrote: "Proud people breed sad sorrows for themselves." While pride can motivate a person, it can also bring great difficulties. Do you know anyone who is overly proud and unwilling to ask for help?

7. Libby's relationship with William had many of the problems first relationships often do: She thought she should have a boyfriend without yet knowing who she really was and what she wanted out of life. Have you experienced this yourself?

8. Raine and Stefan met as children, as did Libby and William, yet Raine and Stefan's relationship has endured. Why do you think that is?

9. This story is an homage to Jane Austen's books and characters. If you are a Jane Austen reader, which is your favorite book of hers and why?

10. Part of the fun of writing this book was thinking up a dream wedding. What would be your dream wedding or party?

Acknowledgements

Many thanks as always to my family who act as draft readers, sounding boards, and idea helpers. In particular, thanks to my husband who indulged my desire to visit historic estates in England as research for this story. Not only did he accompany me, he drove us all over the place including some tiny roads where we weren't meant to be. Getting lost with him is still a delight after all these years.

Thanks to Brandon Miller for reading the manuscript and giving me encouragement to keep going when I was considering trunking the work.

Thanks to Ella Gilbreath for her image she provided of Libby for the cover. I had a clear image in my head and Ella managed to capture that exactly.

Thanks to all my writer friends who may not even realize the amount of support they provide. Writing is a solitary process but keeping spirits up while navigating the publishing landscape takes a community.

About Dee and her other books

To find out more details about any of my books, check out my website http://deegarretson.com To sign up to receive my monthly newsletter and the occasional notification about new releases, go to http://deegarretson.substack.com

I write for both children and adults. One of my middle grade books for 8 to 13-year-olds, WOLF STORM, published by HarperCollins, is the story of Raine and Stefan as young actors the first time they met. I had fun imagining them as adults for this story. The book was a Scholastic Book Club selection and nominated for three state awards lists.

I have one historical mystery published for adult readers, DEATH ON THE SEINE, set in 1878 Paris and featuring a young art student, Clary Ashton, who gets caught up in a web of international intrigue.

My two young adult historicals are set during World War 1 and published by Macmillan. ALL IS FAIR could be described as inspired by Downton Abbey but with spies and some daring escapades. It was a

Junior Library Guild Selection. GONE BY NIGHTFALL is set at the beginning of the Russian Revolution and was inspired by The Sound of Music.

My other middle grade book, WILDFIRE RUN, also published by HarperCollins, is the story of the president's son trapped at Camp David with his friends when a wildfire causes the security systems to go haywire. The book was also a Junior Library Guild selection and nominated for ten state award lists.

I've also written 14 Boxcar Children books for Albert Whitman Publishers, which was a great thrill for me to be part of such a treasured series for young readers.

Before turning to writing, I did landscape design and taught landscape horticulture classes at a technical college. I have a degree in International Relations, which has helped tremendously in my writing, and a degree in landscape horticulture. When I'm not writing, I'm reading, gardening, watching old movies and traveling.

To find out more about any of these books, check out my website at deegarretson.com or scan the QR code to be taken to it.

www.ingramcontent.com/pod-product-compliance
Lightning Source LLC
Chambersburg PA
CBHW051957240626
47153CB00005B/1797